MELISSA HOPE

Mendota Heights, Minnesota

First Edition
First Printing, 2021

Book design by Jake Nordby
Cover illustration by Juan Manuel Moreno
Interior illustrations by Jake Nordby, Pixabay

Jolly Fish Press, an imprint of North Star Editions, Inc.

Library of Congress Cataloging-in-Publication Data (pending)
978-1-63163-443-7

Jolly Fish Press
North Star Editions, Inc.
2297 Waters Drive
Mendota Heights, MN 55120
www.jollyfishpress.com

Printed in the United States of America

For Cedric,
my redheaded prince

NOA'S MAP

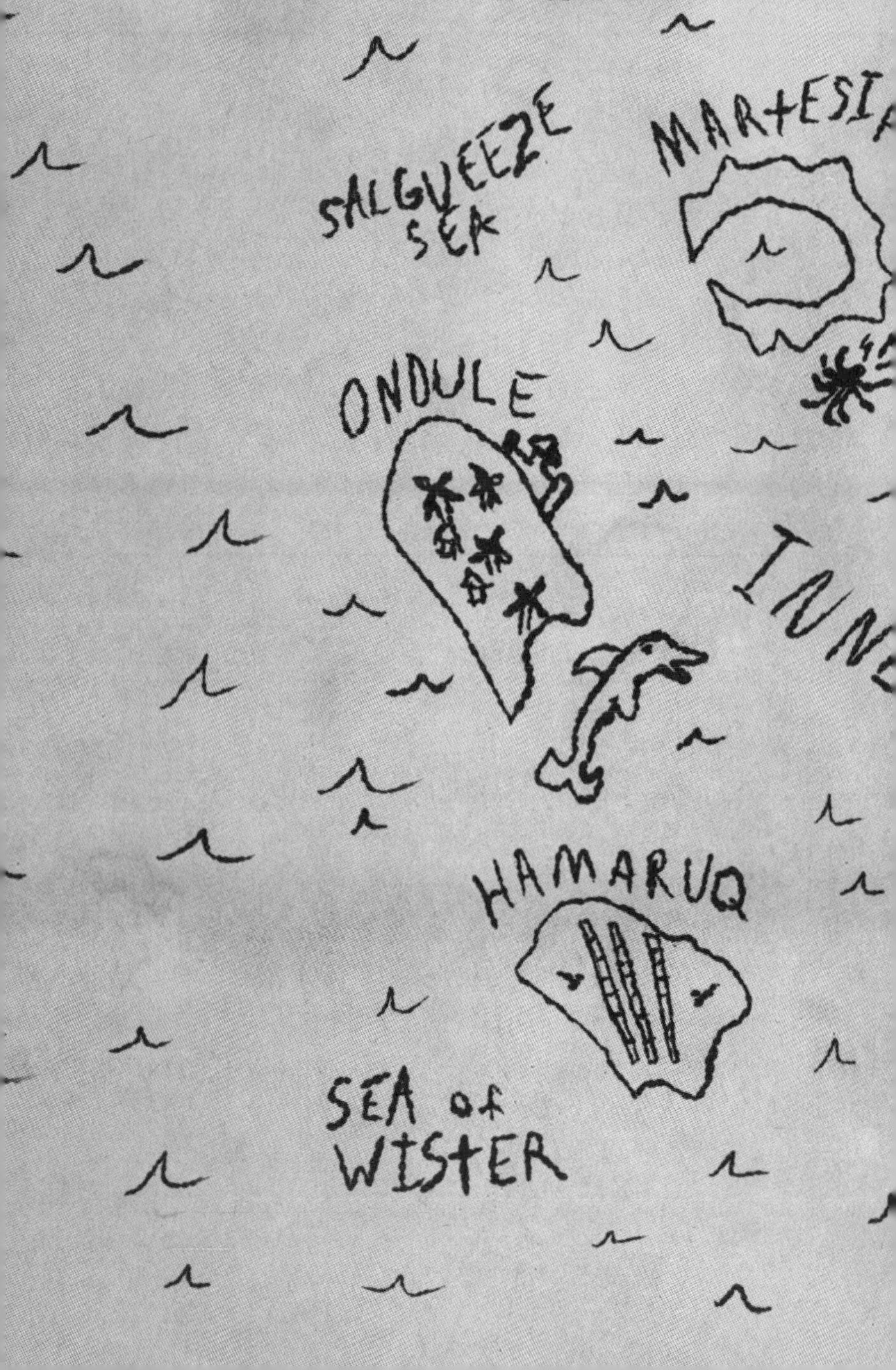

CHAPTER I

SECRETS IN THE SAND

Noa traced his finger down the page until he found it—a diagram of a snail. No, correction: Ondulian whelk.

Sunlight roasted his bare feet so that he had to rotate on the sand like a rotisserie hog. Beside him, waves gently rolled in, shimmering each time their frothy tops dipped into a trough. Shimmering right into his eyes.

"Ugh," he huffed, looking up from the page. He frowned at the sea. Sunlight wasn't the culprit; there was something shiny beneath the water.

Something stirred in Noa's chest, the kind of feeling he got every time he wanted to know something. Snatching up his book, he stepped into the sea for a closer look. Waves licked his rolled-up breeches as he waded forward. When he reached a drop-off that stopped him from going farther, he called for his younger brother's help.

"Come here, Dagan!" he hollered, lifting his book above the advancing tide.

His brother surfaced at the cliff base, shaking water from his hair. Behind him, the rope from which he'd swung bounced playfully in the breeze off a lopsided palm tree. They had discovered the frayed, braided cord upon arrival to this hidden beach. Of course, Noa had examined the rope's safety before letting Dagan swing from it. The sea knows his brother wouldn't check it himself.

Dagan gazed longingly at the rope before swimming toward Noa.

"You should try the swing," he cooed, floating placidly to Noa's side. Noa pushed him under in response, and the boy came back up, choking on his laughs. "Are you *really* such a puffpot that you won't have a bit of fun? Go on."

"We're *supposed* to be researching. And puffpot isn't a word."

Dagan tsked as he stood up in the water and slicked back his hair. "Exactly what a puffpot would say . . . so, you found the snail for your project?"

"You mean *our* project?" Noa corrected, glaring at the pineapple-head he called family. "I'm not writing this by myself again. And I've told you, it's called Ondulian whelk." He flipped his book around to reveal the spiral-shelled snail of which he spoke.

Dagan snorted and flicked the page, splattering droplets over the diagram. "You've found one then?"

"No," said Noa, pulling the book safely against his chest. He pointed at the glitter beneath the surface. "I've found something else."

Side by side, the brothers were the definition of opposite. Dagan's toned arms and dark features contrasted sharply against Noa's lean body and auburn hair. Without knowing better, one might suppose Dagan's build resulted from a life on the high seas, but of course, that wasn't so. No child had left the island in the thirteen years Noa had been alive, regardless of their status.

Dagan's gaze darted from the sunken glitter to Noa's dry shirt. "You want me to fetch it for you?" he asked, amused.

"You're already wet."

"Am I?" Dagan slapped his soaked sleeve over his brother's shoulder, but Noa shoved him off.

"Just do it . . . please."

Snapping his suspenders with pleasure, the boy dipped underwater only to resurface momentarily with a frown. "It's a necklace, but it's stuck under a rock."

"Well? Can you get it?"

Dagan sighed and dove below for a second attempt, splashing Noa as he went down. He came back up and shrugged.

"I can't," he said, wiping the water from his eyes. When he looked up, Noa was glaring at him, drenched and shaking water from his book. Dagan chuckled guiltily. "Oops."

"You owe me a new book," said Noa, smacking him across the head.

"Whatever." Unfazed, Dagan rubbed the sore spot and

slicked his hair back the way he liked it. "Take mine if you insist on being a keener. I haven't opened it yet."

Noa rolled his eyes and returned the soggy book to shore. Then he ran back into the waves and dove under to retrieve the necklace himself.

Noa couldn't be blamed for his "insufferable need to know everything" (their words, not his), especially when it came to the ocean. Knowing precisely what slimy, spiny, and toothy things swam beneath him was the only way he felt comfortable enough to swim. Obviously.

Under the water, the pendant remained stuck under a white rock like a ball and chain held a prisoner. Noa scooped away the sand and pulled the rock toward his chest. With a muffled pop, it broke free.

He froze. This was no rock.

"SKULL!" he squealed, bursting through the surface. Frantically, he dropped the skull and wiped his hands against his breeches. "I touched a *dead* man!"

Dagan gawked. "What? Let me see!"

He swam to Noa's side. Together, they stared at the empty sockets and rotting teeth sitting below the waves, panic weighing into silence. Now, with only the rustling palm leaves above and the whoosh of the rhythmical surf, they waited. They waited for a long time—conceivably, for an adult to swoop in and shelter them from what they'd seen—but no one came. No one even knew where they were at that moment.

"I can't believe I touched it," said Noa, peering down.

"You think it's someone from Ondule?"

Noa shuddered, shaking his head. "We would know if they were. It's probably a sailor from another island who fell overboard."

"And drifted all the way here?" asked Dagan, amazed.

Noa shrugged, still shaken. He was used to people asking him questions because he often knew the answer. No other kid on the island could recall a fact quite like he could, or at least the book where one would find the information.

When he finished explaining which ocean currents could have drifted the body to their shores, a lecture Dagan may or may not have asked for, a large wave slopped against his waist, drawing his eyes back to the water and the shimmer below. He didn't try to grab the necklace again. The rest of the bones were down there.

Perhaps it was the effects of standing in the heat, or the gnawing guilt that had started to sneak into his stomach, but Noa couldn't leave the pendant alone. What if no one else knew about it? What if the pendant gave a clue about the person who died, and Noa could find the family and give it back to the rightful owners? Wasn't that the noble thing to do?

Noa's mother had left all her things in a trunk when she had passed away three years ago. Sometimes Noa asked the servants to unlock it just so he could smell her again on the dresses . . . or hear her voice again as he read the notes she had scribbled into her books . . . he couldn't take that away from someone else.

Cursing under his breath, he plucked the pendant from the sea and sloshed onto the warm sand, examining the symbol stamped into the cold metal. Encased in a circle were two arrows—one short, one long—and two "C" curves.

Noa scratched his head. "Why does this look familiar? It's not a kingdom seal."

"Is it a family crest?" asked Dagan, leaning over to see.

Noa shook his head.

"Maybe sailors wear pendants on other islands to show which ship they belong to," Dagan suggested.

Tide washed over Noa's feet and pulled the beach out from under his toes. Not far away, the skull's oval cranium had sunk back into the rippling sand.

"We should go," Noa decided.

"D'you suppose Father knows about this?" Dagan asked.

Noa laughed. "Oh sure, our father, who sends search parties out if we're ten minutes late to dinner, knew a dead guy was on the beach and decided to leave it. A little surprise for the morning swimmers."

"No one swims here," said Dagan, rolling his eyes. "It's too far from the village and hard to reach. You almost fell down the cliff yourself."

"You *tripped* me," Noa corrected, straightening up. He picked up the soggy book, shoved the pendant into his breeches pocket, and trudged across the sand to the cliffs. Dagan followed.

Dust covered Noa's coconut-husk sandals as he scaled up the cliffside, sometimes on all fours. "We need to find out what this symbol means. Then we'll know who it belonged to," said Noa, gripping a fern to pull himself up the rock face. "Salaso can help us."

Dagan groaned. "The librarian? Must you turn *everything* into homework?" He slipped past his brother without waiting for an answer and darted up the path. Noa continued at his own pace, grumbling under his breath.

At last, the trail plateaued. Clumps of jungle vegetation replaced the white rock.

"Fall asleep on the trail?" Dagan mocked, despite still catching his breath. "The faster we run home, the sooner you can do your book-search thing."

Noa slumped on the ground. *Run?* His thighs still burned from the climb. No longer near the water, the humidity was stifling, weighing down his clothes and sticking his fingers together. Normally Noa sheltered from the sun in the one-room school hut with the other island children, bending over his slate to make sure he spelled words like "exasperation" correctly as Dagan shot spitballs past his ear at the younger kids seated up front. However, classes for the week had been canceled.

His sister's royal birthday ball was tomorrow. Since the whole island would attend, there were many preparations underway.

Wiping his arm across his sweaty face, he turned to the horizon. Rolling waves extended as far as he could see. Out there were five other island kingdoms, each doing their part to provide resources for the realm to which they all belonged: Aztrius. A number of theories had surfaced about the realm's beginning. Some believed that hundreds of years ago, a ship had journeyed from a distant land and crashed in the shallow reefs, forcing its passengers to settle here. Others thought the realm of Aztrius had simply always existed. And others, though the idea was utterly absurd, claimed merpeople chose to give up their lives at sea to cultivate the lush jungles and sandy beaches.

Noa wasn't sure if he believed any of these theories, although he did know this: no one who left the realm ever came back. Even within the realm, the turquoise waters could turn treacherous within an hour, swallowing ships whole. Thirteen years ago, the king had passed a rule that no child could leave the island and, on this at least, Noa was happy to oblige.

"I wonder what killed him . . ." Noa mumbled, leaning back on the rocky ground. "A storm? Maybe a waterspout . . ."

"A mermaid! Or maybe a magic—"

Noa glanced at his brother's cheeky grin. "Don't be dumb. Magic is scientifically improbable."

"*Magic is scientifically improbable*," Dagan mimicked.

Noa clicked his tongue impatiently. "You're a true jester," he remarked dryly. Then he pointed to the beach below. "*That's* what happens to people who leave their islands. The ocean isn't a fantasy world of mermaids and sea monsters. It's just fish and water. And it holds no mercy for loggerheads like you."

Dagan crossed his arms. "Discuss that in book club, did you?"

"Hey!"

"Hey, what? You started that stupid group."

"It's not stupid," said Noa indignantly. "We have parties all the time."

"I would hardly call inviting grandmas over for seaweed cakes a party. Just because you haven't read about something doesn't mean it doesn't exist. You wait, I'm going to be the first to discover a mermaid."

Noa frowned. "Good luck."

Standing up to leave, Noa brushed off the dirt sticking to his wet pants.

Something below caught his eye. Squinting at the beach, he could see the skull glowing in the sunlit water like a white orb. Near it, the swing swayed above the sea. From Noa's place on the cliff, it almost looked like . . .

Uneasiness welled inside him. He scanned the beach again, swallowing hard. The crooked palm hung over the waves, casting an ominous shadow over the skull. How had he not recognized it before?

"Dag," he whispered, "I don't think that's a rope swing."

———————————

The boys shoved palm fronds aside as they dashed through the jungle. Above them, fuzzy monkeys scattered at the commotion, cramming fruit into their mouths before bolting to higher branches.

"Should we tell someone about the noose?" asked Dagan.

Noa ran beside him, shaking his head. "Not Father. He'll ban us from coming back."

"Someone was hung until dead back there. Don't you know what they'll do to us for keeping it a secret?" Dagan stopped to catch his breath, then glided a forefinger across his neck.

Noa laughed. "Oh please."

"Well, we'd need more than my smooth talking to get us out of that one," said Dagan, brushing imaginary dirt off his shoulder. "It's against the law to kill."

"Not if that someone committed murder, piracy, or treason," Noa pointed out.

Dagan thought about this as he rested on a carpet of ferns, crouching in the undergrowth. "You think the dead man is a bad guy?" he asked, intrigued. "What if . . . what if he worked for an evil sorcerer who rode sea monsters and . . . and sunk ships! Then the pendant could have the sorcerer's powers!" He rubbed his hands together, a mischievous glint in his eye. "You win. Let's keep it."

"I didn't say we were going to keep it."

Noa had learned from years of experience not to encourage his brother's ideas unless he was prepared for another near-death experience. He still needed time to recover from last month's viper incident, although the nightmares had stopped.

"One: sorcerers aren't real," said Noa flatly, counting on his fingers. "Two: magic's not real. Three: sea monsters aren't real. Am I missing anything?"

"Social skills, for starters . . ."

Noa rolled his eyes.

"I thought that old ruler, the Death King, found a way to live forever," Dagan went on, slightly distracted by the mob of ants biting his feet as they defended the home he sat on.

Noa pulled Dagan from the bushes and helped swat the ants away.

"Obviously not, since he's dead." He flicked an ant off his brother's ankle. "Magic is for stories. Hold still."

Dagan winced and shrugged. "Would be nice to ride sea monsters, though."

The brothers meandered through the undergrowth—carefully avoiding village trails, so as not to be slowed down by anyone they knew—until the bay's blue-green water peeped through the trees.

The castle sat strategically on a cliff overlooking the bay. Its white stone, the island's most crucial trading resource, sparkled like sunlight reflecting off a wave. Towers shot into the sky, fully encompassed by a high wall with ramparts.

Noa rushed through the open gate, glimpsing the ships anchored in the bay as he entered. The last time he'd been on a ship, he'd convinced Dagan to crawl inside a cannon based on the premise people shot themselves into the ocean for fun. It took the crewmen nearly an hour, and one bucket of coconut oil, to pull Dagan free from the barrel. That was years ago, though, back when they were allowed on the ships.

"Don't say anything about the pendant," said Noa, hurrying through the courtyard. "Father hates surprises, especially coming from you."

"*Excuse* me? It's not my fault your science experiment exploded in Father's face."

"Did you add a *spoonful* of black powder when I said add a *pinch*? Then it's your fault."

Dagan pointed an accusing finger as he ascended the stairs. "Well, it didn't help you insulted his grammar in the middle of him punishing us."

Noa was baffled. "If I were going around saying my sons were 'edacious' for blowing up the cookhouse when I meant 'audacious,' I would want someone to tell me. It made no sense in the context!"

A small girl called after them, bouncing up the courtyard steps to where her brothers stood. Her hair, raven-black like Dagan's, had fallen almost entirely out of her braid, and she pushed it away from her face as she spoke.

"Alya dropped this off for your project," she said, reaching into her apron and pulling out a spiral shell.

"It's Ondulian whelk!" Noa took it and dropped the shell into his breeches pocket. It clinked beside the pendant. "Thank you, Lana."

"You'll be at my fitting, right?" Lana asked, changing the subject. "Bonnie is surprising me with a new dress. I hope it looks like one of Momma's."

Dagan nudged Noa in the shoulder. "See? Surprises are fun."

"Yes, I'll be there," said Noa, in answer to Lana's question.

Anxious to put the pendant somewhere safe, he and Dagan turned on their heels and sprinted up the spiral tower, rounding the corner so fast they collided straight into the somebody Noa didn't want to see.

"Confound it, boys!" their father cried. Scrolls flew from his arms and rolled across the floor. Noa scrambled to pick up the rolling parchment. King Titus looked very much like an older Dagan. His cloak did little to hide his belly, which sagged over a thick belt, and when looking at him straight on, it was difficult to tell where his black beard ended and the chest hair protruding from his tunic began.

"Where have you been? The whole castle has been up since dawn to prepare for King Edjlin's arrival tonight, and I've only just completed the inventory of crops we'll have this fall," Titus complained, massaging his temples.

Once a day, Noa caught his father massaging his temples as if he had a bad headache. Noa suspected this was due to him insisting he know where his children were at all times. His numerous kingly duties kept him from being with them himself, however, so Titus assigned the staff to babysit instead.

"Father, you've known Edjlin since you were kids. He won't mind if the castle is dirty," said Dagan, attempting to be helpful.

"Must I remind you the entire kingdom will attend your sister's birthday ball tomorrow? Unless you want your mousy blanket flapping on the laundry line when your classmates arrive, we have work to do." Titus patted his robe and checked his pockets. "I feel like I'm forgetting something . . ." he mumbled.

Noa hadn't forgotten the ball's date, for it conflicted with his monthly book club and they had needed to reschedule. It was, however, a mistake to tell his father this.

"Book club? I thought we discussed spending more time practicing the sword," Titus whispered, turning an embarrassing shade of red. "You're twelve now—"

"Thirteen," Noa corrected.

"Then act like it," he snapped, suddenly stern. "What will it take for you to stop hiding behind your books? One day you shall become King of Ondule. Our people shall look to you for more than your wit, but for your strength in the face of fear. I know the likelihood . . ."

Noa's eyes glazed over in boredom. He had heard this lecture countless times. It didn't matter how often his father shoved him outside to learn archery or sword fighting or whatever it was that day; life between pages was more exciting than real life. Until today.

Giving up on his lecture, Titus sighed, adjusting the scrolls Noa had replaced in his arms. "I see you've been swimming. Which beach did you attend?" Dagan glanced sideways at Noa, a knowing look which Titus caught. "Oh boys, you weren't swimming in your skivvies again, were you? I've just about had it with all the complaints."

"No, we weren't," Dagan promised. "Even if we did, the cliffs would have hidden us."

Titus paused, a storm forming beneath his burly brow. "Cliffs? Which cliffs?"

"North," said Noa.

"South," said Dagan.

The boys looked at one another.

"South," said Noa.

"North," said Dagan.

Heat rushed into Noa's cheeks. "What we mean is . . . it was the north part of the south cliffs. Wilson was with us, don't worry."

Dagan nodded vigorously in agreement.

It wasn't the proudest moment of Noa's life when he and Dagan had invented the fake chaperone, Wilson, but seeing as it allowed them freedom to go where they wished, they weren't ready to confess. Just yesterday, Wilson had gotten Noa out of a farmer's meeting with his father, giving Noa an extra two hours to read in Salaso's Scrolls while Dagan, by the looks of his muddy trousers, had spent his free time catching frogs again.

"That's what makes it fun," Dagan had said, after Noa told him the frogs were deathly poisonous.

Titus looked at them, scrutinizing their guilty faces. "All right, confess. What did you do?"

"Nothing. It was already there," said Dagan quickly.

"What was already there?"

Dagan chewed on his lip, the realization of his mistake showing on his face. Then he buckled. "The rope . . ."

"*Dag*!" Noa complained, furious.

Titus looked confused. "The rope . . . at the beach?" He stroked his beard thoughtfully, then his face changed. "The noose is still there?" Noa's heart flipped. "It should have been cut down years ago. I can't believe Wilson let you find it! You didn't find anything else, did you?"

Dagan shifted uncomfortably under his father's gaze. "Noa did find—" He stopped, catching Noa's warning glare.

"*Well?*" Titus turned his full attention on Noa. Noa reached into his pocket. His fingers wrapped around the circular metal and traced the pendant's unfamiliar design. The last thing his father needed was another reason to worry. Telling him about the dead man at the peak of his stress seemed like a poor choice, especially if Noa wanted to party late tomorrow night.

"I only found this." He handed Titus the spiral shell. "It's Ondulian whelk, for my school project."

With a sigh of relief, Titus told him to keep it. "Stay away from that beach until I can sort this out," he warned. Then he returned to his usual, frazzled self. "Oh . . . oh dear. Ohhhhh dear. I knew I forgot something. I've left Lady Gumpett alone in the throne room. She came hours ago . . . accursed monkeys stole her petticoats again . . ."

And he was off, tearing down the hall, the scrolls bouncing in his arms as he disappeared around the corner.

"Why didn't you tell him about the pendant?" whispered Dagan.

Noa shot Dagan a cross look. "You should have kept your mouth shut."

CHAPTER 2

SHADOW ON THE SHIP

The afternoon sun shimmered above the treetops as the village loomed in front of them, flags sporting gold-and-blue lighthouses rippling atop the gate entrance. Cobblestone roads replaced the spongy forest floor, and townhouses and shops lined the bustling streets, carrying scents of freshly baked bread and hog manure.

"Father doesn't know about the body. He thinks we only found the noose," explained Noa, stepping around an overfed lizard sunbathing on the street. They had stashed the pendant in Noa's room for safekeeping and were on their way to the library to find out what the symbol meant.

Dagan strolled beside him, popping dried papaya in his

mouth and staring absentmindedly at a shop selling pet hermit crabs.

"He acted funny, didn't he?" he said thickly, fruit balled up in his cheeks. "Almost like he was . . ."

Hiding something? But neither boy dared say this out loud. He was their father, and the honorable king, for that matter.

A plump woman carrying several bags strode across the street to meet them, almost tripping over her dress. Dagan gulped the fruit whole before she could see.

"B-bonnie! What a surprise!" said Dagan. "Don't you look nice today! Did you do something different with your hair?"

"Ha! Don't go buttering up to me like that, young man," the nursemaid replied, with a disapproving look. "I didn't raise you to be a thief, did I? I can see my dried papaya stuck in your teeth!"

Dagan's grin instantly vanished.

She set down her bags and landed a smacking kiss on both of his cheeks, then turned to Noa and fussed over his hair sticking up in the back.

"Why aren't you wearing a hat? Are you trying to look like a human lobster?"

"You never make Dagan wear one."

Dagan leaned in. "That's 'cause I don't look like I suntanned under a strainer," he teased, flicking Noa on his freckled nose. Noa slapped him in retaliation, and suddenly they were wrestling on the ground.

"Oh, *honestly!*" said Bonnie, breaking them up. "You should both wear hats. Now look here. Look what I've just bought."

She pulled out a wooden marionette from her bag. The

puppet wore a cream dress and had strings attached to its limbs to help it move. "It's for your sister's birthday," she said, hardly containing her excitement. "Do you think she'll like it?"

Noa's stomach dropped. He couldn't believe he'd forgotten to buy Lana a gift.

Bonnie read his expression. "It's fine, dear. You can give your sister the puppet," she said, though he could hear her excitement deflating. "I've knitted a pair of socks she'll like just as well." Dagan rubbed his hands together at the easiness of taking credit for the gift, but Noa shook his head.

"It's all right, Bonnie. We can stop by Woode's Custom Whatnots before we go home." Even though Noa was dying to know more about the pendant, his sister came first. She would not easily forgive him if he forgot about her special day.

"I'll take that pup—" began Dagan, but Noa cut him off.

"We can *both* find gifts. Right, Dag?"

Dagan grumbled.

Bonnie sighed in relief. "If you insist, but I want you back in the castle for the feast with King Edjlin. He should arrive soon. And don't forget your sister's fitting is right before we eat," she warned. "She truly values your opinion."

Noa took Dagan by the arm, and they disappeared into the bustling crowd. Before heading to Whatnots, Noa stopped to check his mail.

"I'd like to see my box today, Edsel," said Noa, leaning against the mailroom counter. The familiar scents of parchment and ink nearly overpowered the crowded place. Outside, birds with tube backpacks sat in cages, ready for long-distance letters.

Behind the mailroom counter were hundreds of thin doors about a half foot in height, each painted with a golden number. When opened, the doors revealed a small pipe waterway where a bottle floated inside containing the mail. The waterways connected to each house in the village. They floated down the hill and accumulated in the mailing center, then sorted to the proper recipient.

Noa eagerly passed over his key as a teller handed a message in a bottle to the lady beside him.

"I'm sorry, Master Noa, but your box is empty today. Perhaps a letter will come tomorrow," said Edsel kindly. Noa sank onto the counter. "Would you like me to open your brother's box as well? It's quite full."

Edsel glanced at the window outside where Dagan had snuck away to a group of younger girls, casually rolling his sleeves above his biceps.

Noa scowled. "No, his head is fat enough."

Stepping back into the sun, he headed to Woode's Custom Whatnots across the street. A bell dinged somewhere in the shop, and a boy Noa's age with a bulbous nose and shaggy blonde hair came to the front.

"I knew you'd forget Lana's birthday," said the boy.

"Shut up, Bones."

Bones grinned, sitting back in his chair to carve something small. "Is that any way to treat your best friend? You're so dramastic."

"You mean dramatic," Noa corrected.

"That's what I said. Did you know Bonnie bought a puppet

for her today? I'll bet she'll say it came from you," said Bones, pity now evident in his voice. Bones was the first kid to treat Noa like a normal person instead of a prince; it only took an afternoon of grass whistling and catching beetles to solidify their friendship.

After examining the puppets, miniature ships, and building blocks, Noa returned to the front, unsatisfied. His sister deserved something more unique than those toys, something special.

"I should have bought that book last week!" he said, slumping onto a stuffed monkey. He thought of *The Completed Edition: Mer-Tales of Aztrius*, the perfect children's book which had sold out last Thursday. "Kids love that make-believe stuff. I used to read mer-tales all the time with my mother when I was little."

While a younger Dagan climbed palm trees outside, Noa would hide in the wardrobe to read, imagining descending a kelp stock to the ocean floor where treasure littered the ground and a giant monster slept.

Suddenly, he spotted the thing Bones carved in his hands: an oval locket.

"Bones! Why didn't you show me *that*?" he asked, jumping to his feet.

Bones brushed the wood shavings away. "You want it? How much will you give me?"

"I can give you four pargents," said Noa, digging into his pocket for the coins.

"Throw in a loaf of Bonnie's coconut bread, and you've got a deal," said Bones, hopping off his chair and taking the money. "Just give me another hour to finish it."

Noa slumped comfortably back into the monkey's feathered stuffing, basking in the load lifting from his shoulders. An hour. He would use the time to research the pendant at the town library, Salaso's Scrolls. He was becoming more confident he'd seen the symbol before, and if he was good at anything, it was retrieving information from the many pages of a book.

Just then, Dagan burst through the door and slammed it shut behind him, his shirt ripped and stretched from the mob of girls outside.

"I offered *one* girl a tour of the castle tomorrow night, and suddenly they all wanted one!"

"I give up," said Noa, hanging his head.

Dagan straightened his shirt in a dignified manner (which was rather tricky seeing as most of it hung off his chest) and smoothed his licorice hair. "At least I talk to the girls on this island. Remember Alya . . ."

Fire swept into Noa's belly. "What about her? Why do you always have to bring this up? I don't like her. I mean, I like her, but I don't like her like *that*. We're friends. That's it."

"I was just going to say it was nice of her to give you that shell," said Dagan, a smile lifting at the corners of his lips.

"Oh."

Before Noa could justify himself, Dagan burst into a fit of laughter, swiftly joined by Bones.

"Don't worry, your secret's safe with me. I won't tell anyone about the love letters you send her."

"They're not love letters," Noa insisted.

"Don't you talk enough at school?" Dagan held up an

imaginary parchment and quill. "'Dear Alya, what were you thinking about in history class that one minute when you weren't talking to me? Love, Noa.'"

"'PS,'" Bones added. "'I want to kiss you on the lips!'"

Noa scowled. "Grow up."

The laughing restarted, this time with added kissing sound effects. Noa crossed his arms, unamused, and headed for the door.

"Wait. We'll stop, we'll stop," said Bones, wiping away tears. He cleared his throat to show his maturity had returned. "So, Dagan," he said, picking up his woodwork. "Noa just bought my locket for nearly five pargents."

"*Five pargents*?" Pretending to stab himself in the heart, Dagan collapsed on the floor as if dead.

Noa nudged his brother in the leg. "Get up. When you stop giving me your old stockings for my birthday present, I'll buy you something nice too."

Bones plucked a wooden boat from the shelf and held it above Dagan. "Care to buy something for your sister as well?" he asked, tempting him with the toy.

Dagan shook his head. "I got her a locket."

"No, *I* got her a locket," said Noa. "Buy your own present."

"Come on," protested Dagan. When Noa didn't budge, Dagan put his hands behind his head and closed his eyes. "Fine. I don't need your dumb locket. I'll give her a better present."

Noa knew what that meant. "Not the smiley-face rock again," he begged.

"She loved it last year."

Noa needed to get away from his brother before his laziness rubbed off. He left Dagan the task of picking up the finished locket while he scurried off to research the pendant. Squeezing through the group of schoolgirls outside, he swiftly headed to Salaso's Scrolls down the street.

"Mr. Salaso?" Noa called when he entered the library. He scanned the cluttered room. Books in every color and level of dustiness crammed together like mussels on a rock. Noa took one off the shelf and breathed in the musty scent of its pages. It was his favorite smell.

A balding man with round spectacles entered the room from the back, balancing an extremely tall stack of books in his arms. He peered out behind them.

"Master Noa! I wondered if I'd see you today!"

"I'm looking for books on Symbology," said Noa, reshelving *Beach Erosion for Beginners*. "Er—can I help you with those?"

"No, no, I can manage," said Mr. Salaso, plopping the books on the counter. He smiled at Noa. "Symbology, you say? What kind?" He climbed up a wooden ladder leaning against the bookcase to read the titles at each rung. "*Traditional Symbols: An Illustrated Volume*; *Flags of Aztrius*; *Signals in the Sky: Constellations and Their Symbols*—there's an entire row here on symbols in literature . . . does anything catch your eye?"

"I'll take them all," said Noa eagerly.

———————————

Noa found Dagan in the bay an hour later, watching the ships dock.

"I couldn't find *one* thing on the pendant's symbol," said Noa, kicking the deck in frustration. "I don't understand. Are you sure you haven't seen it too? That would narrow it down—I could count the books you've read with one hand."

The bay's seaweed stink perfumed the air. Ropes held creaking vessels to the docks and sailors passed lifeless fish among themselves for drying or salting. Under their feet, the tide filtered through the slimy green pilings.

Sitting up on a pillar, Dagan tossed Noa the finished locket, then covertly folded his arms in a way that made his biceps stand out. "I only read pictures, thank you very much," he said, without a hint of shame. Then he noticed a sailor carrying a salted carcass. "Look at the size of that meat!"

Noa paced beneath him on the dock, smacking a mosquito on his arm.

"It's deer. Father bought some for Lana's birthday tomorrow." He pocketed his sister's gift, then glanced nervously at the setting sun. He didn't want to be late for dinner.

Dagan rubbed his hands together. "Deer, eh? From Valkaria? I wonder if someone lost a hand trying to catch that thing."

"Deer aren't mean, they don't—never mind." Noa shrugged in defeat. He had tried to make Dagan read *Animals of Aztrius* countless times, but Dagan could never get past the first page ("Where are the pictures?"). Truth be told, there was a drawing of a deer on page two.

"I'm going to see Valkaria one day," said Dagan, with a determined eye on the horizon. "I'll see all the islands. Then I'll sail to the unknown. No one will stop me."

"Don't be foolish. There's nothing outside the realm," said Noa, waving his brother's ideas away.

Waves rolled in from the endless horizon, crashing on themselves as they neared the sand. Noa had seen the ocean in a storm: toxic black clouds hanging above, wind blasting the sand, and water blowing past its bounds. If Dagan would risk being caught in a storm on the open ocean to see the other islands when he could easily learn about the islands from books, it proved just how dim-witted he could be.

A two-mast ship dropped anchor nearby. On the cliff above it, a lighthouse beamed light over the dusky, purple water, revealing the bustling men on deck. Painted in cursive letters on the stern was the ship's name: *Evangeline.*

"It's King Edjlin's ship—he's here."

"They look like a cheerful lot," said Dagan, watching the scowling crew. "Do you think the sailors have ever seen sea sprites?"

Noa's palm smacked his face. "For the last time, those aren't real! It's sailor superstition."

"Says who?"

"Look it up. If they existed, we would know."

Dagan clicked his tongue impatiently. "We haven't searched the entire ocean yet. They could be out there."

"Fine," said Noa, giving in. "I'll believe in sea sprites, or any other mer-tale creature you wish was real, when I see one."

A longboat full of men neared the shore, including one wearing a crown, unmistakably King Edjlin. Ondulian guards met them at the beach. Dinner would begin not long after King Edjlin had settled in his chamber.

Noa's gaze returned to the foreign king's ship. Immediately his eyes found a figure in the window of the cabin.

It was a man. Noa was too far away to see his face, but he could see the man wore a tricorn hat. Was the stranger looking at Noa too? Then as quickly as he'd appeared, he was gone, dissolved into the darkness of the ship's interior.

". . . don't you think? Noa?"

Noa snapped to attention, turning to his brother in surprise. How long had Dagan been talking?

"We should go home, don't you think?" Dagan repeated, clearly annoyed. "Father won't like it if we're late."

Noa searched the ship's windows one last time before he complied. Several paces down the beach, a thought entered Noa's mind: If King Edjlin was on shore, who was in his cabin?

Flying up the spiral stairs, Noa passed arrow slits overlooking the ocean until he reached a door and entered.

His bedroom resembled a library destroyed by a hurricane. Scrolls and books lined the shelves, as well as his desk, bed, and every other nook available, even competing for space with a collection of stockings on the floor. Noa hurried to the wardrobe across the room to find something to wear for the banquet.

When he was halfway through dressing, Bonnie announced from the other side of the door that dinner would be postponed an hour to let King Edjlin bathe.

"Can't he wait?" asked Noa, when he opened the door with his shirt on backwards.

"He insisted on having 'time to think,'" said Bonnie, scanning Noa's cluttered floor with a disapproving look. "He looked rather distraught, I must say. I expect he's had a hard journey, so *no Wilson excuses tonight*. King Edjlin has traveled far to see you." Bonnie knew all about their make-believe chaperone. She saw through their scheme faster than a poisonous frog could jump out of Dagan's reach, but seeing as she was already worn thin taking care of Lana and chaperoning them to school and sword practice and this and that . . . she had agreed to keep their secret safe so long as they told her where they ran off to.

"Goodness, Milly! Not again!" Bonnie cried when a maid rushed in, begging Bonnie to help with an explosion in the kitchen.

"I don't know what happened!" the maid wailed, globs of red sauce splattered in her braids.

The two women hurried down the hall gathering their skirts, but not before Bonnie called over her shoulder to "Comb your hair before dinner!"

Noa ran his fingers through his hair once and called it good. With new time to spare, he pulled a hand-drawn map from a barrel and unraveled it on the desk, smoothing it out with his hands.

Before him were all his favorite hangouts: the castle gardens, the abandoned tunnel in the quarry, a beach with dolphins (although his drawings more accurately resembled deformed sharks), and a swimming hole labeled *Capture the Conch Lagoon*.

His mother had been the genius behind starting the maps. Together they had traced the outline of the island.

Tempted to draw the noose, he eyed the blank cliffs. Risks always follow penning a secret in writing, but putting ink to paper was the best way Noa could untangle his thoughts.

He picked up his quill.

Once the tip hit parchment, ideas flowed freely. Pathways, secret castle tunnels he'd found with Dagan, caves, and anything else that might help him uncover how a hanging went unnoticed were inked onto the parchment. He even pulled out a second map of ocean currents, calculating potential drift paths the body could have taken before floating back to the beach.

"Noa, you didn't come!"

Noa practically jumped out of his seat at the sight of Lana. She stood in the doorway, tears spilling down her cheeks.

"I waited for you for hours!" she sobbed.

It took Noa a moment to remember what he'd forgotten: the dress fitting.

"Shh, Lana, didn't you get my letter?" he asked, thinking fast.

Lana wiped her eyes, confused. He lifted his sister in his arms and carried her to the bed, wiping her tears with the corner of his sleeve.

"It must have gotten sent on the wrong pipe . . ." he muttered. "Blasted mail. It said I would be late because your birthday present arrived and I needed to pick it up."

He pulled the oval locket from his pocket, and her sobs subsided.

"For me?"

He smiled and nodded, thanking the tides he had something for her on time. Clicking it open to reveal its hollow inside, he clasped the tiny fasteners around her neck.

"I guess I can forgive you," she said, admiring its carvings though her eyes were still puffy and red. "It's much nicer than the smiley-face rock Dagan always gives me." Somewhat sheepishly, Lana added: "I didn't try my dress on yet because you weren't there. Can we go now?"

Noa kissed her on the head and nodded. They left together. As soon as they entered her chamber, pushy servants swept her away to unbutton her dress.

A warm night breeze whistled through the open window where Noa had leaned his chair against the wall.

"You're wearing a birdcage to the party?" he asked, when a servant crossed the room carrying a hooped contraption. Several women giggled from behind the divider.

"Psssst! Noa! Noa Blackburn!"

Noa's heart leaped into a triple-back handspring. He knew that voice. He peered around the room, searching for its owner.

"Out here!" came the voice again.

Noa turned to the open window and found Alya hanging off the windowsill.

"Alya—!"

"Shhhhhh! I don't want them to see!" she said, hoisting herself up and sliding into the room. Two braids divided her thick chestnut hair, shaping her face and drawing out her dark eyes. Being a blacksmith's daughter meant soot got everywhere, and the black smears on her cheeks were no exception. Noa hid her with the curtain, a goofy grin on his face.

"How did you climb the castle walls?" he asked in disbelief. Alya was always besting the boys in athletics. Dagan seemed to be the only one who came close to beating her, although Noa pinned it more on body mass than skill.

"I passed Dagan on the way up. He showed me how to climb the tree and get past the guards," she said, lifting a lumpy bag off her shoulders.

Noa couldn't bring himself to ask where Dagan was sneaking off to at this hour. Sometimes the less he knew about his brother's mischief, the better. He peeked around the curtain to see if Lana had come out of the divider yet, but she hadn't. They were still fussing with strings and buttons.

"I was out with the dolphins today," she said. "Look what I found by the old shipwreck."

Gingerly she lifted the flap of her bag and pulled out a porcelain bowl. Noa ran his hands over its painted surface. When he tried to return the bowl, she pushed it back into his hands.

"See the hands in the water? I think it's a picture of the blue men!"

Noa peered at the bowl with new skepticism. The blue-and-white designs painted the bony, webbed hands of a creature reaching from the waves to the ship above.

"You didn't need to sneak in to show this to me."

Alya laughed. "Have you *met* your father lately?"

She had a point. The death of Noa's mother changed their father in two significant ways: He never let Noa, Dagan, and

Lana go anywhere without supervision (thank goodness for Wilson), and he had become fiercely adamant they understand that magic and mythical creatures were not real.

"Fair enough," agreed Noa, all-at-once aware his shirt was still backwards. He hid it discreetly with his crossed arms.

Her eyes sparkled. "Do you think it means the blue men are *real*?" Noa scoffed, and she leaned back. "What? If they're real, maybe other creatures are real too. Creatures with healing power . . ."

She drifted off quietly, and Noa was reminded he wasn't the only one who had lost a loved one.

"You sound like Dagan. The blue men are as real as deer with fangs. It's sailor superstition."

Her face fell. She snatched the bowl back and stuffed it into her bag without another word.

"It's not a bad thing," whispered Noa, trying to save the conversation. "They're monsters who drown sailors, aren't they? We don't want them to be real."

Lana's voice called him. He glanced imploringly at Alya before jumping out from behind the drapery and sitting in his chair.

"I'm here," he assured his sister. "Just dropped something by the window."

Alya snorted from behind the curtain.

Lana stood in the center of the room surrounded by hand-maids and dressmakers. Her royal blue gown puffed out around her hips, and white flowers adorned her cuffs. She looked like a miniature version of his mother, with black hair instead of red, and it filled him with sadness.

"You don't like it?" she asked, nervously twisting the locket chain around her finger.

"I do . . . you're beautiful." His mother had been beautiful too.

Lana's smile returned. "I can't wait to show Alya."

Fluttering warmth returned to his stomach. "Alya? She's not here, what are you talking about?"

Lana giggled. "She's going to sit with me at the festivities tomorrow. Maybe after she sees what a good brother you are, she'll let you marry her!"

Noa nearly fell out of his chair. He rushed toward her and slapped a hand over her mouth. "*Lana!*"

"I mo moo mike er!" Lana told him, her voice muffled under his hand. She peeled his fingers away to speak. "Your face turns red every time someone talks about her. See? Like it is right now!"

Noa covered her mouth again and apologized to the women around them. "She's joking—JOKING!" he added extra loudly in the window's direction.

Lana scrunched her nose as she removed his hand again. "I want you to marry her. Then she could stay in the castle and share my room."

Noa looked heavenward. "Plan Dagan's wedding instead."

A maid checked the time, and all of a sudden they were buzzing around Lana once more, rushing to remove her birthday celebration gown and return her to the one she would wear at the banquet for the foreign king. While they worked, Noa slipped away to the window.

"Don't listen to her—" he began, reaching behind the curtain, but all that remained of Alya was the whistling summer breeze.

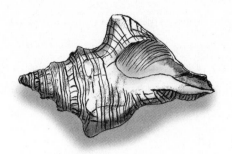

CHAPTER 3

THE UNINVITED GUESTS

"Titus, you old dog!" Edjlin bellowed, arms outstretched as he strode into the dining room. "Good to see you!" The pair collided at the door, laughing and slapping each other on the back. Titus was always happier when Edjlin came to visit. It was as if, for a moment, he could return to a time before he'd lost everything. Before he'd lost her. Edjlin knew the feeling, for he had lost a son before Noa was even born, and it was this shared pain that had drawn them closer in the last few years.

Adjusting his cloak, Titus led Edjlin to the table. If Noa had one word to describe Edjlin, it would be hairy. Half of his long blond-gray hair had been tied back, while the bottom half blew behind him as he walked. Four braids were woven into his beard, and they each shook as he greeted those present.

"Noa, my boy, I hear you have a Capture the Conch game tomorrow? I hope I can bring you good luck," he said, shaking Noa's hand. "I can't say I remember the rules . . . you'll have to teach me again, I'm afraid."

"Don't worry, it's simple," said Dagan, entering the room with one pocket suspiciously lumpier than the other. Noa wasn't sure when Dagan had returned from his little escapade outside, but he was almost certain a croak had just emitted from his brother's pants. "All you have to do to win Capture the Conch is capture the other team's conch shell and bring it back to your base. That gives you one point. First one to three wins."

"Ah yes," said Edjlin, as he settled into his chair and flapped his napkin. "It's quite impressive to see you do it all underwater. I must say, those air sticks are just the sort of thing you'd want in a tight spot! Breathing underwater with a single bite into its wood? Brilliant! I'd like to shake the hand of the one who discovered that plant."

"That would be me," said Titus, with a grin. He clapped his hands, and the soup arrived.

Later that night, Noa lay on his bed reading. He flipped through *Courting with Class,* absentmindedly plucking his brow hairs as he read, until his thoughts drifted to the events of tomorrow. The Capture the Conch game would start off Lana's birthday celebration, followed by a ball later that night. His stomach flipped as it did before every game at the thought of playing the final game of the season alongside Alya, their star player.

Someone knocked softly. Bonnie entered. Strands of hair had strayed from her bun. She plopped on the bed beside Noa with a steaming bowl for him to wash his face.

"I tucked Lana in bed. She's sleeping."

Doubt it.

"Best you go to bed as well. It's a big day tomorrow," said Bonnie. She handed him the bowl, and he splashed water over his face.

"Can you tell Father not to come?" Noa asked, wiping his cheek with the towel. "I always play worse when he's there."

"Nonsense."

"People will be cheering with joy all around him; he won't like it."

"Noa . . ." Bonnie warned.

"What? Doesn't he have a 'kingly duty' to fulfill? He's always lecturing me that they're never-ending."

"I know what you're doing. You can't keep pushing him away. What your father did wasn't right, but it's been years. Forgive him, sweetie. If you don't learn to forgive, you will always feel like you're running from something."

Noa scoffed.

"It was a grim time for us all when the Queen passed, and we each dealt with it in our own way."

"He *abandoned* us."

In every storybook Noa had ever read, a person's darkest

hour showed their true character. He wished he could say his father's darkest hour had made him realize how much he loved the family he had left behind, but it hadn't.

Bonnie kissed Noa on the forehead. "He's coming to the game whether you like it or not. There are more ways to lose a parent than through death. I hope you will not let your stubbornness make you lose your father as well."

Noa scrunched a pillow under the nape of his neck once Bonnie had left and stared at the ceiling. She didn't understand. She didn't stay up at night, wondering why she no longer had a mother to come in and say good night. She didn't know how much it hurt to have a father who would rather lock himself in his quarters for months to mourn than sit down for breakfast with his kids.

He wasn't sure how long he lay awake before his door creaked open. Lana slipped into the room, hopping onto his bed in her nightgown, begging for cake.

"Why are you still awake?" he mumbled sleepily, pushing the courtship book under his pillow before she read the title. "I was never allowed to stay up this late when I was your age. Besides, I was banned from reading for an entire week the last time I snuck out. I can't risk getting caught again!"

Lana tugged on her braids impatiently. "Just one piece of cake? Please? Please? Pleeeeease?"

He was about to object again when he remembered his promise to Bones: coconut bread and four pargents to pay for the locket, that was their agreement. He grumbled in defeat. "Stay in your room, all right? I'll be right back."

Noa tiptoed downstairs in his nightshirt to the castle cook-house outside and snagged a piece of lemon cake cooling under a cloth. He nibbled the end for a taste and wrapped up the rest, then took a loaf of coconut bread from the bread bin and carried it outside.

Torches lit his path up the courtyard stairs and back into the castle. He could hear his father and Edjlin in deep conversation down the hall. What part of their talk couldn't wait until morning?

A pair of patrol guards strutted into the hall. Noa pressed into the shadows until they passed, then slipped away toward the throne room. A sliver of light from the open door lit the wall, and he peered inside.

"The Battle of the Mines may have stopped the tyrant Death King, but I fear the realm is growing unbalanced once again," Edjlin said, studying Titus's grand figure. The fire nearby had reduced to a slow burn, and all servants had left the room. "If we wish to avoid a repeat of the Death King's reign, where laws were worth no more than sand and pirates plundered freely, we must . . ." He hesitated. "We must use the map."

Titus gripped the handle of his mug. "The map does not work on our timeline or train of thought. I no longer look at it."

"The Map Keeper refuses to consult the one possession he has been appointed to protect?" blamed Edjlin. "Already pirates attacked my ship on my travels to Martesia!"

"I am protecting the map by keeping it here. The only way thieves could enter my kingdom is if I opened my arms and invited them in."

Embers made Edjlin's face glow orange. "That map is crucial for the future of Aztrius. Mark my words, Titus, the venom prevails with him. We cannot ignore the significance of this!"

Titus glared his disapproval. "Venom? Is that why you want the map?"

Edjlin placed his hands on the table and leaned closer. "We both know if word gets out you have the map, matters shall turn sour . . . fast. Don't be a fool."

Titus recoiled. He stood up, his bear-like figure blocking the fire's light. "I know my place. I suggest you remember yours. I believe it is time you are shown to your chambers."

Noa leaned away from the doorway and hastened down the hall, his palms sticking to the warm, wrapped cake in his hand.

The next morning, the lagoon's crisp air did little to calm the lively crowd filtering through the trees. Surrounded by his Capture the Conch team, Noa plunked himself on the banks to discuss the strategy before the match.

"Vim said their new play is impetrible," recalled Bones, taking a bite of the coconut bread Noa had brought him.

"*Impenetrable*, not impetrible," Noa corrected.

Bones answered through a mouthful of bread. "Thath what I thed."

They watched Vim Trawling, the opposing team captain, spit orders at his teammates while he pushed a pair of specs over his egg-shaped head. Vim's family sold bait and tackle, so he often smelled of dead fish and rubbery crustacean claws. Since the day Noa had joined the village school three years ago, Vim had been trying to get rid of him. He was rarely kind to anyone, although he had a particularly strong desire to return Noa to a shut-in life in the castle.

A boy on Noa's team with tight curls complained, "This team cheats."

"They use our bubbles to find us, and then they attack. They don't even try to grab the conch," said his identical twin, Fig, who was either best friends or worst enemies with his brother, depending on the hour. As Deviators, Pan and Fig confused players from the opposing team to slow their progress in snatching the conch. The twins' most successful diversion yet (popping octopus-ink bombs next to the other team's players) was still discussed among the younger children in reverent tones.

"The team will want to celebrate after the game, so let's agree on our Wilson story now," Dagan told Noa as he tightened his swimming trousers. "I say we go with the he-was-behind-you-the-whole-time bit. That way Father feels guilty for not noticing. He's usually more agreeable like that. Uh oh, not it," Dagan added, nodding to a younger, chubbier boy running toward them. As expected, the boy tumbled to a stop at their feet and instantly begged to play.

Noa exhaled deeply. "Good morning, Aaron."

"Morning!" the boy replied gleefully. "Can I—?"

"No, you're not old enough to join the team."

"But I—"

"Besides, the Sharktooths are the worst. They never play

fair," said Noa. He stood up and steered the disappointed boy back to the onlookers.

The game was easy enough for even Aaron to understand. Each team tried to steal back their conch and return it to their base, and each player had a specific role in achieving this: one Watch to guard the conch, two Deviators to distract, two Seizers to seize the conch, and two Shaders to protect the Seizers. Noa was a Shader; Dagan was a Seizer. Alya was a Seizer too.

They neared the opposite end of the lagoon when someone ripped Noa's equipment sack off his back. Aaron and Noa whipped around.

How the opposing team's captain had managed to sneak up on them, Noa didn't know, but he clearly had more rat-like qualities than his face.

"Give it here," Noa demanded.

"'Property of Noa Blackburn,'" Vim recited, ignoring Noa's outstretched arm. He read the team name sewn into the bag and snickered. "You call yourselves King Conches? Well, ain't it nice the island know-it-all and his pudgy sidekick are bonding over sea slugs."

Aaron peeked out from behind Noa. "Not sea slugs, *shelled gastropods*," he corrected.

Noa blushed, deeply regretting telling Aaron that information.

Sneering, Vim shook the bag, listening to the items inside clink together. There were air sticks for breathing underwater, weight to help Noa sink, a blowgun and ammo to "tag" people from the other team, and a belt to hold it all around his waist. And of course, his official Capture the Conch specs made with clear mussel shells to allow him to see underwater. Vim dumped Noa's bag upside down, spilling these contents onto the sand.

Noa glared but said nothing to this. He would not give Vim the satisfaction of telling an adult. It's what Vim wanted, to make it harder for Noa to go anywhere without being watched like a baby.

"Ain't ya mad?" taunted Vim. "Gonna run to your nursemaid for help?"

Noa glanced at Bonnie on the banks of the lagoon, holding Lana's hand as his sister walked across a trail of mossy rocks. It was then Alya came around the jungle path, jogging with her bag of equipment on her back and her hair a sooty mess. "Aaron! You were supposed to wait for me!" she called, skidding to a halt at Noa, Vim, and Aaron's feet. She regarded the three boys quizzingly. "Am I interrupting?"

"I was just helpin' Noa pick up the things he dropped," explained Vim in a syrupy voice. He handed over the bag with a wicked grin. "I'll see you both in the water."

"How can you *stand* him?" asked Noa, watching Vim leave.

"He's not so bad," she said soothingly, helping Noa pick up his things. "He always gives me free squid for the dolphins." Alya's eyes suddenly gleamed. "Noa, you must see the dolphin carrier I've made! Now I don't have to return to shore when I find something."

Noa remembered the last time he swam with Alya. Thinking he could impress her with his front stroke, he invited her to the beach, only to be upstaged by a pod of dolphins she had trained using whistles and hand signals. She had even designed her very own underwater whistle in her father's smithy, melting and pounding the metal into shape herself, and all she had to do was drag the device through the water to call the animals to her side. Eventually Noa had to retreat to the shady palms to avoid sunburning his pale skin, occasionally waving to remind her he was still there while she and the dolphins searched for treasures in the sand.

By the end of this daydream, they had reached their team at the banks.

"Have the captains hidden the conches on their respective sides?" asked the moderator when both teams had gathered around her. Dagan and Vim nodded together. Noa suctioned his clear mussel shells over his eyes and checked his weight belt to ensure everything was in place. Blowgun? Check. Ammo? Check. Air sticks? Check. "Right then. No fighting underwater. If you are hit and fail to surface immediately, you will be disqualified."

Everyone nodded to the routine speech. The horn blew, the crowd cheered, and the game began.

The lagoon was liquid sky beneath the water, clear and bright, making it easy for the crowd to view from above. Boulders littered the bottom, air sticks growing in between them like quills on a porcupine, and everywhere girls and boys dodged in and out of sight to capture the other team's conch and bring it back to their base.

Under the water, Noa bit off the end of a tree nut, shoved it into his blowgun, and blew hard. The nut fizzed through the water until it hit a Sharktooths boy square on the shoulder, and the boy was out, surfacing immediately with the spiny nut clinging to his jersey.

Noa needed a breath. He reached for an air stick from his weight belt and bit down. His teeth punctured the soft wood, and he inhaled the pocket of air trapped inside.

It wasn't long before they scored with Dagan's signature move of stampeding to the end, but soon the Sharktooths struck back with two points in a row. Titus hollered praise to Dagan as he emerged smugly carrying the conch with another point. They were now tied with the Sharktooths, two-two. The moderator dipped a red flag in the lagoon to alert those still underwater the round had ended, and both teams huddled on the sand to strategize for the final point.

As the moderator readied the seashell horn to her lips, Vim shouted at them from across the lagoon. "I hope ya *slugs* are ready to lose!"

"You bet!" yelled Bones, punching the air. Instantly he blushed upon realizing what he'd agreed to, and Dagan smacked him on the side of the head.

"Bones, you fool."

The horn blew to announce the last round. Noa stole a glance at Lana cheering on the rocks, "King Conches" written on a large banner above her head. In the palm fronds behind her, King Edjlin's tan beard peeked through the green vegetation. Why wasn't he watching the game? The king was talking with another man behind a bush. Then the two left in opposite directions, King Edjlin returning to the castle.

"Get in the water! Noa, go under!"

Noa refocused. Waving her arms to get his attention, Lana pointed to the game. Quickly, Noa dove under, instantly immersed in a frenzied battle. Tree nuts fizzed through the water in all directions. Someone attacked Noa from below, but Alya came to his rescue. Back-to-back, Noa and Alya unloaded their ammo on the opposing team, sending Sharktooths players to the surface with spiny nuts clinging to their jerseys.

Ahead of them, Dagan swam to the Sharktooths' conch. Noa and Alya followed. Then suddenly Alya was gone, shot in the arm and forced to surface. Panicking, Noa darted into the reeds after his brother, but Dagan the pighead bolted to the conch without checking if the coast had cleared. Tree nuts fizzed through the water in opposite directions, striking Dagan and the enemy player, leaving Noa alone.

The conch's pink lip sparkled under the waving sunlight. With Alya and Dagan out for the round, this was Noa's chance to take it. His stomach knotted when he thought of the praise that would follow him bringing in the winning point—and being able to shove the winning conch into Vim's smug face.

He went for the shell.

Both his hands grasped its prickly body as he kicked feverishly with his feet. In a matter of seconds, pain pricked his side and it was over. He was shot.

Vim Trawling emerged from behind a nearby boulder, lowering his blowgun as bubbles floated from his smug smile. Noa surfaced empty-handed to a wild crowd. His entire team had been shot, making them automatically forfeit the last point. The Sharktooths had won.

Staggering away from the water, Noa threw his equipment down with unnecessary force. He searched the crowded banks for Dagan, but the boy had already squeezed through the horde of people and disappeared with a guard up the jungle path to the castle. Passing the twins, who were threatening to booby-trap Vim's house with coconut bombs, Noa pushed through the villagers and started up the jungle path alone.

Noa paid little attention to his feet stumbling along the beaten path. His mind kept wandering to things he could have done better in the game, or straying to the audience where his father watched in disappointment. Edjlin hadn't watched the game at all. Had he known how it would end and wanted to spare Noa and Dagan the embarrassment?

As he neared the castle, Noa heard his father's voice calling after him. "Noa, wait!" he said, catching up. They rounded the path that led to the entrance. "Where is your chaperone?"

"That's what you care about?" Noa scoffed, lengthening his stride through the courtyard. "Why do I need one?"

"You know it is for your safety," said Titus, frowning. "Why must you fight me on everything?"

"*You* don't have a chaperone. *Edjlin* doesn't have one. I saw him return to the castle alone during the game!"

"You saw Edjlin?"

The pair ascended the stone steps of the courtyard. Titus followed Noa up the spiraling stairs of the nearest tower as Noa explained what he'd seen.

"It is not our place to question the affairs of Edjlin," concluded Titus. "Edjlin may do as he wishes. He is a king."

"Crown *me* as king, then," said Noa, entering his chamber. A servant had lit a fire in the fireplace, bringing warmth to Noa's cold, wet clothes. "It's the only way I can do what I want. I'm tired of chaperones, tired of Capture the Conch . . ."

"I created that game to teach you strategy, teamwork, and to prepare you boys for what's out *there*," Titus hissed, pointing to Noa's window. Ignoring him, Noa slipped behind the divider and peeled off his clothes, replacing them with a plain shirt and trousers.

"There are no round twos in life," continued Titus from the other side. "I worry the stories you fill your head with are making you forget this."

Noa emerged and collapsed facedown on his bed, listening to the crackling fire. The last thing he needed right now was a lecture.

"You are top of your class in school and your royal tutors often learn things from you, yet you avoid real-world experience that would solidify your knowledge."

Noa didn't move from the bed. He thought it was rich of his father to say such a thing. It was Titus who first made Noa fear the world by making rules they could never leave the island. The one time Titus had broken his own rule, someone lost their life.

". . . perhaps if you spent more time with me and less time . . . what's this?"

"Hmpf," came Noa's muffled reply through the pillow. Titus said nothing more, so Noa lifted his head.

His father stood in silence over his desk, examining the maps Noa had drawn about the body from the beach.

"Don't look at that!" said Noa, jumping to his feet. "It's nothing!"

"Secret passages to the docks? Ocean currents that lead away from the island?" Noa stared at his father, his heart drumming in his chest. "You're running away?"

"No!"

"Then, explain this," said Titus, pointing at the desk. "Why do the currents lead to this beach? What else did you find there?"

Noa swallowed under his father's viper glare. After a moment or two of silence, he resigned, telling him about the skeleton and the mysterious pendant.

Titus's stare sharpened to a point as he held out his open palm in silence. Bitterly Noa complied, opening the drawer which held the pendant and handing it over. Titus took one look at the necklace before closing his fist around it.

"You kept this from me? Your own father—your *king*?" He suddenly looked around. "Wilson was with you, wasn't he? A fine job he's done watching over you! Where is he? I'll have him locked away for his disloyalty!"

Noa threw his hands in the air. "Wilson's not real! We made him up!" he blurted out.

"WHAT?" said Titus, outraged.

"You wouldn't let us go in our own courtyard without someone watching. What did you expect?"

Immediately Noa regretted what he'd said, but he had little time to process the damage when Dagan waltzed in. Completely failing to read the room, he asked if he could shoot off coconut bombs at the twins' house to get his mind off the disappointing game.

"Now before you say no," Dagan added to an already fuming Titus, "we'll have plenty of water in case of a fire, and don't worry, Wilson will be there the whole time."

Noa swore steam had started blowing out of his father's ears. Titus's face contorted, his cheeks flushed, his thundering voice stuttered, "GET—OUT—NOW!"

Dagan scampered away as fast as his legs could take him. Titus shoved the pendant into his robe and snatched the maps on the desk. In one sweep, he had gathered the rest of the rolled parchment from Noa's bin. Homemade charts, essays, and diagrams were crinkling under the power of his grip.

Before Noa realized what was happening, Titus had tossed the scrolls into the fire.

"What are you doing!" Noa screeched, rushing to save his life's work. He tried to pull them from the flames, but Titus blocked him.

"It's for your own good—"

"No! You have no right!" He shoved his father's arm aside and threw himself down to fish the remains of paper from the hot, curling ashes.

"You may be my son, but I am still your king. I'm sorry, Noa..." said Titus, sounding repentant. "It's time you put away your childish fantasies. I wish not to speak of this again."

Noa looked at the bits of charred parchment scattered on the floor in front of him. Titus made his way to the door.

"I hate you," said Noa, with all the feeling in his chest.

Titus paused at the door but said nothing. Unable to stand his room any longer, Noa fled the moment his father was out of sight. He shoved a notebook and quill into his Capture the Conch bag and sprinted outside to the one place he still felt he belonged.

It was nearly sunset when Noa emerged from Salaso's Scrolls. He felt much better after losing himself between the pages.

Outside, villagers bustled about closing their shops, hurrying to prepare for the celebration of the princess. Every villager was expected to attend the ball. Noa found Alya sitting on a bench outside the library, and he drank in everything from the red sash around her waist to the curls straying from her bun.

"I know my hair is cravy," she apologized when she caught him staring as he walked toward her. "Crazy-wavy . . . I tried to fix it," she added, tucking a loose curl behind her ear.

"I love it," he whispered. He rarely saw her change from her gray frock and leggings, and by the lack of soot on her dress and the extra inch of fabric dragging on the ground, he assumed it had once belonged to her mother. "You look even better than normal—not that you normally look bad!" he added hastily, blushing.

She smiled politely. They were quiet for several minutes before Alya asked if he was all right.

Noa shrugged.

"It was an unlucky round. We'll win next season," she assured him.

Noa shrugged again, this time a bit heavier. He had spent hours among books, and while he felt a little bit better about the devastating loss of his maps, Noa still had no lead on the pendant from the beach. And between that, losing Capture the Conch, and fighting with his father, he didn't even want to think. He most definitely didn't want to talk. Alya seemed to understand.

"Do you want to go on a walk?" she asked. "We can catch the sunset on the water if we leave now."

Noa agreed, and they strolled down the path to the bay below.

It was hard for Noa to keep from staring. He'd never seen her like this. Once she caught his eye, but he quickly averted his gaze to the trees behind her as if he was searching for something until she looked away.

Sunlight sparkled on the water like red confetti. Tide foamed around their ankles as they walked.

"Did you know there are such things as black beaches?" asked Noa, breaking the silence. "All the sand is black like ashes from a fire. It's made from tiny pieces of volcanic rock."

"Did you read that somewhere?" asked Alya, looking up at him.

Noa nodded.

She left the water and slumped into the cool sand. "You are something else, Noa Blackburn. You must have read every book in Salaso's library."

"Not *every* book." He had, though, at least twice.

As the darkening void above brought out the stars, he

crunched into the sand beside her. They listened to the waves, watching them curl onto shore in a stampede of froth.

"Sometimes when it's quiet like this," said Alya, "I pretend I'm a grown-up. No more school, no more Lady Penebe telling me to sit up in my chair. I want to take over the smithy when my Pop dies. What do you dream about? I'm sure you can't wait to be king."

Noa said nothing. He didn't need to dream of becoming king, for it would happen whether he wanted it to or not. His destiny was set. It wasn't easy to attend school with Alya and the other children and know one day his duties as king could separate them back into different social classes, despite the king himself arranging for Noa, Dagan, and Lana to mingle with the people.

What Noa did dream of was autumn afternoons picnicking in the garden beside his mother. With his baby sister asleep in the empty basket and his brother climbing the orange tree nearby, Noa and his mother could cuddle together on the grass and read book after book . . .

"I think you'll be a great ruler," Alya assured him. "You're smart, kind, creative—when you're king, no pirate in the realm will dare challenge you."

Noa stroked his chin. Pirate? The pendant . . . the symbol . . . a pirate!

He sat up. "Piping pufferfish, *that's* who the skeleton is."

"What skeleton?" she asked in alarm.

Noa clasped his hands together. He really shouldn't say, but it was Alya. He could tell her anything. He described what he and Dagan had found at the beach, then, ignoring her gaping mouth, explained why it made sense.

"The Death King caused the Battle of the Mines, right? When the Battle of the Mines ended, soldiers didn't know how to fit back into society; they only knew how to be warriors. Many of them turned to piracy after that, joining the pirates of the outer seas, and my father led the movement to bring all pirates to justice."

"Yes, I remember," said Alya, scratching her head. "We learned that from our assigned reading last month, *The Island of—*"

"*—Antiquity: A History of Ondule.*" Noa finished her sentence. "I reread it today in Salaso's Scrolls, but I didn't make the connection. My father held executions on our island, but my mother didn't approve of the death penalty. He must have hidden the execution."

Alya looked skeptical, but Noa ran his hand through his hair. "Pirates are the one thing my father hates. It's no wonder he took the pendant," he mumbled under his breath.

A chilled wind flowed through their clothes, tingling their skin. Alya scooted closer. Noa stared at the sea, not wanting to appear too excited about her new position.

"I have to tell Dagan. He'll kill me if I don't."

Alya laughed. "It's too late for that. You should have seen how mad he was when he found out you were missing. With you gone, he's probably worried Lana will start trying to braid his hair."

They both gasped.

"Lana! The party!"

"Maybe we haven't missed too much," Alya panted, running beside him down the beach. They neared the cliffs, and a distant orchestra echoed from the castle.

Clunk clunk. Clunk clunk.

"What was *that*?" Noa slowed, squinting into the dark bay. A longboat floated at the base of the cliff below the castle, knocking against the rock. Moonlight shone over the men inside, who were starting to jump out and climb the rocks.

"The entire village is at Lana's party," whispered Alya. "I don't think that boat belongs to this island. Look." She pointed ahead.

Noa followed her finger until he saw two unknown ships bobbing in the waves behind the longboat, black flags flying at their sterns. He gasped.

"Pirates!"

"Stay down, or they'll see us!" Alya hissed, pulling him into the damp sand. Grit coated his front, clinging to his forearms and knees as he crawled across the beach toward the trees. The anger Noa had for his father morphed into fear. Were the intruders here to kill the king?

"We have to warn my father."

In the security of the blackened jungle, they scampered up the steep path to the castle.

"Where are the guards?" asked Alya, out of breath. She surveyed the empty castle wall above her.

"Keeping watch inside, guarding the halls against guests. You remember what Pan and Fig did last year, don't you?"

"The pillow fight in your father's chamber? I remember," she said heavily, and she followed Noa to a clump of bushes. "What are we doing here?"

"We'll never reach my father fast enough if we have to push through crowds at the main entrance," he said, pulling vines and tree branches away from the castle wall. "This is a secret passage to my father's chamber. Dagan found it when he was seven."

Alya helped him tear vines from a wooden door in the ground until she found a rusty latch. The door groaned as she pulled it open, and they dropped into the hole.

Stale air swallowed them. "Alya?"

"I'm here," she whispered.

"It's not far," he assured her, feeling the stone wall to guide him. "There's a stash of emergency weapons stored behind the coconut mead barrels in the cellar. Grab as many weapons as you can carry and hand them out to guests at the ball, just in case. I'll find my father."

They stumbled awkwardly in the dark until their eyes adjusted, and they could see the staircase that led to the king's room. The orchestra's muffled music played in the throne room above. To their right, a different hall wafted the fermented smell of drinks aging in their barrels.

Noa wiped his dirty palms on his breeches and reminded her not to enter the throne room through the trapdoor.

"Trapdoor is secret," she repeated. "Got it. Be careful, Noa."

Inside the king's chamber, Noa could no longer hear the orchestra's lively melody. In the dark, he felt around him, brushing over a conch shell and a feather quill on the table before

64

he bumped headfirst into his father's bedpost while trying to find his way to the door.

Without warning, a thick arm seized him around the neck. Noa squirmed and kicked. He hollered for help, but a hand slapped over his mouth and muffled his screams.

"You'll never find it!" the man snarled in Noa's ear.

Despite the giant palm squashing his lips, Noa managed to get out, "Fa-er?"

"Noa?" The grip relaxed, and Noa whirled around.

Titus stepped back against the wall, his bushy hair a black halo around his face.

"How did you—? Never mind, you must leave before they come." Titus hurried past him to a canvas of the island hanging on the wall and began feeling around the edges with his bear-like hands.

Noa watched him suspiciously. "You know about the pirates?" he asked.

"They aren't just pirates. Quick! Bring me my dagger."

Noa snatched a dagger from the desk drawer. Titus peeled off the canvas with the blade's tip, but not before Noa noticed a familiar symbol on the canvas. It was the symbol from the pendant.

"Why is *that* on there?" Noa asked, pointing to the symbol. Titus ignored the question. Instead, he reached inside the hole he'd made between the canvas and the frame and pulled out a rolled piece of parchment.

"Take this," he said, shoving the parchment and dagger into Noa's hands. Then he pressed the canvas back onto the frame until it appeared as if nothing had been inside at all. "Listen to me. This is a map. Above all else, you must keep it safe. Do you understand?"

Since pirates invading the island was slightly more important than their fight earlier, Noa nodded. "Yes, Father."

"You cannot destroy it."

"I won't, Father."

"You *cannot* destroy it," Titus repeated. "It will not rip. It will not burn."

Noa scrunched his brow in confusion. What paper didn't burn?

"There's more," said Titus, cupping Noa's hands in his own. He held his son's gaze. "I need you to follow the map. You're good at following maps, best on the island, and now more than ever you must do it . . . it is your time to protect your people. This makes little sense to you, I know, but you can save us all if you leave the island now and follow where it leads."

Had Noa heard his father correctly?

"Leave the island? Without you? But . . . the ocean . . ."

"The ocean is perilous, yes, and everything I've done has been to protect you and your siblings from it, but I fear there is more danger for us all if you stay. We need you. You know more facts than all my libraries put together—use your knowledge to find your way."

While this may have been true, Noa stared at the rolled parchment, a sickening wave of fear rising in him. There were a hundred ways he had imagined his father looking him in the eye and telling him he needed him, but this was not one of them.

For a moment, he considered his father had gone mad. No child left the island. That was the rule, the rule *his father* had made. And it was one of the only rules Noa believed in too.

Plus there was the matter of sailing. He hadn't been on a ship in years, let alone sailed one on his own, although his extensive research on the subject would help. Was his father, who had never allowed Noa to leave the castle without a chaperone for fear he could get hurt, honestly suggesting that Noa take on the ocean by himself?

He squeezed the map and looked at his father. "Where will it take me? The map . . . where does it lead?" A clash of metal resounded from the hallway.

"You will see soon enough," said Titus hurriedly, trying to push Noa toward the secret door. "Don't open it until you are alone. My son," he added, suddenly woeful, "I'm afraid our world is not what you think . . . forgive me . . . forgive an old man for thinking he knew what was best."

This made Noa pause, and he felt a fire ignite like a match inside him. The last time Titus said he knew best, Noa's mother paid the price. He didn't want the map any longer.

"I'm not following this," he said, dropping it on the ground. "You haven't even told me where it—"

Another clash of metal and the roar of men's voices came from behind the door. Titus shoved Noa into the tunnel and tossed the map in after him, a pleading look in his eyes.

"Save us, my son. Follow it until the end."

The door slammed. Noa heard the curtain sweep aside to cover the passage. Within seconds, the door of his father's bedroom crashed open. In the darkness, Noa pressed his ear against the keyhole and listened to men burst into the room, many recognizable by their drawling accents as the pirates Noa grew up reading about in stories.

"What is the meaning of this? These are my private chambers. I order you to leave at once!"

"I'm afraid they can't do that, Titus."

"Edjlin . . ." whispered Titus. "This is not who you are."

"Where is the map?"

Titus didn't answer.

"Don't be a hero. I have your lovely party guests surrounded as we speak. I know you have it, and I know it is in this room. You slipped up too much when we were young, telling me all your family secrets, but now it's time. Give it to me."

"It's not here."

Edjlin's limping steps came closer: a war injury Noa had never had the chance to ask him about. "Titus, be reasonable."

"Why are you doing this? Why now, on Lana's special day? I thought you cared for my family!"

"Of course I care, but I cannot wait any longer. You know why I need it. And this day is the only event of the year your entire island is occupied in the castle. Your generosity to the people of Ondule has left you defenseless, and for that, you have only yourself to blame."

Noa heard a slap through the door.

"Tell us where be the map!" said an unfamiliar voice.

"Rot in the sea, you filthy pirate!" hollered the king.

Another slap, but this time Titus seemed to retaliate. Crashes and bangs resounded from inside his chamber. Noa sat in horror behind the door, his mind racing so fast it paralyzed him. Where were the guards? Should he go in and help? Should he run away as his father wanted?

Then Titus howled in pain, and Noa knew it was over.

"We got 'em, boys!"

"Hit him again!"

Noa couldn't peel himself away. His knees were trembling, and nauseating spurts of adrenaline coursed through his veins, turning his grip on the map to soft butter. But he couldn't move. What would become of his kingdom if he stayed? What would become of him if he left?

His father could tell him. His father loved to tell him what to do and claim he knew best, but then it was not his father's fault that Edjlin had betrayed them all. Even a man like his father did not deserve to be stabbed in the back by his best friend.

"Psssst! Noa?"

Noa jumped. Alya had returned from the cellar, and through the flickering torchlight he could see a bow and quiver on her back. Had she already handed out the secret stash of weapons to the party guests?

Her face told him everything: she had been too late.

"They've taken everyone hostage!" she whispered frantically. "I didn't know what to do!"

Noa's heart sunk at the thought of Lana in the throne room with neither her father nor himself to protect her, but the noise from his father's bedroom stopped him from any attempt at replying. Noa and Alya crouched together on the stairs. Inside the room, pirates opened drawers and overturned tables, looking for the map.

"Ah yes, the painting. I should have known," said Edjlin at last.

The sound of ripping canvas echoed across the stone walls, followed by a long, uncomfortable pause. Then, smashes of furniture against stone erupted from the room as Edjlin cursed in rage at the empty hiding spot.

"Titus! GIVE ME THAT MAP!"

A deafening bang exploded against their eardrums, throwing Noa and Alya back. Someone had thrown a heavy object, a piece of furniture perhaps, and it had smashed against the secret door behind the curtain. The hollow sound which rang out was followed by menacing laughter.

"What've we got 'ere? Another way out?" said a pirate.

"A secret door!" said Edjlin. "Until I have that map, I am taking control of this kingdom. Some leaves are fated to fall, Titus. Thus, I'm afraid your fall is now."

Footsteps approached. Noa and Alya fled. Deep within the tunnel, their feet splashed, echoing alongside their panting in the darkness.

"What's happening?" gasped Alya, climbing out of the tunnel into the muggy night.

Crickets orchestrated their wings among the cicadas, oblivious to the frenzied pair. Noa followed her outside and tied a vine through the latch to stop anyone from following them. It felt like he was trapping his family with every bad man on the island, and to say it made him ill was an understatement.

"This is all Edjlin's doing."

"King Edjlin? Isn't he our ally?"

"He *was* our ally!" Noa bowed his head, trying to think. "We need to hide."

"People are trapped in the castle," Alya protested. "My family's in there!"

"I can't help them!"

Or could he? Should he keep the map? One toss over the cliff could stop Edjlin from getting what he wanted. Noa would face the same fate as everyone else on the island.

Thoughts did somersaults in his head . . . leaving his people felt cowardly, like something his father would do . . . but his father had also said using the map would save them. Could he truly save everyone by doing this one thing? He wanted to. He didn't want to let his family down. Not again.

Noa stared at the lighthouse on the edge of the cliff, his father's last words replaying in his mind: *Follow it until the end.*

"Noa? Are you listening to me? What do we do?"

Noa blinked back into awareness. He spoke without a moment to change his mind.

"We're leaving the island," he said. "Tonight."

CHAPTER 4

FIRE SHIPS

Few times in his life had Noa run full speed through a jungle without swatting away the spiderwebs first, and after regurgitating the mummified mayfly from his throat, he vowed he would never do it again. A cluster of Edjlin's soldiers sprinted down the path after them, their armor clanging with each step. Noa and Alya ducked beneath mail waterways and raced into the village to hide.

"Are they gone?" asked Alya, peering around a barrel.

"Who's gone?" said a voice behind them.

Noa and Alya spun around.

"Dag? You got away!"

"Got away?" Dagan repeated, confused. "I thought the point was to *be* with Lana on her birthday. I've been looking for you for ages. Thought you fell asleep inside Salaso's Scrolls again."

Squinting at Dagan in the dark, Noa realized his brother's hair was coiffed into a perfect lick and he still had a starch crease in his dress shorts. Not even Dagan could maintain a look of such finery if he had escaped the castle and run through the steamy jungle like they had. Alya's wired curls spiraling around her sweaty face were proof of that.

"Dag, the castle is under attack . . ."

"That cockroach-licking traitor!" roared Dagan after Noa told him everything. "Where does this map go? Doesn't Edjlin have enough treasure?"

"I'm not certain it leads to treasure. Edjlin said he wanted some kind of venom, and then he called father a Map Keeper. If Father had been entrusted to guard this map, it must be important, and it leads off the island."

"I'm coming with you," said Dagan without hesitation.

"You will *not*. If I die, you will be heir to the throne." He leaned closer for a better look at the kerchief around Dagan's neck. "Isn't that mine? I've been looking for that!"

"Priorities, Noa," Dagan reminded him. "You think I'm going to stay here while you go on an adventure? Get over yourself."

"*Pardon me?*"

"I don't need your permission. It's my kingdom too. Besides," he added, with an air of superiority. "I know you want me to come."

Alya ended the charade with a single word. "Come."

They sprinted down the street and snuck into Alya's home to gather supplies. Swords, daggers, and bows hung on the walls above bins of arrows. The place smelled of smoke from years of blacksmith work: not foul, but almost sweet, like burnt honey.

"You'll want better shoes," Alya said, noticing Noa's sandals. "I'll be right back."

She left to the cellar. Seconds later, they heard her scream.

"Alya!" Noa cried, jumping down the stairs after her. Instantly he was boggled by the sight before them.

Two oil lamps lit a long table, and twelve boys sat huddled around it. Playing cards were dealt in front of each boy next to mountains of banquet sweets which they were using as gambling money.

"Well, fry me a flounder and cook me a cake," said Dagan, marching to the edge of the table. "You should all be at my sister's party!"

The boys looked self-consciously around the room. Even Vim was present.

"Neither of you are there," said Bones, avoiding their eyes as he shuffled the cards.

"It was a bust anyway!" said Pan.

"A flop!" agreed his twin, Fig. "All of our parents bought her the same *Mer-tales of Aztrius* book. We could have made a fort with all those copies. Our parents actually think that's what we're doing right now—making a fort in Noa's bedroom. We figure we have another hour before they notice we've left."

Alya put her hands on her hips. "So, instead you decided to invade my father's smithy?"

"We didn't *invade* it," said Bones. "Aaron invited us."

Alya glared at her little brother, who cowered in his chair.

A familiar, shiny object lay on top of the gambling sweets. Noa made his way toward it.

"Where did you get this?" he asked, picking up the pirate pendant.

"Oi, got to play if you want the winnings," chimed Pan.

"We nicked it from a room in the castle," said Fig proudly as he discarded his cards. "I fold."

"My *father's* room?" said Noa testily.

"Course not," Fig laughed. "We wouldn't risk doing that again. The bed had blue blankets."

"That's my father's room," said Noa dully.

Fig thought for a moment, then smacked his twin on the arm. "I *told* you his blankets weren't red. Noa's blankets are the red ones."

Noa's blankets were not red at all, leaving him very curious to know how many rooms the twins had broken into before giving up to play cards.

"You know . . . this could work," said Dagan, chewing on his nail. "We have enough here to fight back."

Alya shook her head. "We are not fighting back. We're leaving the island."

"Leaving the island?" repeated Chaston, twisting his blond ponytail around his finger. Noa knew little about the quiet older boy, except that he belonged to one of the biggest families on the island and routinely supplied the twins with coconut bombs.

Excited chatter spread around the room. Noa lifted his hands to quiet them, then explained pirates had invaded. Much like

Dagan, the boys stared. A few chuckles circulated through the group.

Pan smacked his lips thoughtfully. "This is some special training, isn't it?" he said, casually pulling a king of hearts from inside his afro and exchanging it for a two of spades. "Royal flush," he declared, spreading his hand of hearts on the table. Groans rose from the group as the twin pulled in his winnings.

"Wait, so what's happening?" said Bones. "Something about pirates?"

Dagan pounded his fist on a pair of tens. "Weren't you listening?"

The baker's son, Jonath, plucked dough off his sleeve and rolled it between his fingers in irritation. "Stop playing around," he said.

"We're not playing around," said Noa, his voice rising. "Don't you get it? Our families are locked in the castle. Alya and I have been running for our lives through the jungle! We have to leave to find help!" The more Noa said it, the more it angered him. He had known Edjlin his whole life. How could the king betray them?

A murmur broke out among the boys. Some threw their cards on the table, and many of them were standing up now, so confused they didn't know what to do.

"It's against the law to leave the island at our age!"

"Why do you have special privileges?" asked another.

Alya pushed through the grumbling group and dropped a pair of high-ankle boots at Noa's feet, instructing him to put them on and stuff a dagger in each boot like she'd seen her father do. Noa hadn't noticed her gathering supplies. He did as he was told, clinging to the chance to disappear from the crowd.

Soft jingling echoed above as he tightened his laces. It grew louder, and then Noa heard footsteps shuffle upstairs.

He reared up in panic. "They're here!" he hissed.

No one moved at first, but the terror in Noa's eyes made each of them snap into action. Boys jumped out of their seats to hide. Aaron had to be pulled from the table by the twins when he wouldn't stop stuffing pastry winnings into his pockets. Boys sidled in between boxes of dried pork strips and jars of pickled beets before Alya plunged the cellar into darkness.

Creeeeeeeeeeeeeak. The door opened.

Hiding beneath the stairs, Noa covered his mouth to quiet his breathing. Bones crouched beside him and silently pointed up. Then he motioned for Noa to help him grab the guard's feet through the stairs. Noa hesitated. It was too risky. One wrong move and the guards would have possession of the map. Everything his father did to protect it would be for naught.

Two guards stomped down the steps, pausing right above Noa's red locks. Before he could stop himself and against his better judgment, Noa lunged through the stairs with Bones and yanked the soldiers' feet from under them. The men yelped. Armor crashed as they tumbled down and lay sprawled at the bottom of the steps.

"Everyone, upstairs!" Noa shouted. Dagan rushed from his hiding spot behind the laundry, flinging Aaron's skivvies off his head. Boys squeezed out of cupboards and fell off shelves before bolting up the steps after Noa.

"Ahhh yeah, this is better than Capture the Conch," said Malloch, the sailor's son, after they locked the guards in the cellar. "They looked like real soldiers!"

Noa pushed through the crowded room to find the twins, who owned a small fishing boat. They wasted little time in determining how many people could fit on it and what that meant for the ones staying behind, and soon Noa, Dagan, Alya, and Aaron were preparing to leave. The others huddled around the twins as they discussed acts of sabotage they could inflict on the unwelcome visitors.

"Malloch, Chaston, and Vim, you handle the ground traps," instructed Pan. "Leave the canopy net to us. It's tricky to set up."

Noa creaked open the door to peer outside. The coast was clear. When they were ready, he led the boys into the empty streets toward the bay.

Shattered glass glinted in the moonlight beneath a broken mailing pipe. Water gushed out of its thin spout to the road below, carrying broken mail bottles across the street to the busted house doors. The Pigeon Post had been overturned, its sign tossed several feet away.

Smoked mango and pine smells began to fill the night air. At first, the aroma smelled pleasant, but it quickly became overpowering until Noa found himself coughing to catch a full breath.

"Do you see that?" Alya asked, coughing and pointing ahead.

Noa followed her gaze to a warm glow from the bay. It couldn't be morning yet. A blast echoed in the distance. Noa rubbed his watering eyes and sprinted into the trees until he reached a clearing, at last witnessing the origin of the glow.

The bay was on fire.

Noa stared slack-jawed at the flames consuming the fleet. The others soon joined him. Black snow rose above the bay and sprinkled over the island. Ship masts toppled, ablaze, detonating their explosive cargo, and hulls crackled as they began to sink.

"Mango wood . . ." Noa sniffed the air now reeking of acrid mangoes, smoke, and the burning oil drenched over the ships. He should have known he was smelling mango wood. Every ship was made of it.

No one else spoke, or, it seemed, remembered how.

An explosion sent wood splinters showering onto the docks, where Noa located the twins' fishing boat ablaze on the water. Leaving the island was proving harder by the minute. He tried not to look at the castle, where fighting had broken out in rebellion on the castle walls. He didn't want to picture Lana in the chaos. As soon as he could, he promised he would return for her.

"Not everything has been destroyed," said Dagan, pointing across the bay with one hand, his other hand shading his eyes from the flaming bay. "There."

Across the flaming bay next to the castle cliff were two ships. Behind them, a third ship's silhouette appeared in the dark.

"Is that—?" Noa began.

Dagan grinned. "King Edjlin's boat? Yup. If he wants to take our ships, then we will take his."

"You ain't serious," said Vim haughtily. "Ya can't sail the *Evangeline*!"

Bones stepped forward. "You'd need at least ten people to sail it. There are fifteen of us. We're coming with you, right boys?"

A rebellious spark ignited in the boys' eyes. They each agreed to come. Noa readjusted his sack carrying the map with new determination, then knelt on the ground.

"The *Evangeline* is the farthest out to sea. The other two ships are dropping people on the banks here and here," he said, drawing a diagram in the dirt with his finger. "She should be empty, but we'll need a diversion from shore just in case. That's where you come in." He nodded to the group of boys around him. "Once you see us sailing the *Evangeline*, stop the diversion and wait at the West Dock."

The twins immediately began plotting to trap oncoming soldiers in fishing nets.

"How d'ya expect to reach the *Evangeline*?" asked Vim, his hands on his hips. He'd been the only one who hadn't agreed to help. "You ain't swimming."

In the bay, another explosion from the royal fleet sent wood showering into the water below.

"Leave that part to us," said Dagan, slicking back his hair. He turned to Noa and Alya. "Let's go."

Alya squeezed inside a crumbling building behind Noa and Dagan. "If this collapses, we're all going to die," she said nervously.

Moonlight streamed through cracks in the lighthouse stone. Noa squished against the wall. He'd almost lost it when he realized where Dagan was taking them, but he had to admit his brother was right. They needed a diversion, and no one would expect them to hide right under the castle's nose.

"Don't light a fire," Dagan jested, eyeing the gunpowder barrels stacked in towering heaps around them.

Sandwiched between the wall and Dagan, Alya hissed, "Move *over*, Dagan, I can't breathe! What was your father thinking putting all this gunpowder here? The lighthouse is falling apart. Ouch! That's my foot!"

Noa leaned against a stack of barrels to give Alya more room. "You didn't expect him to store gunpowder in the castle, did you? Not after what happened when he was our age."

"He accidentally blew up the west wing!" Dagan explained happily, in answer to Alya's blank expression. "That's where I got the idea!"

Noa nodded. "See? It's much better here. The lighthouse has weathered storms for over a century—" Noa looked at Dagan, all at once aware of what had been said. "What do you mean that's where you got the idea?"

"My idea to blow up the lighthouse," explained Dagan, grinning.

Noa and Alya gawked.

"*WHAT?*" they said in unison.

"Clever, don't you think?" Oblivious to their stunned expressions, Dagan unraveled the tied-up barrels, wrapping the rope around his forearm. "Don't worry, by the time it blows up, we'll be climbing down the cliff."

Alya gasped. "*That* cliff? It's suicide!"

Noa didn't know why he was surprised. This was a typical

idea from the brain of his brother. "This is just swell," he said miserably. "Just. Swell. We'll never leave the island alive."

"Listen to my whole plan before you mope around like I've ordered a death sentence," said Dagan, hoisting the coiled rope over his shoulder. "You and I can climb down to the ships—just like they do at the quarry—and swim out to the *Evangeline*. Once we're there, Alya will blow up the lighthouse as a diversion. There's no chance Edjlin will notice his ship leaving the bay if he's putting out the fire up here."

At the mention of her blowing up the lighthouse, Alya produced a look that could cut through stone. Noa was quiet for a moment before he admitted they didn't have time to come up with a different plan.

"Unbelievable," she scoffed, waving her finger at Noa. "You always say the lighthouse is a historical landmark. It's the symbol of our flag!"

Noa groaned. "Believe me, if I had a better idea, we'd be doing it already." Then he had a better idea. "What if we blow up the cliff too? It will crush the ships below!"

Dagan couldn't contain his glee. "Spittin' pies—you're as mad as me!" he chirped, but this proved too much for Alya, and she angrily spread her arms out in front of the door.

"You've both lost your minds! You'll blow up the whole castle!"

"I have crazier ideas if you want," Dagan pointed out, sidling to the door until their noses almost touched. "Your job is easiest. We need muscles to go down the cliff."

Alya glared at his face, still just inches from her own. Then she pinched his gut, and he squealed in pain.

"Oops," said Alya, batting her eyelashes.

"Break it up," said Noa. "Alya, when you see us swimming to the *Evangeline*, that's your cue to blow up the lighthouse. Then meet us at the docks."

Alya shook her head.

"The ships are right next to the cliff," Noa went on. "Edjlin knows we've never found the sea floor there, and he's using it to his advantage."

"But what if—?"

"If anything goes wrong, we'll jump into the water. It won't hurt us." Noa stole a sidelong glance at his brother before returning his attention to Alya. "Use an arrow to light the barrels. You have the best shot of anyone on the island. It's all right. You can do this."

She stared at them, fingering the string of her bow, which hung on her shoulder. Ever so slightly, she moved away from the door.

CHAPTER 5

THE ONE-EYED PIRATE

"**H**urry *up*," Dagan whined. Crisscrossing the rope over his legs and back in a makeshift harness, he squatted to begin his rappel. "Someone might see us!"

Noa followed Dagan's instructions and weaved the second rope around his own body. His hands couldn't stop shaking. He glanced at the two ships moored below, then at the *Evangeline* another three hundred yards out to sea, seriously doubting the sanity of their recent choices.

"I will see you jump off the ship, won't I?" asked Alya nervously.

"Mm-hmm." Noa couldn't even open his mouth after seeing the distance; his lips had suddenly gone numb.

Alya embraced him, letting him breathe the smoky scent of her hair.

"Steady . . . steady . . ." Dagan instructed moments later when Alya had left them alone. He inched carefully over the edge.

Noa's stomach somersaulted. Feeding the rope through his thighs, he leaned back and inched over the lip of the cliff until the overhang left him dangling in the air, the line tightening snuggly against his groin and shoulders. Dagan descended with such enthusiasm that Noa briefly considered his brother was insane, but at least they weren't dead yet. *That* was something to be excited about.

The breezy air developed into a warm wave as they lowered. Most ships had scorched and sunk, but some still flared, the fire rapidly consuming any wood set in its path. Noa's sack felt like a boulder on his back. Sweat coated his raw palms as the rope slid through, but the pain was nothing compared to what he felt in his heart. His home. His family. He was at war, and his entire island depended on him to save them.

"It's farther than I imagined," moaned Dagan, when the rope ended a couple of yards above the crow's nest. Seaweed surf below cradled longboats full of men, unaware of the boys above them.

SNAP.

Noa looked up at the broken thread protruding awkwardly from its yellow braid. In a voice much higher than usual, Noa asked, "How strong are these—?"

A second frayed end popped off his rope. Dagan hollered at him to swing to the crow's nest.

"On the count of three, we both let go!" said Dagan, jiggling his rope until he could push off the rocky cliff. Noa didn't want to look down. At this height, a fall would most definitely break every bone in his body, unlike what he'd told Alya.

A third *Snap!* announced Noa's rope had only one strand left to hold him. Dagan counted. Kicking the rope off their legs, the boys rebounded off the cliff and swung into the air toward the ship.

"Someone's in the crow's nest!" Noa cried, as they swung back like a pendulum for the last time.

"Too late!" shouted Dagan.

The force of the rock wall shocked through their shoes and sent them soaring toward the mast. Noa's final strand of rope snapped like the crack of a whip. He couldn't help but scream as he flew through the night air and slammed into the railing. It knocked the wind out of him.

Dagan tumbled inside the crow's nest and barreled into the sailor. He struggled with the crewman, then *pop!* Clutching his nose, the sailor toppled backward and bounced off the diagonal shrouds into the water.

"Help!" Noa gasped, hanging over the edge.

Dagan pulled Noa into the crow's nest, gawking at his own strength. "I just knocked out a grown-up!"

Looking around, Noa realized the sailors aboard this ship were Edjlin's army. The ship next to theirs belonged to pirates. And the *Evangeline* . . . well, he hoped he was right that the *Evangeline* was empty.

"Do you think they heard the splash?" asked Dagan.

"Man overboard!" the crew shouted from below, as they tossed the fallen crewman a rope.

They had heard the splash, all right.

Noa's hands were hot enough to fry an egg. The rope had torn his skin raw. He ripped the bottom of his shirt and wrapped it around his sticky palms, wincing at the sting, then did the same to Dagan. The metallic odor from his brother's rope-burned hands turned his stomach.

Tying the fabric in a knot, Noa turned Dagan's attention to the topgallant sail above them.

"If we cut that sail off the beam, I can get us off the ship. It's something Captain Herring did in book three of *Hazardous Heroics*."

"*Hazardous Heroics* . . ." Dagan repeated thoughtfully. "Wait a minute . . . is that the stunt we were trying to do when I broke my leg?"

Noa cringed guiltily. "Don't worry, it will work this time. We just need a bigger cloth."

Dagan narrowed his eyes. "If I break anything, you're dead meat."

Noa pulled a dagger from his boot and bit down on the blade, then carefully climbed up the beam and started sawing at the fabric sail. Nerves buzzed inside him. High. He was very high up.

"Be careful!" he hissed when Dagan followed him onto the beam and nonchalantly let go to fix his hair.

Suddenly, an arrow whizzed over Noa's head and dug into the mast above them. Noa shouted at Dagan to hurry. The ratline shook. Men were ascending with swords in their mouths.

"They're coming up!" Dagan yelled. The boy scurried back into the crow's nest and began cutting knots off the ratline as fast as they could. Men fell in thuds, followed swiftly by the ratline itself. It dropped to the deck like a deadweight.

Another arrow whizzed past Noa's ear, throwing him off balance. That action caused him to see the explosion first.

A white cloud burst on top of the cliff. For a split second, there was silence. Then the deafening eruption of gunpowder and snapping rock filled the air.

"She did it! She blew up the lighthouse!"

"But we're not off the ship yet!" Dagan cried.

Pieces of lighthouse rained down around them, smashing onto the deck or splashing into the water, and a deep crack had formed beneath the cliff's overhang. Panic rose from the two ships. People began abandoning their posts and diving into the sea.

Noa tore the sail off the beam and thrust it into Dagan's arms as he clambered back into the crow's nest. With shaking hands, they each grabbed two corners of the rectangular fabric. If he had calculated correctly, they would glide down to the water just like the character from his book. At least, that was his hope.

"JUMP!" Noa screamed. They dropped down . . . down . . . down toward the deck. Catching the wind as they fell, the sail inflated and carried them slowly through the air.

"It's working!" Dagan cheered.

"I know it's working! Now lean left!"

Gliding lopsided over the water toward the *Evangeline*, wind whistling in his ears, Noa was unable to keep the grin off his face. Stars above them reflected off the water below, lighting their path. He couldn't believe it had actually worked.

"THIS IS AMAZING!" Dagan hollered into the night.

Behind them, the cliffside smashed onto the ship with a deafening crunch. Ocean flushed over their heads, and Noa's grip slid down the cloth. Blinking through the salty shower, pain searing through his hands, he held the fabric as though his life depended on it. Because it did.

With a rock fall that large, he knew it hadn't ended. As expected, the wave came next.

Water rushed under their toes in the biggest tidal surge Noa had ever seen. Noa lifted his feet to avoid dipping them into the crest of dark water. Moving on, the wave slapped the starboard side of the nearby ship and swept away the pirates on deck. Then it moved on and smashed into the *Evangeline*'s bow, flushing water all the way to her stern.

"DID YOU *SEE* THAT WAVE?"

"Shut up! There might be another—"

The second wave clipped their feet, spinning them around. Dagan let go first, pulling Noa down with him, and they spilled into the sea.

Muffled silence cloaked Noa the moment he dipped into the black, shapeless depths. Salt seared into his cuts and scrapes, his rope-burned palms the worst of them all. A debris cloud engulfed him when he surfaced, and he spun around in the bobbing swells, coughing and looking for Dagan. Dust settled into the sea, revealing the timber giant mooring in the dark. Clinging to the ship's barnacles was his brother.

"Over here! I've found the gunport." Dagan jerked his head to the opening above him.

Noa swam over and grasped the prickly barnacle casings. Sharks often gathered around docked ships because of the waste thrown overboard, and this thought crossed Noa's mind when another wave splattered over him.

"Let's make one thing clear," said Noa, spitting out the liquid salt. "If we ever come up with ideas like that again, spear me."

"Are you reelin' me in? I want to do it again!" Dagan lifted himself into the gunport and slid over the barrel onto the floor of the lower deck. Then, as an afterthought, poked his head out and said, "I'd have a serious talk with your girlfriend, though. She tried to kill us."

"She did not," said Noa, following after him. "And she's not my girlfriend. She must have thought the man falling overboard was us swimming away."

"Whatever you say, fish lips," said Dagan, puckering his lips to make a kissing noise.

The spacious lower deck held twenty cast-iron cannons on each side, all facing out to sea. Straw mattresses in wooden bunks lined the walls in between the guns, separated by flowing canvas sheets. The entire place reeked of a mixture of seaweed and sweaty men.

Noa tiptoed around the bunks. Water left over from the enormous wave dripped onto the rungs of the ladder. The ship lurched forward, and the sound of rushing water resonated from the gunports. The *Evangeline* had set sail.

"Where did you get that? Put it away!" said Noa when Dagan

jogged toward him wearing a spare breastplate and helmet. The armor was so big he could practically swim in it.

Dagan shrugged. "It might come in handy." He climbed the ladder and poked his head above deck, then dropped down a moment later. "There are nine or ten soldiers watching the shore on portside. Portside is left if you didn't—"

"I know what portside is," Noa snapped.

"We can't let the ship reach the cliffs. They're trying to rescue their men."

Noa climbed up the ladder to see for himself. Just as Dagan had explained, soldiers were glued to portside, bows at the ready.

"Around thirty feet to that guy . . . probably another fifteen to that guy . . ." Noa calculated under his breath. "And the barrel would go there . . . dropping over there . . ." Ideas clicked like keys into locked doors, opening new possibilities to stop the enemy crew.

Ten minutes later, Noa and Dagan were suited up in oversized armor, rehearsing Noa's plan to send the entire crew into the sea. Noa had never read of a character in his books doing the stunt he was about to pull, but it seemed like basic science. Weight sinks. Anything caught in its way would go down with it.

"Ready?" asked Dagan, tilting his helmet back so he could see.

Noa hid his sack under a mattress for safekeeping, then tied rope between two heavy barrels. He rolled one barrel to his brother and nodded. "Ready."

Up the ladder Dagan went, the barrel under his arm. Noa followed, holding the tail end of the rope and his own barrel.

The armor hung loose over Noa's shoulders and weighed him down like a bag of rocks, yet no one paid attention as he chinked across the deck. Smoke strangled the shoreline as arrows flew across the water toward the ship, landing dangerously close to the men on board—but it was the diversion Noa had asked for.

Noa lugged his barrel to the last man in the archer lineup, the top of his helmet just barely reaching the height of the man's shoulder. Quickly, he signaled to Dagan that everything was in place.

"You there!" a red-faced captain hollered at Dagan. "Put down that barrel and grab a bow! We're under attack!"

Noa froze. *Not Dagan!*

"Did you hear me, soldier?" the captain barked, his buckles rattling as he stomped closer. Others looked Dagan up and down suspiciously. "Fire at shore! That's an order!"

For a moment, Dagan didn't move. He stared at the captain like a mosquito ogles at lamplight. Then he shook it off and snapped into action. Shoving the barrel into the man's arms, he pushed him over the railing, and the man splashed into the sea. At once, the rope started tightening. Noa tossed his own barrel over the side. It caught soldiers in their backs and slingshotted them over the rails into the water.

"The ship is ours!" Dagan cheered. "Oi! Back to shore or I'll drop this on your head!" A soldier clinging to the gunport took one look at the cannonball in Dagan's hand and let go, falling into the passing waves.

Noa scanned the rustic masts and flapping sails of their victory, amazed his idea had actually worked. With a jolt, he remembered no one was steering the moving ship. Hurrying down the gangway of the main deck, he tore off his armor and threw it to the side.

Then he heard a deep, rumbling voice.

"I suppose you think yer smart, outwitting me crew?"

A man stepped out from the shadows of the captain's quarters. He was dressed in a burgundy overcoat, and a black eye patch covered his right eye. Scars meandered across his face. Noa's eyes flicked from the sword on his waist to the tricorn hat on his head. Instinctively, he knew it was the man he'd seen on Edjlin's ship the previous day. Backing away, Noa abandoned his attempt to reach the wheel.

"Whoa there, Mr. One-Eyed Creepy Man," said Dagan, when the pirate unsheathed his sword. Noa glanced nervously at his brother. "Give up. Your crew's long gone."

The pirate's lips curled into a sick smile. "How rude o' me to not give a proper introduction," he said coolly, his golden earrings swaying as he approached. "They call me Weston."

Noa's mouth dropped. "Weston, the Pirate?"

"Privateer now. I be working under the reign o' King Edjlin," said Weston, flashing a broken-tooth smile.

Noa caught a sword from Dagan and brandished it in front of him, his rope-burned hands baking in their bandages. "You should be in jail," he said through gritted teeth.

"Aye, King Edjlin visited the prison, you see, and asked me to work for 'im. I'm a free man now. Tell me, as me first customers, how do ya feel about trade cards? I'm thinking of advertising me business. Which one sounds better? *Plunder Without*

Blunder—Send Word Now to Get What's Yers, or *Steal the Loot Before Ya Get the Boot—Call On Your Neighborhood Privateer*. Eh?"

"How can you *live* with yourself?" Noa asked in disbelief. "Don't you feel bad?"

Weston smirked. "Never."

Dagan looked the pirate over. "My father told me stories about you," he said, taking off his helmet. "Didn't expect you to be so ugly."

Weston's snarl looked as if it might bite. Then he paused. "Yer father? Oh, this be too delicious. Black hair, sturdy build—yer the king's son, aren't you?" He eyed Noa's red hair, then turned away without interest. "Yer father ruined me life and the lives of many others," Weston went on, his eyes narrowing on Dagan. "I'm simply returnin' the favor."

Heat rushed into Noa's cheeks. "No one was safe at sea with you plundering and terrorizing every ship! You deserve a prison cell."

A spasm of irritation flitted across Weston's face. "He murdered me friends, servant boy, is that not the same?"

Servant boy?

"And yet, revenge is sweet. King Edjlin says Titus has kept many secrets . . ."

Weston absentmindedly tugged a chain around his neck, drawing Noa's attention to the familiar pendant attached to it. Noa stood his ground, eyeing Weston's smug smile with a glow of discontentment. Arrows from shore flew over their heads once again, barely missing them. If their friends on shore weren't careful of their aim, the diversion could easily turn deadly.

"Aye, 'tis a shame yer never gonna know what's out in the sea before you die. What's *really* out there. How's about we have ourselves a little duel? Winner keeps the ship."

"How's about not?" said Noa, moving protectively in front of Dagan.

The pirate licked his lips. "I didn't say you had a choice."

Weston struck with his sword. The brothers split apart and skirted around the pirate, rejoining in the safety of the captain's quarters. Weston followed them inside. He yanked books from the shelf and threw them at their heads. Then he jumped onto the desk, but the boys slid beneath it and escaped out the door.

"Never killed a man before, have ya?" Weston taunted, catching up to them. "Too afraid to fight, eh? I'll make you see the backside of a shark's tooth."

Dagan scratched his head. "Come again?"

"I'm going to kill you."

"Ah."

Weston pointed his sword at their chests. Arrows from the diversion group on shore showered the deck with no intended target, digging into the mast or flying straight past to the water. Noa stared down his blade, the heat growing as they neared the blazing fleet. They had to steer the ship away, or they'd be doomed to crash in the fiery bay.

Quick as lightning, the pirate swung and they jumped away, tripping over their feet. Noa fell on his back, banging his head against the deck, and there was a howl of pain—yet it wasn't Noa who had cried out.

Squinting through white stars, Noa watched Weston pull a

bloody arrow from his arm. The pirate staggered backward. It took Noa a moment to understand that one of the diversionary arrows from shore had hit the pirate.

"Mark my words," Weston huffed, wincing as he steadied himself against a deadeye. "We will meet again." Struggling to pull himself up the railing, he flopped over the side, barely making a splash.

Dagan reached the wheel first and pulled it hard over. Cargo rolled to the opposite end of the deck as the *Evangeline* cut into the sea away from the flaming ships and sailed broadside to shore.

Wiping his brow, Dagan laughed. "See? You can't learn everything from books."

They sailed parallel to shore, scraping the charred crow's nest of a sunken ship as they neared the dock where the others awaited their return. Noa gazed at the hazy horizon, the bloody stains on his bandages spreading like watercolor paint. How could he leave his people, his sister, with traitors and pirates? His eyes met Dagan's, and he knew his brother wondered the same.

At the sight of the group, Noa threw a rope. It slapped the water, and boys dove in to scale the ladder on the vessel's side. Alya was nowhere to be seen.

"Grab hold! We can't stop!" Noa instructed to those remaining on the docks. Then he caught the nearest boy as he came up the ship ladder. "Jonath, where's Alya?"

"I thought she was with you," the boy answered, shrugging.

The sound of screaming made him turn. Edjlin's men emerged from the trees. Kids scattered in panic. The twins activated a fishing-net trap that heaved a handful of guards into the jungle canopy, then jumped into the sea with Aaron close behind. A pair of guards dove in after them.

"There she is!" cried Jonath, pointing up. Running down the hill, Alya stopped at the cliff's edge out of breath, then notched an arrow in her bow and shot at the water. The guards swimming after Aaron and the twins were not deterred, so she jumped, plummeting through the air and then vanishing beneath the waves.

"Hurry up! They're behind you!" Noa called to Aaron and the twins.

At last Alya surfaced, and Noa couldn't believe what he saw. Racing through the water, Alya clung to the dorsal fin of a speckled dolphin. As she neared, Noa spotted the dolphin whistle around her neck. Of course, she had called the animal to her side.

Reaching the boys, she slipped off to let the dolphin tow them to the ship.

One by one, Noa yanked the boys over the railing by their belts. The twins tumbled onto the deck, dripping wet and exhausted. When Aaron toppled in, Noa reached over the side for Alya, but she wasn't there.

Alya hugged the ladder, doing something with her hands that Noa couldn't see. Beneath her, a guard clung to her leg, his lower half dragging in the wake. She lost her footing and fell, disappearing under the sea with the guard in tow.

"ALYA!" Noa shrieked. She resurfaced in the ship's wake, and he climbed the railing to dive in after her. "Hold on!"

"Don't!" she hollered back as she treaded water. "They need you!"

The guard swam to her, and she met him, turning herself in. Noa's stomach dropped like a rock falling to the bottom of a well. He couldn't leave her behind.

"No! Get off her!"

The moment he readied himself to dive in, he was yanked back inside the ship by none other than Alya's little brother.

"Get—off—me!" Noa cried, prying Aaron's pudgy fingers apart.

"Don't go!" he squealed, struggling to keep Noa wrapped up. "You have to save our parents. If you leave, none of us have a chance!"

Noa broke free and staggered back. Only eight boys had made it onto the ship, not including himself and Dagan. His chest heaved with each labored breath. His eyes were bloodshot and stinging; his heart, a palpitating drum, burned with hatred.

Alya had made it to land and was now being led away in the direction of the castle. Noa stared at the shrinking dock as smoke rose from the bay behind it, smothering his home and smearing the moon with gray.

Bones stepped forward, wiping the dripping water from his eyes.

"What do we do now, Captain?"

CHAPTER 6

THE UNLIKELY SEESAW

Noa's head spun. What in the king's name was he doing? He didn't belong here. The ocean was a dreamer's trap. Too many of his people had left home with promises of new land, sunken treasure, or greater trade alliances, only to be swallowed up in storms or beached on long-forgotten sandbars. His own mother had left once, and that choice had been one of her last.

He stared blankly into Bones's face without an answer to give him. Waves crashed against the hull as it plowed through the water, and his legs wobbled with the lurching ship.

Head bowed, Vim whispered mournfully, "We ain't got a chance without Alya. She was a better fighter than all of us put together."

Scuffles broke out between the sailor's son, Malloch, and the twins over who was allowed to handle the freshwater barrel. As Noa dashed around the rocking deck to sort it out, he became acutely aware of how uncomfortable he felt. His neck was hot and sweaty, his stomach felt queasy, and his head had started to hurt behind his eyes. Massaging his temples while he slowed to a walk, he tried to focus on the steady night horizon.

Please don't throw up, he begged himself.

"Let us wash our hands! We're sticky from the salt water!" complained Pan.

"We don't know how much is on board," explained Malloch. "My father is a sailor, and he says it's bad luck to start a journey without knowing the supplies."

Noa motioned for the twins to step away. "Count the inventory before you wash your hands in any water."

"I ain't recallin' voting you captain," said Vim, joining the crowd. His friend, Chaston, trailed behind, tightening his blond ponytail.

"Ahhh, Noa has the map," said Malloch.

Vim glowered. "I don't see no map, and Noa ain't no sailor."

Noa thought of the map hidden under a mattress below deck. Chewing on his lip, he pressed his bandaged palms against his neck to cool himself down and stop the nausea.

Malloch piped in. "Don't worry, Vim. King Edjlin lives two days from here. If he packed for a return journey, she'll have enough on board for another two days. So unless we travel more than that—"

"More than two days?" said Vim, gawking. "Where do ya plan on taking us? Valkaria?"

A fearful murmur echoed around the circle. All the boys were present now, save for Dagan who held the wheel steady on the quarterdeck, listening to the conversation below.

Noa clutched his stomach, trying to hold back what he knew was coming.

"We're risking our lives at sea," continued Vim. "We should go back—EW!"

Noa sprinted to the railing just in time, spraying sick against the hull and into the water. Waves licked the sides of the ship, disintegrating his mess into the ocean's bottomless stomach. The circle of boys backed away. Vim took one look at Noa hurling over the side and laughed.

"I'm not callin' ya 'Captain.' You ain't got the murkiest idea how to run this ship. We'll be dead before dawn. I say the leader is the eldest, and that's me." He swung his arms around in tight circles. "Come on, then. Let's fight for it."

A sour, burning taste lingered in Noa's throat. Wiping the sick from his mouth, he imagined the misshapen purple prune he'd resemble if Vim's knuckles found their way to his face.

"Stop it, Vim," said Bones, stepping between them. "This isn't helping."

Vim pushed Bones to the side, sneering at Noa, who was steadying himself on the shrouds. "What's the matter? Are ya 'fraid to damage your perfect prince hands?" Noa turned around and glared. "All right then, let's have a vote. All you cowards who ain't willin' to go back to save the island, say 'Aye.'"

Noa wanted to punch Vim square in the face. The prospect of being called a coward had deterred everyone from answering.

"Good! It's settled. We're turnin' round," said Vim.

On the quarterdeck, Dagan jammed the wheel into place, then marched down the steps to where Vim stood, rolling up his sleeves as he neared.

"Noa has the map. He's the captain leading this ship."

"I can handle this, Dag," said Noa testily.

"He's also your prince," continued Dagan. "You're a mutineer if you're against him, and I'll throw you overboard myself if that's the case."

"I said I can handle this!" said Noa, raising his voice. "We're not going back." He turned to Vim. "Vim, you're an idiot. The castle's overrun. The fleet is ash. We can't go back to the island alone, and if you want to try, be my guest."

He gestured to the water. Vim held his ground, staring venomously at the brothers in silence.

"Listen, Edjlin knew what he was doing," Noa continued, balancing his wobbling legs in the speeding ship. Why was he the only one having trouble finding his sea legs? "He invaded when the entire island was busy at the celebration. One thing is sure—help is out there, not back home. Since the Treaty of the Seven Kingdoms is still in place, the rest of the realm is obligated to come to our aid. We just have to let them know we need help."

For their last school project, Bones had carved a wooden puzzle in the shape of the seven original kingdoms to demonstrate how they had come together and agreed on a system of balance: if one island invaded another, all other islands were obligated to help. Noa recalled Bones had gotten a top grade, one of the few times he matched with Noa.

Malloch placed his hand on Noa's shoulder to steady him. "Perhaps we ought to make headway to Martesia. It's the closest island to us, only a day's journey. Once we explain to King Pontus what's happened, he will send armies home to put Edjlin back in his rightful place."

The boys murmured amongst themselves. Noa liked the idea, but his father's counsel to follow the map nagged at his mind. He would not abandon his people. Was following the map the best way to save them? He cleared his throat tentatively, the acidic taste of vomit lingering in his throat, and announced he would view the map before choosing a heading.

"Right then. Check the map while we sail," agreed Dagan. He returned to the wheel without another word.

Vim scowled. The others acknowledged the plan with new hope.

Remembering Malloch had helped test-sail ships with his father, Noa asked him to organize the group to hoist the rest of the sails. "Can you teach the others? I want all canvases blowing."

Malloch agreed eagerly, blowing a clump of hair from his eyes, and began calling out instructions as he pointed to rope by the railings and the main mast. Line stretched everywhere; it even steered the ship in a collaboration of pulleys from the rudder to the wheel. Everyone watched with relief. At least someone knew what to do.

"Keep your wits about ya, *Your Majesty*," snarled Vim, striding past to help hoist the mainsail. "It will be your fault if the whole island is destroyed when we return, and I'll be ready when that time comes."

Noa swallowed, surprised to find his throat as dry as a conch cracker.

———————

"It reeks of your underpants down here," said Fig, sniffing the air.

Pan snorted. "At least I wear underpants."

Foul odors engulfed Noa as he climbed down to the lower deck after the twins. He had come to retrieve the map, while the twins were already busy counting the food supply. In the stuffiness below deck, the uncomfortable warmth that accompanied seasickness crept up his neck again.

Lifting the mattress to the nearest cot, Noa felt a cold fist close over his heart. The map was gone.

"The map!" he shouted, throwing the mattress off the cot. "It's—!"

Pan and Fig started giggling behind him. Noa whipped around to see the mischievous twins holding his belongings in the air.

"Give me that!" he snapped, yanking the sack away. He rummaged inside until he pulled out the map and relief flooded over him.

"Tried the old under-the-mattress trick, I see," said Pan.

"Bless him, he's got so much to learn," said Fig, shaking his head. Then they both burst into laughter.

Noa scowled and sent them away to finish counting the supplies.

By himself, Noa found a cooking pot and placed the cold metal on the nape of his neck. His nausea lifted almost instantly. Ten minutes later, he returned to find the twins wrestling on the ground, Fig's head pinned between Pan's thighs.

"Cut it out, will you? What supplies do we have?"

The twins bounced up and held up their fingers to count.

"We found one barrel of these biscuit things, three parcels of salted pork, one jar of pickled eyeballs—"

"It's pickled onions," explained Pan, after seeing Noa's shock. "They only look like eyeballs."

"Two cabbages and a couple of these orange potatoes . . . yams, are they? A couple of yams. Oh, and one, two, three, four, five—"

"Six," added Pan, counting on his fingers.

"*Six* barrels of palm beer," finished Fig.

That wasn't nearly enough to keep a crew fed and hydrated. It appeared King Edjlin hadn't planned a return journey after all.

"Thank you, Pan, Fig. It's time I see what's on this map."

As Noa spoke, another sickening feeling bubbled in his stomach, one that had little to do with the rocking waves. He knew maps better than almost anyone on the island. What if this one was different? Weston's words replayed in his mind:

Yer never gonna know what's out in the sea before you die. What's really *out there.*

Where did the map lead?

———————

Stumbling through the darkness of the captain's quarters, Noa navigated his way through the shadows of furniture. His hand rested on a wooden matchbox lying on the desk, and he struck a match. Light illuminated rows of books and barrels of rolled-up parchment. It reminded Noa of his bedroom.

He lit an oil lantern hanging from the ceiling and reclined into a cushioned chair behind the desk. A wax-seal stamp proved what he already assumed: this was also Edjlin's private cabin. He pushed aside the books Weston had thrown at them and smirked as he read the titles: *The Seventy Stupidest Things to Try with Saltpeter* and *Sailing Fundamentals for Landlubbers*. No pirate would need these books. He doubted most even knew how to read. The books were obviously Edjlin's, and Weston had unknowingly led Noa straight to the information he needed to sail the ship.

Noa rolled out the yellow map on the desk, flattening the creases with his palms. It was completely dry. Was it waterproof too? To his surprise, it looked like a standard map of the realm. The circular formation of islands appeared no different than the larger map hanging behind him on the wall: the west held the island kingdoms Hamaruq (Edjlin's kingdom) and Ondule (Noa's kingdom); Martesia, Zapphire, and Malibis (where the Marooner's Market and Justice Isle were located) were in the middle; Blightip and Valkaria occupied the east.

Noa flipped the map over. The other side was blank.

His heart quickened. There were no directions. Had they washed off? He dumped his Capture the Conch equipment onto the desk, looking for more clues, but nothing came. He brought the map to the lamp's heat, but it remained the same. No invisible ink. No directions.

Noa slumped into the chair, speechless. Had his father used him as bait? Bait to lure away Edjlin's men while he carried the real map?

If there even was a real map, he thought. Noa didn't know what to believe anymore. He had let himself trust his father again, and this was the result.

The door banged open. Dagan burst into the room.

"What does the map say?" he asked, swinging the lamp light in Noa's face.

Noa shook his head. "Nothing. It's useless. It's—"

He stopped, eyes widening in awe. The realm on the map had vanished. In the corner of the map, black ink surfaced like blood oozing from a wound, forming a star. Noa blinked, afraid he'd imagined it. The parchment continued to draw a compass rose with eight points, and the north point glowed royal blue.

"Impossible," he breathed. "How did it do that?"

Dagan peered down. "Do what?"

The compass which had materialized in the right corner glowed brighter still. "How did it draw the compass—it's glowing!"

"Give me that." Dagan leaned over the desk and pulled the map from Noa's hands. The instant the parchment touched his fingers, the compass disappeared and the map of Aztrius came back. "What are you talking about? Nothing is glowing."

It was at this moment Noa realized the rarity of the item he was holding. The map was *changing* to show them different things. He held it once more, and his suspicions were confirmed:

the glowing compass returned, spinning to stay north when he moved it around.

Perhaps his father hadn't lied after all.

Dagan stared from the parchment to Noa in wonder. Then he frowned.

"No fair. Why can't I see what you see?"

"I don't know," Noa admitted. He searched for a true compass, and after finding one in the desk drawer, he compared it with the glowing compass on the map. "Perhaps it changes if it falls into the wrong hands . . . Ah, see? Both compasses align north—the one on the map is accurate. It's unbelievable. It's just like magic."

Dagan folded his arms. "You don't believe in magic."

Noa shook his head in amazement. He knew he didn't believe in it. What logical explanation was behind the map's power?

A sly smirk appeared on Dagan's face. "I guess this makes you the mad one in the family."

"I thought you believed me . . ." said Noa, deflating slightly.

"I do, but Father gave *you* the map. He would only give a magical map to someone who was crazy enough to follow it. Plus, you see things I can't. Mad, I tell ya."

Noa thought for a moment. "What if I'm *not* crazy enough to follow it?"

Dagan guffawed. "You *are* mad! That map tells us how to save our island. After everything Father went through to hide it, you don't want to follow it?"

Noa brought his eyes to the heavens. "I'm mad if I follow it and mad if I don't," he confirmed.

"Well, Father said this map could help our people. Not following it would just be selfish."

"You think *I'm* selfish? Do you have any idea how many times I've had to save your fat behind? 'Look, Noa, I caught a poisonous snake!' 'Oh Noa, you're just in time to see me tie myself to a wagon and roll myself into the ocean!' 'Watch me do a backflip off the roof!' If I were selfish, you'd be dead."

"Whatever."

"This map doesn't make any sense. I'm not going to follow it just because Father asked me to. He can't throw this on me without explanation and expect me to know what I'm doing. Whatever I decide, it will be for the safety of us all. It's not just you whom I have to protect now, it's all of them too," he said, pointing to the door.

Just then, the ship shuddered with a crunch and thrust the boys onto the floor.

"Now what?" Noa picked himself up, stuffed the map inside the desk drawer, and bolted outside.

"We ran aground!" Malloch shouted, his voice high with panic. The main mast's white canvas inflated sporadically with gusts of wind. "It's too dark out. I can't see. I think we're stuck on a sandbar."

Noa groaned.

"I found the lead line!" Jonath called, rushing to the quarterdeck. Jonath held out a coiled rope with a lead tip. Knots in the cord marked fathoms (about six feet worth of line) to measure the water depth, and the tip told them what rested on the ocean floor. His strong, baker's boy arms threw the lead piece over the starboard side. Sooner than expected, the cord gave slack.

"Three fathoms!" he called back to them, reeling in the rope. The cylinder tip poured out watery sand when it clonked on deck, a promising sign, for if it had been rocks beneath them, their ship would risk tearing a hole in the hull.

"Check the other side to see which direction the sandbank is sloping," Noa suggested.

"Check the other side, Jonath!" hollered Malloch. The lead line plunged into the water on portside, and they counted each arm's length of rope as it sunk.

Noa gasped. "Seven fathoms! We're on the edge of a drop-off!"

As if on cue, the ship groaned and teetered side to side in the smoky wind.

Dagan smacked the wheel. "Burning ash! We're stuck on this wretched sand, and the tide is going down!"

Noa paced the width of the ship. Low tide would strand them on the sand for hours. They couldn't afford that. He'd read enough books about sailing to know how much time that would cost them, although he already realized experiencing sailing was much different than reading about it. He needed a mentor to teach them how to return the ship into open water. Or at the very least, a manual . . .

"Wait here—I may know something that can help," he said. Bolting into the warmth of the captain's quarters, Noa used the lamp light to find *Sailing Fundamentals for Landlubbers*, which

Weston had thrown at them earlier. Turning to a section on careening, he read:

Careening: the act of beaching one's ship and setting it to the side for maintenance, repair, or caulking.

He scanned the paragraph for something to help. Words like *High Tide*, *Draught*, and *Tackle* stood out to him, and when he'd finished reading, he had an idea.

Returning to the deck, he found the group in a heated argument once again.

"Ain't never shoulda left!" Vim shouted.

Dagan sneered. "Like *you* would do any good back there. I've never seen anyone run away so fast to save his skin."

Vim lunged toward Dagan, but they were quickly pulled apart by the others.

"Stop it! Both of you!" said Noa, running closer, the book pressed against his chest. The waves splashed against the ship, barely louder than the boys' heaving breath. "I think I know how to get us off the sandbar." All eyes turned to Noa. "We don't have the tide in our favor, but in careening, it's not just the tide that beaches the ship, it's the cargo. The lighter the load, the easier she floats."

"You want us to throw things overboard?" asked Aaron.

"Exactly. We'll start with the guns on the main deck. Everyone helps!"

The group dispersed to the cannons and began pushing and heaving them over the edge. They'd only managed to push off three in a half hour and were now sweating so hard their clothes looked as wet as when they'd jumped in the ocean.

"This is taking forever," moaned Aaron, wiping his forehead.

"What if we try rocking the ship instead?" asked Vim's friend, Chaston, as he tightened his ponytail. "If we fire all the starboard guns, the force should rock the ship into deeper waters. What do you say?"

Noa had had enough explosions to last him a lifetime, but Dagan looked eager for another go.

Below deck, a gun sat at each gunport, its cold cast-iron barrel facing out to sea.

"Gunpowder goes in the barrel ends," Chaston shouted, as the boys each found a cannon. "Put the cloth in afterward and jam it in—*not with your hands, Pan!* Use the rammer!" At the end of the lineup, he found Aaron, who had somehow managed to tangle up his legs in rope. "The rope is the only thing keeping the gun from rolling back and running you over, Aaron. Tie it back!"

Noa helped Aaron free himself and set up his gun. Then, confident Chaston had things under control, Noa skittered up the ladder to check on Malloch and Jonath. He found the sailor's son and the baker's son staring at the night horizon. A shadow contrasted against the haze of the burning island: the silhouette of a ship.

"They're following us," said Malloch heavily.

The only ship that had not been burned in the bay or smashed by a falling cliff was the pirate ship. A bang erupted, followed by a distant splash. The enemy ship had opened fire.

"Chaston, when you're ready. We've got company," said Noa, sliding down to the lower deck. "Ugh! What's that smell?"

"Aaron threw up," Chaston explained, rolling his eyes. "Nerves."

Noa looked to the middle of the deck where Aaron was bent over his sick. The others had backed away as far as they could manage without abandoning their guns.

Chaston gave the signal. Sparks zapped on the wick of the cannons ("Two pargents says they'll give up if we fire your stinky trousers at them," said Fig from a nearby barrel). Then . . . *KABOOM!*

The ship rocked violently backward. Noa's ears burst. Dagan and Chaston pointed at each other angrily, cannons trickling out smoke behind them. All Noa heard was the constant ringing in his ears. By the time he recognized voices again, the boys had swarmed to reload their cannons.

"Stop!" he cried, pulling Chaston to the side. "Untie the cannons and set them off again. We need the weight of the boat to shift, right? If the cannons roll all the way to the other side, I think they'll give us the push we need."

Chaston considered the idea—*BOOM. SPLASH.*

"It's worth a try," he concluded at the sound of the enemy ship's fire, and he sprinted down the row, dodging Aaron's mess. "You heard him, boys! Untie the guns and load up!"

Boys ripped ropes off the barrels until each cannon sat unattached on the starboard side. Chaston checked each one for a proper reload, making sure the boys sponged each cannon first to avoid premature fire. Just as he finished reminding Fig not to stand behind the gun unless he wanted to be run over, an explosion echoed in the distance.

Noa flew backward into a barrel of palm beer. Wood splinters sprayed past his face. They'd been hit. Each of their own guns sat untouched. Noa glanced around wildly for anyone who might be hurt, knowing it wasn't the cannonball but the splinters that were the deadliest.

"We still need to fire!" he yelled, lifting a flailing but unharmed Fig from the floor. Boys scrambled to their guns. Aaron had flown into his mess and now had sick smeared across his back. Soon all the cannons were lit. Guns exploded and flew to the other end of the ship. The floor tipped as the cannons switched sides, but then it started to tilt back.

"It's not going to work!" someone shouted.

"Everyone to portside!"

Noa led the pack to the opposite end. Boys scrambled to get out of the way of a smelly, barf-covered Aaron as they ran to the other side. The floor tilted with their added weight, then a sand-scraping sound emitted from beneath the ship and the floor bobbed back to a level position.

"We're floating again!" Malloch cried from the main deck, barely audible above the cheering below. The twins slapped their hands together in an apparent secret handshake. Aaron collapsed beneath himself, sobbing in relief.

A cannon-sized hole in the hull revealed the choppy water below and the ship in the distance.

"They won't make it past the sandbar until the tide rises," said Noa.

As if on cue, a cannonball splashed in their wake. The enemy ship already looked smaller as they sailed away.

"We can't keep this up for long," said Noa, returning to the helm with Dagan and a true compass. His gaze returned fearfully to the ship on the horizon. "I've had enough close escapes for one night. Malloch, set a course for Martesia."

"Aye, Captain." Malloch took the compass from Noa and turned the wheel slightly. The ship creaked and shuddered as the sails caught the wind and it sped toward the distant island in the dark.

———————————

Moonlight spilled into the captain's quarters. Dagan slumped onto the couch to sleep, yawning and burying under a blanket, while Noa lay on the only bed, the moldy stench of the mattress making him question if he should have offered to take the couch.

He thought guiltily of Malloch alone at the helm, a blanket draped over his shoulders and tucked around his neck, but the sailor's son had insisted they rest for a few hours before sunrise. Noa had stayed with him until the enemy ship's twinkling dot disappeared on the horizon. With the currents on their side, they would arrive in Martesia by noon tomorrow, and Malloch, Noa had now realized, was more than capable of managing the helm on his own.

However, it was the map that held Noa's true attention. He pictured the glowing compass once again before pushing the thought away. They would be safe in Martesia, he assured himself. His father hadn't expected him to sail the seas; that was too absurd—they hardly knew what they were doing!

"Do you think it's odd how we escaped?" Noa asked Dagan, who was almost asleep.

Dagan rubbed his eyes. "Eh? I wouldn't say odd. Brilliant, more like."

"I mean with Weston. He's one of the last surviving pirates in Aztrius. We should have died at his hand."

"Meh, Weston is clearly out of practice. Two against one proved too much for him, and he fled. Everyone knows pirates are cowards at heart."

Noa clicked his tongue. "I suppose . . . I forgot to tell you something earlier." Dagan grunted and rolled over, a sign he was still listening, though barely. "I saw a pendant around Weston's neck. It was definitely the same as the pendant we found on the beach."

"Yeah?" Dagan asked, opening one eye.

"I recognized the symbol." He fidgeted with his thumbs. "The tapestry in Father's chamber had the symbol as well. It's where Father hid the map before giving it to me." He waited for Dagan to reply, but Dagan said nothing. "What do you make of it?"

Dagan yawned before mumbling, "Coincidence? Look, I'm tired. Can we talk about it tomorrow?"

Without waiting for an answer, Dagan rolled onto his stomach and started to snore.

Noa's brow furrowed in thought, though his eyelids, like lead blankets, begged to tuck him in for the night. The ship creaked and groaned around him, plowing through the water, while half-empty medicine bottles clinked in the cupboard. Too many worries flooded his mind: pirates, the castle, the map, the

116

pendant, sailing, Lana, Alya . . . the list was exhausting. At least he knew villagers would gratefully give their lives to protect Lana, their only princess, from harm. It was Alya who needed protecting; she was the kind of girl who wasn't afraid of trouble even when she was on her own to face it, which often she was.

Listening to Dagan talk in his sleep ("Ladies, please, one at a time—"), he rotated to his side and drifted off.

Alya and Lana played on the beach in Noa's dreams. Then sand swirled around him until he could no longer see. His father's voice thundered inside the whirlwind, ordering him to follow the map, but the girls were screaming for him in the distance. He swatted the sandy air to find them, stumbling, lost in the churning mess.

CHAPTER 7

SUGAROOMS AND STOLEN GOODS

Sunlight spilled into the cabin the next morning. Noa rolled out of bed and stumbled across the room, rubbing the sleep from his eyes. Burning anxiety fluttered in his chest, remnants of a bad dream, he assumed, but he couldn't remember any of it. He had half expected to be awoken in the night by treacherous seas or news of pirates, but through the checkered windowpanes, an empty ocean lay calm and serene.

Noa unlatched the window and swung it open to ventilate the room. Warm wind blew inside, flapping the canvas drapes around his bunk.

Passing a painting of a boy with different-colored eyes, Noa made his way to the door, then spotted a book he had never seen before. A twinge of pain shot through his rope-burned hands as he reached for the unfamiliar cover and scanned the title.

"*Sea of Kings: A History of Aztrius*," he read aloud. Ondule didn't have this book, or he would have read it already. He slumped into a chair and flipped through it, stopping at a paragraph circled in ink.

Soon after Gravner Hallowbit took the throne, he discovered the remains of the last Leviathan of the century (see footnote) and extracted venom from the deceased creature. At high cost, Hallowbit experimented on himself using the Leviathan venom, only to learn at the end of his trials the destructive properties within it. Hallowbit, referred to by many as the Death King, died in his chamber from overconsumption of the venom, ending the Battle of the Mines fought on his kingdom's soil. Upon investigation, it is believed Hallowbit depleted the entire source, as it was never recovered.

Noa read the footnote.

Leviathans are reptilian creatures containing poisonous fluids within their saliva. They commonly inflict injury through biting or spitting (see Men and Monsters, *Chapter 8). When consumed, Leviathan venom creates a prolonged life of double the average human. It is also believed to contain the ability to bring back the dead.*

A diagram of a venom-filled vial marked the page beside the footnote, with a question mark inked in the margin. Noa leaned back in his chair. Leviathans didn't exist, did they? He stared curiously at the question mark.

"Land ho!" Malloch hollered from the quarterdeck. Yanking on his boots, Noa darted out the door.

It was clear the moment Noa stepped outside that the sense of danger from yesterday's attacks had dissolved into nervous excitement for their arrival in Martesia. On deck, Dagan and the twins sword fought with splintered wood from the cannon fire ("I chased Weston until he fell to his knees, begging for mercy," Dagan bragged.). Bones zigzagged between them carrying tools, off to fix the hole made by the cannon fire. Beside the foremast, Chaston, who was always keen to blow something up, had lit the fuse to a dud to practice stopping it with his bare fingers. Next to him, Aaron babbled about what Martesia would be like to an uninterested Vim, who seemed to have fallen asleep in a hammock he'd made for himself from bed draping.

"Ahhh, can you believe our luck? Perfect seas," said Malloch at the helm.

Noa shaded his eyes to examine the gray island in the distance. "How long until we reach Martesia?"

"Soon," said Malloch, yawning. His eyelids drooped, and red branched through the whites of his eyes. "Oi, Jonath! I said no whistling! It's bad luck! Are you trying to anger the sea?"

Malloch glared at the deck where Jonath stood, frozen in the middle of whistling "A Wave and Toss Be for the Sea, Not for Me." "Eh? Did you say something, Captain?"

Noa almost laughed at Malloch's exhaustion. "To bed with you, all right? Dagan! Take the wheel!"

He steered a reluctant Malloch to the lower deck, veering him away from the twins who Noa overheard plotting to sneak

Martesian girls aboard. When Malloch disappeared down the ladder, Jonath resumed whistling, this time choosing "What the Heck, Let's Swab the Deck." Noa bounded up the stairs to the quarterdeck where Dagan held the wheel.

"You won't believe what I just read," said Noa.

Dagan looked disgusted. "You *read* this morning? Don't you ever pull your nose out of books?"

"No," said Noa irritably, "and be glad I don't. I read what the Death King was after: a Leviathan's venom that could prolong life."

Dagan blinked. "You mean like a giant snake monster?" He faked a cough and mumbled, "Mad."

"Don't be stupid, monsters aren't real," said Noa shortly. "A smaller snake must exist with life-prolonging venom . . . but don't you see? It's *venom*. I'll bet Edjlin believes the map leads to this 'Leviathan' venom, and he wants it to make his life longer too."

"Leviathan venom . . ." Dagan pondered the idea, fixing his hair as he held the wheel steady with his knee. "I can see why Edjlin wanted it. He's an old man, even outlived his son. But spitting sea serpents, Noa, you sound like your head's full of sand."

Noa blushed, feeling rather unlike himself. He didn't know why he felt sure about it, he just did—the venom and the map were connected. Why else would Edjlin circle the paragraph if he wasn't concerned with finding it?

"Explain why Edjlin mentioned venom to Father, then," Noa demanded. He waited, but for once Dagan was speechless. "That's what I thought. It can't be a coincidence."

Wind blew over them, inflating the already-billowing sails.

Noa stared over the vast ocean to the speck of an island in the distance. He just wanted to reach it. The longer it took to arrive in Martesia, the longer his people were hostages. And despite his better judgment, he was developing a strange fondness for sailing. He'd taken to the ship's creaks and groans as it plowed through the watery terrain. It annoyed him how much he enjoyed it.

Noa kicked the deck. "I hate sailing."

Dagan shook his head. "Then go back inside, crabby fatty. Bury yourself in a book."

Noa didn't move. "Once we reach Martesia, I'll tell King Pontus about the map. He can handle it after that."

Dagan gazed at the horizon, steadying the wheel on a straight course. "Are you sure we should go to Martesia instead of following Father's map?"

"We have no idea where the map leads. Besides, we're nearly there."

"I know, but Father said—"

"Come off it, Dag!" said Noa testily. "The longer we're at sea, the more likely we'll fall into Weston's hands. If you complain about Martesia one more time, you can forget about bunking with me on the way home."

Dagan looked at the ground.

Noa added, "Plus, I'm older. I'm in charge."

"Oh sure, being older by one whole year means you know best."

"Exactly, and I can teach you what I know."

"You can't teach me sarcasm, that's for sure."

Noa ignored Dagan's comment. "I know what I'm doing. Martesia is our ally. They will help us."

They wouldn't have to wait long for Martesia's help, for within a few hours they had made it to the island. Martesia's crescent-moon shape allowed only one entrance to the island, and they sailed toward it. Two towers emerged like giants guarding the entry, and as far as they could see, soldiers patrolled the wall surrounding the land.

"All hands on deck!" Noa hollered. Boys spilled out of the lower deck where they had been sheltering from the sun. Malloch stumbled toward the quarterdeck and rubbed the sleep from his eyes, joining the others in awe of the massive gates. Pan and Fig came up crawling on the ground, repeatedly trying to perform handstands.

"He said all hands on deck!" Fig argued when Vim pushed him over.

It took longer than they thought to sail in between the massive open gates, but soon they sliced through the water into a large bay. Noa gasped at the incredible sight.

A shimmering castle stood on stilts tall enough for ships to sail beneath. Villagers floated in bowl-shaped boats in the crystal water, carrying bundles of fresh produce. The castle's dome center split off into three parts where the entire village resided, resembling a three-armed octopus with only one of these "arms" connecting to land. Noa thought the hundreds of glass castle windows were the most fascinating. He'd read about this place, but he'd never seen so much of one material in real life.

"How did they afford that?" asked Dagan, gazing slack-jawed at the sparkling walls.

"Martesia trades expensive spices," explained Noa. "You know, rum powder, smoked honey salt, banana sugar, rose pepperberries . . . if I had my books, I could tell you how they produce them."

"Who needs books? I can ask them myself!"

Organized rows of plants sat on the crescent landscape growing the spices and other essential crops. It was difficult to grow certain spices anywhere else but Martesia's flat, moist land, and Noa recognized channels made from his own island's stone diverting water through the fields.

As the boys reached the docks, the water became so clear that ships appeared to be floating in midair.

"Prepare to make port!" Malloch called, taking the wheel from Dagan and swinging the vessel closer to the docks. The crew assembled on portside, giddy to dock for the first time.

One demolished floating market and near collision with another ship later, the boys decided to drop anchor in the bay. Everyone was anxious, knowing they would soon be saved. Noa organized a group into a longboat and headed to shore, apologizing profusely to the owner of the floating market they had run over. Cursing, the man tried to salvage a basket of floating lemons.

A strange aroma of cinnamon, mint, garlic, and other spices hung in the hot air. Malloch, the only boy with sailing experience, nearly lost his nerve when Bones stepped onto the dock left foot first ("That's very bad luck!"), but Bones paid little attention. He rushed down the dock with the rest of the crew, sprinting toward the closest person in authority they saw.

"They attacked us! Our homes are captured!" They shouted to a man in a violet uniform and proceeded to explain their stories in vivid detail, all speaking over one another. The man didn't even glance above his clipboard. He shook off a disgruntled expression and began reading without looking up.

"Welcome to Martesia, ruled by King Pontus Caraway, son of Albert Caraway III," he recited dully. "I am your Dock Master today. Please line up in an orderly fashion to state your business, and you will be directed to the correct location based on your personal needs."

The group started up again, each boy desperate for the man to understand their predicament.

The Dock Master pulled his eyes away from the clipboard, instantly disappointed at what he saw. "Where is your captain?" he asked, squinting down his long, crooked nose. "I must speak with an adult."

"I am the captain. I need to see King Pontus. It's urgent," said Noa.

"That's above my authority."

Bones shouted from the back of the group, "Then find someone who has authority, ya fat loggerhead!"

The man scowled, then told them to wait. Seagulls flew overhead in swarms, dropping nasty surprises onto the pilings. The boys huddled together to shield themselves from the unwelcome presents. Alas, Bones got pooped on the shoulder just as the Dock Master returned with a woman in uniform. She carried a tiny baby in a sling across her chest. Noa recognized the uniform and octopus badge from his studies of foreign island armies.

"General Narthol, this is the kid I was talking about," said the Dock Master.

General Narthol frowned, patting the baby as she bounced on the spot. "You are the captain of that ship?"

Noa nodded. The general eyed the group with intrigue.

"This is *your* crew?" she asked. Noa nodded again, ducking suddenly when a seagull swooped low. "What urgent matter requires you to see the king?"

"Our island has been invaded!" How many times did he need to say it?

The general straightened up. "I am sorry, young sir, but no one sees the king without authorization." Apparently, she'd decided they were not telling the truth.

"Can't you give us authorization?" asked Noa.

The Dock Master intervened, shaking a purse of money around his neck. "Not for common swabbies like you. That's five vecs for docking your ship, another two pargents for each hour you remain." He tugged on his violet uniform as if to say that was all.

"*Excuse* me!" said Dagan, stepping forward. "We need help!"

"And who might you be?" asked the Dock Master, suddenly amused. "The first mate?"

Dagan puffed up his chest. "Yeah, that's right. I'm first mate to my brother, *Prince* Noa. Didn't I mention our father is King

Titus Blackburn, ruler of Ondule?" The Dock Master's taunting laugh turned into a snarl, and he bowed in respect. The general raised her brows in surprise. "Let us see your king," Dagan said.

"By our royal power, we command you," added Noa, straightening up to match his brother's height. He hated playing his royalty card, but they were desperate.

"You have no power here," the general said calmly.

Noa and Dagan exchanged confused looks.

"This letter from our father must be given directly to King Pontus," said Dagan, taking parchment from his jacket pocket. It had a wax lighthouse stamped on its crease. Noa frowned. When had Dagan snatched one of their father's personal letters? He was the only king in the realm who had that seal.

General Narthol reached for it, but Dagan pulled back. "He demanded we deliver it ourselves."

The woman's eyes narrowed on the parchment, but her shoulders relaxed. "Very well, I will bring the two of you myself. The crew stays."

She marched down the dock to the village streets, patting the baby's bottom as it slept in her sling. Noa followed, then quickly doubled back to instruct Bones and the twins to trade barrels of palm beer in place of provisions for the return home, making himself extra clear they could not afford whatever pranks the twins had up their sleeves.

"When you're done," Noa told Pan, "return the stash of dried mangoes you hid in the cannon so the rest of us can enjoy them."

The twins' faces fell. "Who told you—?"

"Everyone."

"Noa's got a fat stick up his bum," said Pan in an undertone as Noa spoke with Bones.

"Why doesn't he know it?" Fin whispered back.

"Because it's *up—his—bum—*"

"I can hear you," said Noa over his shoulder. "Get to work."

Soon after, Noa found himself bouncing along the streets in a plum-colored carriage.

"I expected a better welcome," Dagan whispered. He stared at the back of the general's head with obvious dislike, then scooted to the edge of his seat. "Move over. You're touching me."

"I am not." Noa sighed. "I expected a better welcome too. I can see why Father never wanted us to visit other islands. They acted like we were common criminals."

They passed shops selling spices of orange, red, and green, the buildings tightly packed between the thin homes. A crowd surrounded a cart selling bags of something greasy. A sign above it read, *Sugarooms! The Sweetest Mushrooms in Martesia.* Women pulled children along and others carried baskets with lettuce and carrots sticking out the end, while boys younger than Noa kicked a ball through the street.

Their carefree manner seemed inconceivable; here they were going about their daily routines while Edjlin held Noa's entire kingdom captive! Had it only been yesterday since Noa felt that free? Not a care in the world bigger than losing a game of Capture the Conch?

After some time, they arrived at the castle's glass dome.

"Please stay here," the general instructed after they left the carriage and walked up a sunlit staircase. She disappeared behind a double door and left Noa and Dagan staring at the doorknobs.

Two huge fishbowls sat on either side of the door. Inside the tanks, octopuses the same purple as the general's uniform propelled themselves against the glass. Their tentacles flashed with blue streaks. Panting from climbing the stairs, Noa leaned closer for a better look.

A girl approached, carrying a tray of drinks. "Don't touch the water unless you want a shock," she warned.

The octopus suctioned itself onto the glass, blue streaks zapping through the water. Noa pulled away. "I've read about electric octopuses. They can kill, right?" Noa asked.

"If someone is exposed long enough," the girl said matter-of-factly.

He accepted the water she offered and handed the other cup to Dagan, who inspected the green plant floating inside.

"Is it customary to serve guests swamp water?" asked Dagan, unaware how tactless he sounded. Noa elbowed him in the ribs.

"Basil water is a delicacy," she assured them.

Noa held up his glass politely. "It looks refreshing. Thank you." He signaled with his eyes for Dagan to taste it, and they drank together. Dagan guzzled his down, smacking his lips with the last drop. Noa gulped his too. It was much more appetizing than the drinking water on their ship, which tasted like old wood.

The girl took their cups and left, and Dagan spread out comfortably on a bench. Behind him, the glass wall revealed the ocean and bustling town. They were several stories high, and white birds soared at eye level. In the distance, darkness marred the sky.

"We're lucky we arrived before the storm," said Noa, eyeing the approaching clouds. From what he understood after reading *Sailing Fundamentals for Landlubbers,* sailing in a storm with their inexperience would most likely prove fatal, especially with an empty cargo. A light ship could roll. Every boat had ballast stones and ballast water in its bilge to weigh it down, but the heavier the ship, the safer they were from tipping.

Dagan nodded nonchalantly and leaned back with his hands behind his head. "I think I should tell the king what happened. Old people love me."

Noa massaged his knuckles nervously as he glanced at the tall, closed doors. "I'm the heir to the throne. It's my job to tell."

"You could make it my job."

Noa snorted. "I don't think so. Do you know how embarrassing it would be if my younger brother spoke for me?"

"As embarrassing as that wonker zit on your face?"

Noa's lips pursed into a thin line. He snatched the letter protruding from Dagan's pocket and smacked it over his brother's head. "You shouldn't have stolen this from Father. It could be important."

"It's not," said Dagan simply. "I found our father's wax seal in the captain's quarters, and I fiddled with it while you were asleep. There's a real nice drawing of a sword inside, one of my best yet."

Noa's mouth dropped. "It's fake? You mean Edjlin had our kingdom's seal? That's illegal! What if the king asks to see the letter?"

Dagan brushed the idea away like a fly in his face. "Don't

you think I thought of that? Relax. Once we tell the king what Edjlin has done, there will be no need for letters."

After what seemed like hours, General Narthol returned and let them in. "Only speak when spoken to," she said, pushing them through the door.

Noa and Dagan found themselves in a throne room at the top of the castle. Sunlight shimmered down in all directions from the dome ceiling, streaming through the violet tapestries which drooped from the glass to the ground.

"Sons of Titus Blackburn, come forward," said an old man at the end of the room. He wore purple and white robes, and his long, silver beard had been tucked into his sash. "I believe you have a letter to deliver from your father."

Without waiting for Noa, Dagan burst into the story of what happened, not even pausing to catch his breath. The only thing Noa could make out was Edjlin's name and the "pow pow pow" Dagan added at the end to show the soldiers had fired at them. He finally stepped back, gasping for air, his face a deep shade of red.

"My dear boy, I could barely understand you!" King Pontus said, resting back in his chair.

"What is wrong with you? *I* was supposed to tell," Noa hissed.

"Now, what do you mean Edjlin invaded? Was he not welcomed as a guest to the celebration held in your sister's honor?"

Dagan blinked.

"Edjlin stopped here just before traveling to your island,"

131

the king went on. "I'll have you know, I quite like him. Are you sure you are getting your facts right, my boy?"

"Your Majesty," Noa answered, "our home has been overtaken. We barely escaped with our lives. King Edjlin tried to steal something from my father."

"Oh no . . ." mumbled the king, shaking his head. "I hoped it would not come to this. Your father has sent you as diplomats to have me on his side, hasn't he? Well, I shall not be a part of this rivalry, especially after I discussed the same matter with King Edjlin only days ago."

What was King Pontus talking about? "You can't trust Edjlin!" Noa protested. He couldn't believe what he was hearing.

"Let me explain something to you boys," said King Pontus coolly, the weight of his robes making him hunch over in his chair. "Each island is a different kingdom, but these different kingdoms create only one realm: Aztrius. To bring peace to this realm, we must all work together, despite our differences. The eldest of you boys shall become king one day, but if your contribution to this realm consists of lies mixed with irrational behavior, then I daresay we may see an end to this peace. Now, I do believe King Titus is a good man. I shall let you leave my home without a single word of this nonsensical visit to your father. That is a bargain you shall not find me offering twice. I suggest you take it and leave."

King Pontus shook his head sadly and gathered up his robes.

"But, our sister and father—the whole island—they're in danger! You must do something!"

"Don't lie to me, boy," warned the king, waving his finger

at Noa. "I've been receiving letters from your father for weeks about his dislike toward King Edjlin, how he believes Edjlin is cheating him in trade, and yet Edjlin, that brave man, traveled all this way to make amends with your father. Edjlin understands the balance of peace we must have in this realm. You shall not pull me into this madness. You say you escaped, and yet here you are, arriving in King Edjlin's ship, with another from his fleet just outside my gates. What fool do you take me for?"

The boys looked at each other in utter shock. Another one of King Edjlin's ships was outside the gates of Martesia?

King Pontus continued, "Do you expect me to believe you came all this way to deliver a letter when you could have sent it by pigeon instead? A faster, perhaps more *reliable* way to send a message?"

Noa grabbed the letter from Dagan's hands and marched toward the king, suddenly understanding. "Your Majesty, there is no rivalry with trade. Edjlin has been forging letters to make you think our father disliked him, but it was Edjlin who deceived you all along. We found our father's seal in Edjlin's cabin!"

He pointed at the wax seal and froze, realizing what he had admitted. King Pontus rubbed his long beard in dislike.

"The letter is a fake?"

Noa gulped.

At that moment, a soldier dressed in a violet cape met the king and whispered something in his ear. A pigeon flapped impatiently on a post behind him. Noa quickly stepped backward, dread overcoming him.

The king rebuked the soldier silently as if to say he was busy, but the soldier pointed to the boys and passed him a letter. King Pontus broke the seal and opened it. Noa's heart stopped when he noticed the yellow seal on the parchment: it was from Edjlin.

King Pontus' face became stern. "How did you come by that ship? Did Edjlin allow you to use it?"

"Well, no."

"You stole it?"

Noa stared wide-eyed at the king. "We had to. You don't understand—"

"Silence!" The king's voice shot through the air like an arrow. He waved the letter at them. "True men do not play the victim. They take responsibility for their actions. I'm severely disappointed your father taught you none of this." Turning to his men, he said, "Guards, it is as I feared. These boys have stolen a ship from King Edjlin and the prized possessions aboard it. From this day forward, they are branded pirates in our kingdom and shall face trial. *Seize them.*"

CHAPTER 8

SCHLUCKING SLIME

Noa felt his jaw go slack. Was this a gag? Did Martesians have a sick sense of humor he had yet to understand? In the corner of his eye, he saw the Martesian guards closing in, but it wasn't until Dagan pulled him away that he fully registered the king's command.

"Stop them!" King Pontus shouted as they escaped through the front door. Noa pushed the pillar holding the tank of electric octopuses onto the ground and it shattered, spilling the animals onto the floor. Admittedly, this was not the smartest idea, for now the floor leading to the stairs was coated in a thin layer of water brimming with deadly voltage.

"How do we get out?" asked Dagan, backing away from the water.

"The servant door!" said Noa, spotting the side door the girl had gone through.

In they went, slamming it shut behind them. Seconds later, soldiers slipped and slid through the spilled water, howling in pain from the electric shock.

Noa and Dagan didn't wait to be found in the darkness on the other side of the door. They scurried through the secret hall, looking for a way out. Smooth, plain walls met them on each side, tightly blocking them in and brushing against their shoulders if they were not careful. A torch lit the hall on the other end, and when they reached it, Noa realized it was another door.

"In here," said Noa, pushing it open and tumbling into the room. They were back in the throne room, coming in from behind the throne. The room was almost empty, except for one guard. The others must have fled down the stairs.

The boys retreated to the servant tunnel as quietly as they could, but the door was gone. Closed. Disappeared into the mirrored glass wall, making it impossible to tell where it opened.

"What do we do?" asked Dagan, panicking. "We're trapped! The entrance has those octopuses!"

"HALT!" hollered the guard. He was hefty, a rare sight in Martesia. As the man charged toward them, the brothers skirted the perimeter of the room.

Noa saw King Pontus peer around his chair, his face livid and shocked.

"Try the window," panted Noa. He wasn't the only one out

of breath. The guard was running at them at the speed of a large turtle, and through his huffing and wheezing, sweat had started to drip into his eyes. He had to pause to wipe his brow every few feet.

Dagan grabbed a nearby chair by the legs and began swinging it against the paneled glass window.

"What are you doing?" cried Noa, jumping back. Outside, the dome sloped out beneath them several stories high.

"What—does—it—look—like?" Dagan said in between swings. The glass cracked but remained in one piece.

"Open the draft pane!" Noa lifted the latch to the bottom windowpane that allowed drafts to enter the room. Cool wind whooshed over his face. The guard closed in. Noa pushed Dagan through the hole and dove after him, then with a choke, hung on the glass by the collar of his shirt. The guard had grabbed his tunic and was holding him back.

"Geroff me!" Noa gasped, wriggling to break free. When he looked up, he realized the guard had tried to dive after him and was now stuck halfway through the window. Soft crackling came from the glass as it started to spiderweb apart, and then with a crash it all came tumbling down, raining on Noa's head. Noa and the guard slid down the hot castle dome on their rears at full speed. Around them, the city sparkled. Noa knew he'd reached the end of the dome when the slope steepened, lifting him off the ground. Free-falling into the air, he smacked a roof and rolled onto the building tops. A pair of window cleaners had to jump to the side to avoid getting hit.

"Aghhh," Noa cried out in pain. He moaned beside a rather

crooked chimney, cradling his bruised ribs, the same spot where he'd hit the railing the day before. "You just *had* to do that, didn't you?" he wheezed to the guard sprawled beside him.

Dagan yanked Noa to his feet, and they jogged across the rooftops. Village streets bustled below them on their right, and the ocean sparkled on their left. They needed to reach the long-boat docked at the road's end.

"I guess it's time for Plan B," said Dagan, sidestepping a chimney.

"What's Plan B?"

"Following that map."

Noa wanted to say, "If we make it out alive!" But he'd just become aware of the guard's heavy breathing behind him. "He doesn't give up, this one!" The overweight man had very nearly caught up, and in a rush of adrenaline, he dove at Dagan. Dagan casually dodged to the side, but the guard, not as nimble as his opponent, torpedoed headfirst into a chimney and knocked himself out, then rolled off the roof into the sea.

"Well *that's just great*," said Noa, peering over the edge. The ocean foamed where the soldier had plunged into the water. "He's not coming up."

"He was trying to capture us!"

"We can't let him die for following orders." Noa thought for a moment, then made his decision. "Take the boat and prepare the ship to set sail. I'll catch up."

"How will you—?"

"Just GO!"

Dagan hesitated, then hurried away. Noa turned around and sprinted back toward the castle.

"You there!" he called to the window cleaners. They backed up nervously against the glass dome. "That man fell in and needs our help! Tie your rope to the chimney. Go on, then!"

With concerned looks, they did as they were told.

"When you feel it tug three times, pull it up."

The window cleaners nodded. Noa gripped the other end of the rope and jumped off the roof. At first, he hit the salty waves in a daze. Then he spotted the soldier sitting on the white sand below. Swimming down, he tied the rope under the man's arms and tugged three times.

Slowly the rope lifted the guard off the seabed. Even under the weightless water, Noa struggled to help lift the unconscious man to the surface. When they broke through the waves, villagers dove in, dragging the man to a wooden landing.

Relief flowed over Noa as water sputtered from the guard's mouth and he took new breaths. But Noa knew he couldn't linger. Slipping back into the water, he swam headlong to the *Evangeline* mooring in the bay.

"All hands make sail!" shouted Noa when he'd climbed aboard sopping wet. He sprinted to help Bones hoist the mainsail. "Let's move, move, *move!*"

"What's going on? Why are we leaving port?" Vim hollered from his place at the rigging.

Noa kept his eyes on the narrow exit. "At your posts! I'll explain once we're outside the gates. Is everyone on board? Where's Dagan?"

"Here!"

"We're all here, Captain!" reaffirmed Malloch.

It took them a moment to get underway. Then they sailed to Martesia's only way out. Black clouds rumbled closer to the island, a wall of rain beneath them. Wind whistled in their ears. Aaron, who'd been watching the sky nervously as he snuck a hand into Pan's bag of greasy sugarooms, now pointed to the village where a mob of soldiers had appeared.

"Are we in trouble?"

Vim glared at Noa accusingly. "They're closin' the gates!"

Ignoring Vim, Noa instructed Malloch to "Bear up!" and the sailor's boy turned the wheel so the ship sailed into the wind. Immediately, they increased speed.

As he stood on the quarterdeck with Dagan and Malloch, Noa's heart blazed with adrenaline. He couldn't believe they were escaping Martesia in such a manner.

The gates started to close.

"Abandon ship!" cried Vim.

"No!" Noa fought back. "We have the wind! We can make it!"

"You're cracked!" said Vim.

The *Evangeline* raced toward the exit. Her hull cut through the waves until the shadow of the gates passed overhead and they were out. Outside of the protected harbor, waves lurched the ship into a nauseating ride. Wisps blew off the whitecaps, and wind gusts shook the sails.

"See?" said Noa, his heart pounding. "I told you we'd make it."

SPSHHHHHH!

Jets of water splashed on them like a waterfall, pouring

down from the top of the gates above and instantly soaking the sails and deck. The crew stood dumbfounded and shivering wet.

Dagan smoothed back his dripping locks. "What's this about?"

A horn blew from the gate, followed by "Fire!" and the whooshing of a catapult. Noa waited for the crunching impact of cannonballs against wood. Instead, he heard sloshing. Five purple balls of slime had landed in the middle of the deck, radiating blue streaks of light.

Noa recognized the creatures at once.

"ELECTRIC OCTOPUS!" he screamed. Electric blue streaks touched the flooded deck, shocking each boy through their sandals. One by one the boys collapsed, convulsing on the main deck.

Noa, Dagan, and Malloch stared in horror from the quarterdeck, the only safe place because of the stairway.

"If you touch the deck, you'll be shocked too!" Noa yelled, stopping Dagan from running down the stairs toward the crew. Another catapult flung octopuses onto the sails, and they slid down the mast.

Noa's throat tightened as he watched the twitching crew. "Where are the bows?" he asked.

"Below deck, Captain!" Malloch shouted, readjusting his grip on the wheel. His knuckles were visibly white.

The *shluck* of tentacles suctioning off the floor resounded across the ship. Noa knew he had to stop the octopuses before it was too late.

Then he remembered he'd left the window open in the captain's quarters.

He tied a rope to the rigging, then threw it over the ship's side. Dagan caught on to Noa's plan and instructed Malloch to keep sailing. Waves almost ten feet high slapped the hull as Noa lowered himself over the edge and into the captain's quarters through the window. Inside, he searched for a weapon.

"The paintings . . ." he whispered, running his hands over the little boy's portrait. He flipped it over to feel the smooth wood on the back. It was *perfect*.

Taking it off the wall, he smashed the portrait on the ground. As expected, the frame broke into jagged pieces, and he passed up the newly formed spears to Dagan, who was leaning off the ship with the rope in his hand. A second painting, this one fully intact, came after it. Then Noa came back up too.

Sitting on the painting at the top of the stairs, Noa gripped a shard of wooden frame in his hand and prepared to slide down to the main deck.

"The longer the boys are in the water, the less chance they'll make it," said Noa, adjusting his rear on the painting. "Bring them below deck when it's safe, are we clear?"

Dagan nodded and gave Noa a push.

Noa zoomed down the steps and skimmed across the thin layer of water, puncturing the octopuses in his path. The moment he stabbed each sac-like octopus, its streaking blue currents disappeared.

A Martesian yacht sailed toward them in the choppy seas. After shocking Noa's crew, the Martesian gatemen were coming to seize the ship. Riding the swells a safe distance away, they waited for an octopus to find Noa and finish him off, but Noa was too quick. He slashed the last octopus, and all electricity disappeared from the soaked deck.

A boy with trousers and mousy hair tucked under a hat came up from below deck, and Noa shouted at him. "Malloch, take the crew below!"

"Captain?" asked Malloch from the quarterdeck behind him.

Noa whipped around. He looked from Malloch to the boy, to Malloch, and back to the boy, at last realizing he did not know the stranger at all.

"Who are *you*?" asked Noa, as he stomped across the deck. "What are you doing here, boy?"

The boy cowered against the mast. "I—I don't want to cause trouble! And I'm not a boy! My name is Ravie. I'm here to help!"

Noa could barely hear her over the flapping sails, loud as the whips of a rug beater. "You're a *Martesian*!"

"I'm looking for a job, yes? You were the first ship leaving the bay."

"You mean you stowed away in our cargo." Noa was in no mood to take pity. "Get off our ship!"

Ravie stared back in horror. "Please don't make me go back. I can help you! I'm a good sailor!"

She was younger than Noa, probably Aaron's age. She couldn't have been more than ten. He glanced at the whitecaps, the foaming swells bubbling with each crashing wave. Could he bring himself to send her overboard?

"Fine. Help him bring the crew below," he snapped, pointing to Dagan. "Then come right back to me and assist with the sails."

"Thank you—"

"Now!"

The girl sprang into action, dragging away a groggy Pan under the arms.

When Noa returned to the helm, Malloch directed his attention to a ship on the horizon.

"We're trapped, Captain," he said in defeat.

Noa reached for the glass to see for himself. A tall figure with a tricorn hat and one eye stood at the helm, staring smugly in Noa's direction. Noa dropped the telescope, stunned.

"Weston followed us from Ondule." Then it hit him. "*He sent the letter to King Pontus in Edjlin's name!*"

"Weston the pirate?" asked Malloch, his brows raising.

"We can't fight back. The whole crew is out," said Noa gravely. "Stay at the helm. We need an escape." He shouted to Ravie, who had returned. "You there! Put out as much canvas as possible. Dagan and I will help."

"Weston's ship is blocking the seas back to Ondule," argued Malloch.

Noa studied the approaching ships around them. Weston's ship advanced from their left, and the Martesian yacht advanced from behind. They were blocked in every direction except the storm, and no one would dare follow them into that. *A light ship could roll.* He recalled the warning from the book he'd read earlier, but their ship was full of cargo now. Cautiously, he took out the magical map from his pocket and pointed to the rumbling clouds ahead. It was already evident from the streaking gray lines that a downpour awaited. Forks of lightning smeared inside the black mist.

"*The storm?*" Malloch's voice quivered.

Rain splattered their faces as they gained speed. Swallowing the lump in his throat, Noa gave the dreaded order: "Yes, straight into it."

CHAPTER 9

SOMETHING BREWING

Water gushed over the main deck and battered the railings. Lightning lit up the monster waves around them before plunging the sea back into an ugly, smeared-gray canvas, followed by clapping thunder. Noa gripped his father's map with both shivering hands. Raindrops bounced off the waterproof parchment as he squinted through sheets of rain at the glowing blue compass and directed Malloch through the waves.

"The sails are reefed!" called Ravie, slipping across the deck toward Noa. She wrung out the water from her cap before slapping it back over her mousy hair. "She'll tip if we leave them open any longer!"

They'd lost sight of both ships in the storm. The focus now

was surviving, and Noa's determination to do so buzzed like a current through every fiber of his being. Everyone on the ship was counting on him. A bolt lit the colossal, frothing waves. Wind and water threatened to tear their vessel apart and send them into a watery grave, but Noa wouldn't allow it. He *must* keep the others safe, keep them alive.

The bow dropped, and all three held the rigging for dear life as the ship skimmed down the back of a wave. Spray splattered their faces like shrapnel. Noa was grateful he had remembered to close the window in the captain's quarters, or else it would be taking on water from the high seas and rain. When they made it to a wide trough, Noa shouted over the churning water for Ravie to head below. There was still much he didn't know about the Martesian girl, but the time for questions would have to wait.

Ravie turned on her heel, slipping and sliding until she disappeared below.

"I think the storm is letting off, Captain!" Malloch hollered from the helm, his tiny arms clutching the wheel to keep it steady.

Like a bubble popping at the surface, Noa's nerves went away. If this was the worst it would get, they were going to make it through the storm. He watched the sailor's son with gratitude. Malloch had known how to steer them through each oncoming wave so they wouldn't tip.

Forked lightning split the sky, electrifying the water, immediately followed by an ear-splitting bang. In other circumstances, Noa would have liked to study the lightning. He was curious to know how storms affected the sea and wondered if any nearby fish were fried, but he stopped himself—*focus on the map!* He squinted through the relentless rain. The compass had glowed blue on the north-northeast corner since their departure from Martesia, and they were struggling to follow it through the storm.

"Keep her steady!" Noa yelled over the screaming wind. They plowed into the rolling swells. Each time, the wheel favored one side, and they had to hold fast to keep her from facing the sea broadside and rolling.

All of a sudden, the map's glow brightened. In the middle of the parchment, ink drew itself into a castle with towers and crenelated ramparts. The only thing strange about the castle was that it appeared to be upside down. Noa held it up for a closer look.

A violent gust tore the map from Noa's hands and blew it down the deck. Noa dove after it.

The deck was awash. The water swept him off his feet, and he slid into the opposite wall. Wiping his eyes, Noa crawled toward the map, which was stuck to the railing. Relieved to find it in one piece, he steadied himself long enough to shove the parchment deep into his pocket. When he turned back on all fours, a voice shouted at him over the rain.

"Spitting sea serpents! It's a bloody mess up here!"

Dagan clung to the rigging, pulling himself through the blasting rain to reach the helm. White water tumbled over the railing and filtered through the scuppers, carrying Noa to the deck's edge. He slid against the wall and stood up to reach Dagan before the next swell rolled in.

"What are you doing here?" Noa hollered at his brother.

Trust Dagan to come running when the chance of being lost at sea had never been higher. "Go back! Get below!"

"I want to help!" Dagan protested.

Noa shook his head furiously. Had his brother gone mad? Any moment, a wave could sweep Dagan overboard. "It's too dangerous!"

Dagan didn't move. He squinted through the spray, trying to make sense of the gray tumult.

"GO *BACK*!" Noa repeated. "I don't need you!"

From the helm, Malloch screamed at them to hold on.

Noa saw the wave a second before it hit. The crest, a white line atop a wall of water, took *Evangeline* at her bow and portside. Noa found himself wholly submerged in green water, tumbling around like seaweed in the surf and slamming into something hard. Pain spiked through his back. The rogue wave drained and sucked him through the railings until he dangled over the ship's side.

"HELP!" he cried. The ship righted herself again. He tried to hold on, but his arms screamed in protest. This was it. He was going to die at sea.

"Take my hand!" shouted Dagan, leaning over the side. Noa reached but slipped off. On the quarterdeck, Malloch hugged the wheel to keep it from spinning uncontrollably. Dagan caught hold of Noa's suspenders, and inch by inch by inch he hauled Noa back in.

"So, not exactly a stroll on the beach up there?" asked Bones.

They were below deck. The storm had passed, leaving its mark on the ship as they sailed through the aftermath swells: barrels had landed onto beds, and anything under the beds had rolled across the floor. It was a miracle the boys had remembered to reattach the guns when they had made port in Martesia. If they hadn't, the three-thousand-pound cannons would have flown across the deck and certainly broke through the hull, an immediate death sentence.

The crew huddled around a communal table near the bow, each boy drinking something hot from a cup. Ravie, the Martesian girl, was dishing out the steaming broth, a quick meal made over the brick furnace in the cookroom.

Water dripped from the ceiling to the blankets wrapped over their shoulders, and plates slid across the table with each rocking motion.

Bones gave Noa a weak smile. "Ravie has been ranting non-stop about our escape, *expecially* from those octopuses."

Noa fought the urge to correct Bones on the proper pronunciation of "especially," but it was neither the time nor the place. Besides, he was too relieved to see him feeling better.

The other boys slurped their soup, blowing steam off the top before swallowing another gulp.

"Well, boys," said Noa proudly. "We've passed through the storm and are heading in the right direction."

"Pray tell, what is the right direction?" asked Vim, slurping from his cup.

"Northeast. We're following my father's map."

"What's in the northeast?"

Noa decided it best to tell them about the castle appearing on the map. "It's not one of the six kingdoms, as far as I can tell, but I believe there is a riddle to it. It's drawn upside down, and that must mean something." Surprisingly, the crew didn't find this as strange as Noa had. They were all tired, and he didn't push the matter further.

Noa sat down at the table and accepted a hot cup, careful not to let it spill when the ship tilted in the waves. He sipped the drink and couldn't help but spit it out instantly.

"We did that too," said Pan, seeing Noa's distaste.

"Couldn't get past the suction cups for ten minutes," said Fig, whose curly hair had frazzled in all directions from the electrocution.

Noa peered into his glass. Inside were floating pieces of purple rubber. "Am I drinking—"

"Octopus? Yes," said Bones, chuckling. "Ravie said the best way to heal from the sting of the electric octopus is to eat one. It's not that bad once you get used to it."

"Electric octopuses are only found in Martesia, d'you know?" said Ravie, spooning another ladleful into someone's cup. "They're our most effective defense."

Vim rubbed his bloodshot eyes. "I can see why."

Now that Noa could hear Ravie correctly without the pouring rain, he noticed she had a distinct accent. All six island kingdoms in the realm of Aztrius spoke the same language, though Noa had learned from his father that separate accents and sayings had come about for each island over time.

Aaron slurped a piece of tentacle, and broth sprayed onto

the cheek of an unsuspecting Ravie, who had just sat beside him with a steaming cup in her hand. Unlike the boys who scarfed down their soups like dogs, Ravie brought her spoon to her mouth with class. She even sprinkled pepper into her cup from a stash of spices in her belongings.

Vim stood up, wiping his hand across his pointy, rat nose. "I'm going to the head. Try not to kill everyone while I'm gone, Noa." His attempt at a sneer looked more like a lopsided smile because of his fatigue. Then he climbed up the ladder and disappeared.

"What's clogging his gills?" whispered Ravie across the table. "You saved his life, no?"

Noa replied, "Don't get me started."

Bones explained, "He's been sour with Noa for a long time, ever since Noa's first day in our school. Noa accidently broke Vim's school project. It was some fish gun or something, I can't remember. Noa offered to help him fix it—"

"More than once," reminded Noa beside them.

"That's right, but Vim was furious. He stormed back home to fix it himself and came so late to school that Lady Penebe made him stand in the corner with his nose to the wall for the entire day."

"That's it?" asked Ravie.

"Oh, you don't know the wrath of Lady Penebe," said Bones, shuddering as he recalled the memory. "When I forgot my quill three times in one week, she made me write the homework down with my tongue. I had to eat cold soup for the next two days, my tongue was so swollen."

Ravie looked shocked. Noa chuckled, wondering if she now imagined a monstrous lady ordering kids to stick out their tongues as she passed out a pop quiz.

When Vim returned, he peered suspiciously into his empty cup. "How do we know we can trust you, Ravie?"

Chaston plunked his cup down and shot Vim a give-it-a-rest stare. "She healed us, Vim. She's on our side."

Vim folded his arms. "For all we know, she could have poisoned us."

The others looked warily at their cups.

"Ahhh, come off it," said Malloch, his freckles tightening around his narrowed eyes. "The soup made you feel better, didn't it?"

Vim sighed and shrugged. He poured more soup into his cup, in no condition to work up an argument.

"Listen," said Ravie, readjusting her cap. "The place I come from doesn't want me. I was tired of it. I didn't know what to do, so I came on the first ship leaving port. Besides, I'm better off alone anyway."

"You came to us for a job?" Noa asked, remembering what she had told him earlier.

"A job?" asked Ravie. "Oh! Right. To find a job, yes." Something about this explanation seemed off, but before he could ask about it, Ravie added, "Besides, I'm the least of your worries."

"Ahhh, but we survived the storm, didn't we?" said Malloch, lifting his mug to toast. The boys cheered and clunked their mugs together.

"No, I'm talking about the rumors," explained Ravie.

Glances made their way around the table.

"Rumors?" asked Noa.

Ravie chuckled and sipped her drink, then observed Noa curiously. "You've heard of the rumors, no?" Everyone shook their heads. Ravie looked taken aback. "There's talk a king wants to bring back the ways of the Death King."

"Which king?" asked Noa impatiently. "Edjlin? It's not my father, is it?"

Ravie blinked. "You're a *prince*?"

"I'm the oldest son of Titus Blackburn."

Ravie scrambled off her seat and bowed. "Slap me with cilantro! I've never met anyone from Ondule, and never a prince! Are you all Ondulians?" she asked, looking around the table in awe. "D'you know, Noa, er, um, Your Royal Highness—"

"—just call me Noa—"

"Oh no, I couldn't. Your Highness, I don't mean to cause offense but . . . I imagined you to look different, yes? From what I've heard of the Blackburn family, I thought you'd look a bit more . . . well, like the boy steering the ship."

Noa didn't even bat an eye. "Yeah, Dagan's my little brother."

Ravie didn't seem to think Noa understood. "Dagan? The one who carried everyone down here?"

Noa nodded irritably. He didn't want to talk about Dagan, the child everyone assumed would one day be king because he looked like their father. Weston made that assumption, Ravie made it too, and worst of all, Noa wondered if they were right to think it.

"You two are brothers?" Ravie went on. "*Blood brothers*? Flour my bottom and stick me in the oven . . ."

"Noa takes after his mum," chimed Bones.

"But . . . if you're a prince . . ." Ravie leaned in so only Noa could hear. "Why are you with *these* fellows? Surely you jest about attending school together, yes? You must have tutors."

Noa fidgeted with the skin around his elbow. "My father thought attending school in the village would help my brother and me cope after my mother passed." He didn't want to say his father also couldn't stand to see them in the castle, walking down the halls Noa's mother walked. It had taken Titus months after she died to even look at Noa, Dagan, and Lana again.

Ravie looked lost for words.

Noa shook it off. "Enough talking about my family. What else do you know about the rumors?"

The boys leaned in anxiously. Even Aaron, who typically had to be pried away from food by force, was so intrigued he forgot to hold his drink, and it slid down the table with the rocking ship.

"My teacher said the rumors were made by bored old men, but when one of our ships was attacked last full moon, people wondered if they might be true."

"Edjlin's ship was attacked as well on his way to Martesia," said Noa, remembering the secret conversation he'd overheard between Edjlin and his father.

"You are mistaken, Your Highness. I heard the sailors myself. *We* were attacked, not Edjlin, by a band of pirates. The captain said the leader was a horrible man with an eye patch. They stole an entire shipment of whale oil."

The room fell silent. Noa's hands balled into fists, his mouth ajar. Edjlin had used that stolen oil to burn down the Ondulian fleet.

"What do Martesians think about *us*?" asked the baker's boy, peeking above his cup.

Ravie sighed. "It's Jonath, yes? Not good. After King Edjlin's visit to our city, people think King Titus Blackburn is the one who turned bad, and that he will try to play victim somehow to gain trust from the realm. I don't believe it, but many do."

Noa's stomach clenched. That explained the Martesians' hostility. And by breaking out of Martesia as pirates, the boys had fed the lies. Their effort to save Ondule had turned into a death sentence, not a rescue mission.

Everyone else seemed to be thinking the same thing. The crew stared at their drinks in silence. Aaron walked around the other end of the table, trying to retrieve his sliding cup, only to have it slide down the table to its original position. The twins began suctioning the octopus's suckers to their fingers to busy themselves.

Eventually, Bones spoke, changing the mood of the room.

"Well, fry me a flounder. If we're outcasts, I say we do it right." He pounded his fist on the table. "We'll sail under our own flag."

Ravie wrinkled her nose. "Fry me a flounder? Do all Ondulians say that?"

"What do they say in Martesia?" asked Bones.

"Slosh my bucket, gulp me some cinnamon . . ." Ravie drifted off self-consciously as Pan and Fig burst into laughter.

"Oi, Pan, slosh my bucket, will you?"

Ravie forced a laugh. "Well, that's not the proper way to use it—"

"Slosh your own bucket, Fig! And stuff your ugly face with cinnamon while you're at it!"

"All right, leave her alone," Bones interrupted when Ravie's cheeks blushed beet red. "Let's talk about this flag. Could we paint a shark on it?"

Noa relaxed as he watched the boys salvage torn bed draping to stitch their flag, ripping the rest to make headbands and neckerchiefs, apparently to appear as "true sailors." He ladled soup into his cup and slipped away above deck.

"That explains it, then," said Dagan, after Noa told him everything. He took another swig of broth from the cup Noa had brought him. "King Edjlin wants to free the Death King and is covering it up by framing Father!"

The smell of rain hung in the air, and the shimmering, moonlit water reminded Noa of the stained glass windows in Salaso's library. It almost looked fake after such a storm.

"You believe the rumors are true?"

"Of course! Spitting sea serpents, Noa, don't you see? Edjlin spoke of venom, *then* we find out the Death King had venom, and *now* there are rumors about someone trying to bring back the ways of the Death King. That's why Edjlin wants the map. He wants the map to lead him to the venom so he can bring back the Death King's ways and live forever."

Noa stared at his brother in the starlight, impressed. But something was missing.

"Edjlin doesn't like the Death King. He fought with Father *against* him. Why would he change?"

Dagan didn't have an answer. Bewildered, they gazed upon the night. A band of stars twinkled across the sky.

A high-pitched squeal disrupted the repetitive swashing waves. It sounded like the squeak of wet shoes. Noa leaned over the railing. The starlight exposed a silver dolphin swimming alongside the ship. Straps were attached to a cylinder container perched in front of its dorsal fin.

"It's carrying a message!"

Noa knew only one person who could train a dolphin to do that: Alya.

Tying a rope around his waist for safety, he unraveled a ladder over the edge and climbed low enough to reach the dolphin, which slipped gracefully through the waves as it tried to keep up. Then he grabbed the pouch, twisted off the cap, and pulled out a tiny, rolled letter. The moment the lid turned back into position, the dolphin bounced away, squeaking and clicking. Noa wondered how the dolphin found their ship, though he didn't bother himself now with finding out how the mammal's brain worked—a *letter* had come. The moment he opened it on deck, his heart fluttered at her perfect, cursive handwriting.

N,

They let me go, but we are being watched. The whole village is being held hostage in our homes. They've taken the mailing pigeons, but I will find a way to send this message.

King Edjlin has your father captive somewhere in the castle. They stood on the castle wall to show the village they are alive.

Lana dropped her locket in the bushes for me, and a message inside said they are confined to their rooms but are being treated fairly. I don't know what King Edjlin is planning, but I hope you are on your way to figuring it out.

—A

PS: Please tell Aaron I love him.

Dagan and Noa swapped glances. By the look of it, Dagan was relieved. Noa felt worse. He should have been comforted knowing his people were alive, but if Edjlin wanted the map, why hadn't he sent all his ships after it? What was he waiting for?

Noa ached to be home, to have things return to the way they were. He pictured Alya working in her father's smithy, sparks flying as she flipped the molten metal and beat it over an anvil. He hoped she had managed to send another letter to a neighboring island—but where? Martesia didn't believe them. Hamaruq, Edjlin's island, couldn't be trusted. Noa didn't know who remained on their side.

He folded the letter carefully. It even smelled like her. The last image he held of Alya falling off the ship and turning herself in scarred his mind. *She's safe*, he reminded himself. *For now, at least.*

Switching the letter for the map, Noa stared at the castle drawing, sure now more than ever the map led to the venom. He still couldn't understand the reason for the castle, let alone why it was wrong-side-up, but for the moment, it didn't matter.

"I'll stay up tonight. Get some rest," he told Dagan. He took hold of the wooden wheel just as the fog rolled in.

CHAPTER 10

AMONG ENEMIES

In the darkness of the early morning, the only light on the quarterdeck came from the map's blue ember. Thick fog covered the water and seeped through the scuppers onto the deck, its gray vapor surrounding Noa at the helm. Noa stood fast, clasping the wheel to keep it steady. The pirate pendant hung around his neck. He'd left it in his Capture the Conch sack for two days, and he now felt it was about time to have another look at it. Tugging the chain with his free hand, he was deep in thought about its meaning. Somehow, he knew the pendant could be useful. After all, he'd seen the same one around the pirate's neck. If only he could trick Weston into thinking they were on the same side . . .

He shook his head, suddenly feeling foolish.

"Your Highness!" yelled a squeaky voice from the main

deck. Ravie emerged from the fog and skipped up the stairs to Noa, adjusting her cap. "I'm supposed to tell you Dagan will take your place soon."

"That's fine. Thank you, Ravie."

Dagan . . . what a lazy bum. Instead of coming up here to tell Noa himself, Dagan had sent up a little messenger. Noa faced the wheel again, only to realize Ravie hadn't left. She peered through a spyglass in the starboard direction. Noa tapped his foot impatiently.

"You won't see a thing."

"I know. It doesn't work," she said, still looking through her spyglass. "Too blurry. I just like to pretend."

"You should go back to sleep with the others." Noa wanted to continue examining the pendant, and he didn't feel comfortable revealing it to the stowaway just yet.

"I've read all about Ondule, but you're the first Ondulians I've ever met. Your people don't travel much, yes? I dream of visiting all the islands in our realm. One day, I want to stand beside Ondule's historic lighthouse watching the sea from the cliffs—"

"Ravie, go to bed." Noa hated to think what rubble remained of his island's precious landmark.

"I can't sleep."

"Try."

"Your Highness, everyone knows trying to make yourself sleep will never get you to sleep."

"Then *don't* try."

"Oh if I don't try to sleep, I definitely won't sleep."

Noa squeezed the wheel a little tighter. The twins' logic had undoubtedly rubbed off on her already.

"Just *go*," he snapped. Regretting his outburst, he added in a kinder voice, "You need rest for tomorrow, is all. I'll ring the ship bell if I need you."

"That's okay. I don't mind keeping you company."

Noa shook his head. At this point, he wondered if Dagan had sent Ravie up to get rid of her.

"Thank you, Your Highness . . . for letting me stay on the ship," she continued, gently closing the spyglass. "I don't belong back there . . . in Martesia, I mean."

"Why not?"

She sighed. "It's complicated." Ravie leaned over the railing to watch the passing sea below. "Nothing unusual in the water tonight? It's the right weather for perishers."

Noa shook his head, smirking. Ravie was still young enough to believe in mer-tale creatures like perishers, a needle-like fish that jumped out of water to impale unsuspecting sailors.

Ravie eyed the water warily, then finally agreed to attempt sleeping again before sunrise. As she moseyed below deck, Noa stared ahead in the fog. *Bah.* He could have used her help spotting sandbanks from the crow's nest, but the girl was driving him crazy. Noa had no idea where he was steering the ship, only that he was following the map. He decided it was worth the risk. At least until Dagan's shift.

He heaved a sigh, wondering how he would have handled sailing at the girl's age. Of course, it wouldn't have been possible. His father hadn't even trusted him to cruise around the island.

Yet in the face of it all, Titus trusted him with the map—a *magical* map. Noa still couldn't believe it. *Magic didn't exist.* His father had pounded the idea into his head ever since he could remember. Why, then, did his father possess something which proved it was a lie?

A loud splash startled him, and he flew forward into the wheel. The ship had stopped. Fog covered his face like a wet cloth, heavy and suffocating without the boat in motion. He hurried through the mist and found that the anchor was no longer suspended from the cathead in the bow but had sunk to the ocean bottom. Noa glanced around uncomfortably.

"Ravie, is that you? Dagan?"

"*What a fineeeee night,*" said a low, chilling voice.

The fog iced the back of Noa's neck.

"Who's there?" Noa hollered into the darkness.

"On a night jusssst like tonight, I met a boy your age."

The voice came from the water. Noa inched to the railing and leaned over the side. His gaze moved from the patch of kelp stuck to the ship's hull to the giant kelp forests floating beneath the dark sea.

"Where are you?" Noa asked, barely above a whisper.

"The other boy didn't sssssssee at firssst, but ssssssoon they all ssssssee . . ."

Noa followed the voice and recoiled in horror, his lips parted in a silent gasp. The patch of kelp had a face, and it was staring right at him.

Noa gawked at the small creature. It looked like a man, except for the distinct likeness to a grisly, bottom-dwelling fish.

Its slippery, blue body was half Noa's size, and long kelp-like hair descended from its bony face.

The moment Noa made eye contact with its large, black eyes, he was transfixed. Moving closer to the creature was the only thing that mattered to him now. Noa leaned forward.

"What do you want?" he asked, staring intently into the creature's eyes. The blue man dug its slender webbed fingers into the wood and climbed ever so slowly up the hull.

"I come to tell you a sssssstory," it said, smiling a black-toothed grin.

"A story? Will it take long?" Noa didn't want to waste time with a story when he could be swimming with the creature instead.

"Shhhhhhhhhhh. You have time enough for this." The creature began. "A boy sssssssailed on his first voyage once, jussssssst like you, to fight againssssssst a man of terrible power, but hissss father forbid him to leave the ssssssship.

"Disssssstraught, the boy was, when I met him. Hissssss father did not believe he wassssss good enough to fight. It wassssss I who convinced him to ssssssstand up for what he wanted."

Noa noticed the creature slither higher up the ship, but he couldn't bring himself to care. His only thoughts were to make the beast happy, and the more he listened, the more comfortable it became.

"The boy fought ssssssssso hard to reach his enemy—"

"Who? Who'd he want to kill?"

The creature's grin curled into its seaweed head. "The Death King, of courssssssse."

The blue creature continued crawling up. Kelp hung around its slimy body. Noa was locked on the obsidian eyes. He couldn't look away even if he wanted to.

Then something pulled on Noa's leg. It was Ravie.

"Your Highness, close your eyes!" she hissed beside him, crouching at Noa's feet. "The longer you look at it, the stronger its control over you will be. It's going to kill you!"

To Noa's surprise, this information only made him want to be with the creature more. He stared into its eyes, daydreaming about what it would be like to live in the water too.

"The Death King could not be sssssstopped. The boy sssss-sealed his fate when he chose to desssssstroy a man who will not allow hissssss own desssssstruction."

The blue man was only a foot away from Noa's face. Bony, webbed fingers reached toward Noa's neck to pull him overboard.

SMACK!

Ravie's spyglass collided with the blue man's face. The creature screeched, breaking the gaze, and fell into the sea.

A heavy haze seemed to lift off Noa. He collapsed. His eyes felt baked.

"What happened?"

"That was a blue man!" panted Ravie at his side. "It's a type of kelpie. It had you in a trance." Boys came on deck after hearing the commotion, their homemade headbands sitting lopsided on their heads.

"Ahhh, all right on deck? We heard screaming," said Malloch, stifling a yawn.

"Everyone to your stations! The blue men are here!" cried Ravie.

Some boys rubbed their tired eyes, while others stretched. They watched Ravie like she'd just said you could walk on the moon.

"What's this about?" Dagan asked.

Ravie tried to crank up the anchor chain, but it was far too heavy. She pointed to Noa, who had begun to stand up, dazed. "We must set sail immediately! We must—will *someone* help me with this?"

But the crew's attention had turned to their disoriented captain.

"What's wrong with Noa?" someone asked.

"Did you say blue men? Like, the creatures from the mer-tales?" asked another.

Ravie abandoned the anchor and hurried across the deck, handing out swords from a barrel, her face pale. "The blue men are no mer-tale; they're the condemned spirits of sailors lost at sea. Sometimes when a man faces death, he will give anything to stay alive. *Even his soul.* Living without a soul is the worst thing in the world. The blue men will do what it takes to make sailors miserable with them."

Noa staggered to the railing where the creature had fallen. He could remember everything now. Waves lapped the side of the ship in the seaweed-filled water. How could he have let this happen?

Behind him, the others were not so easily convinced. Vim had pulled his collar up to make it look like he had no head.

"They can walk on land," Vim told Aaron, rolling his arms like seaweed. "They tie you to the bottom of the ocean until you drown!"

Aaron let out a pathetic plea to leave him alone. When the rest of the crew came on deck to ask what the commotion was about, their bed hair a mess of knots and kinks, Vim pointed an accusing finger at Noa.

"He ain't fit to steer this ship. He's been sleepin' on the wheel, pullin' us off course, and the little Martesian kid is blaming it on some made-up monster."

"Get your head out of the sand, Vim," said Noa, shielding a terrified Aaron behind him, his senses fully returning now. "Ravie's telling the truth. To your posts, everyone, we're leaving these—"

Movement by the railings caught Noa's eye. All at once, slimy blue men flooded the deck. They moved like centipedes, their ribbed bellies low to the ground, their seaweed hair swaying from side to side around their necks as they crawled toward the boys at rapid speed.

"GET BELOW!" Noa shouted.

Scurrying in all directions to find their prey, the blue men swarmed the ship. Kicking one off Malloch, Noa tossed the monster back into the water. The twins fought back-to-back, swiping at the creatures whenever they dared come close, while Jonath tied up a blue man in rope and started mopping the deck with its seaweed head while singing, "What the heck let's swab the deck! More fun for me if I get wet!"

Nearby, Dagan slammed a blue man into the mast and

clonked another on the head with a bucket. Noa came in to help just in time to see Vim pulled overboard.

"Vim!" Noa shouted, sprinting to the edge. More creatures came scurrying, closing in around him.

"Come with ussssss," said one.

Noa averted their hypnotic gaze.

"Like falling asssssssleep. It won't hurt," hissed another, strands of kelp stuck to its bony shoulders.

Vim would be long gone if Noa didn't do something. Looking down, Noa inched closer to a barrel and reached for the coarse rope around its center.

The circle tightened. Noa could almost taste the salt on their skin.

He took his chance.

"NOA! DON'T!" Dagan shouted, fighting off another creature. Noa jumped over the ship's side, barrel and rope in hand, and hit the water with a smacking splash.

The ocean cloaked him in a chilled blanket, seizing his limbs and fizzing up his nose. Noa spun full-circle in a forest of kelp spotlighted by rays of moonlight. Seaweed swayed like the ocean's hair. In the corner of his vision, a webbed foot escaped into the thicket.

Returning to the surface, Noa breathed in the warm air whooshing over him. The barrel bobbed on the waves nearby. A bunch of bananas floated past him, then a pineapple. Had the fruit come from their ship? He snatched the barrel rope and took the largest breath he could muster, then dove back under, pulling the marker of his position along with him.

Slimy kelp brushed his face. He pushed it aside and swam faster, deeper into the sunken jungle. Passing stalks as thick as his arms, he floated over mounds of black mud and rocks littered with blades of fallen kelp and violet sea urchins . . . then, he found him.

Green weeds tied Vim to the seafloor. He squirmed and screamed tirelessly upon Noa's arrival—except the only thing his cries accomplished was a stream of rising bubbles. Noa tried in vain to untie the knots. Then thinking fast, he thrust the barrel rope into Vim's hand and swam down.

As if he swam through a wall, the water changed from cold to ice. His eardrums squeezed into his head. Squishing into the freezing mud, he searched desperately for something sharp, picking up rocks and broken shells, then dropping them to the side. A crab skittered away from the commotion. Salt pierced Noa's eyes.

Grasping a sharp rock, he returned to Vim's side to saw through the reeds. Vim thrashed and kicked for breath. His panic made it harder to work, especially when Noa's own lungs burned for want of air.

Finally, Vim broke loose. Together, they pushed off the ground and rocketed to the surface.

Never had the two gasped louder or deeper in their lives. Noa held onto the barrel, panting in the warm night air, and hoisted Vim above him. Vim hugged the barrel for dear life, vomiting green sea.

"The ship. . . isn't . . . far," Noa assured him, trying to steady his breathing.

The ship, however, was nowhere in sight. Fog enveloped them, making it impossible to see more than ten feet ahead. Noa held the rope and kicked in the direction he imagined the ship to be, moving quickly through the swells despite the baggage he towed. Nothing good could come from lingering, for the creatures would soon realize their prisoner had escaped.

"Where's the boat?" Vim coughed.

Noa kept paddling, pulling Vim along. He hadn't realized how far he'd swum to find Vim.

"This ain't right. We're probably swimmin' away from the ship!"

Noa smacked the barrel. "Don't you know what's beneath us? I'm not waiting around."

Green, freezing waves splashed Noa's face as he pushed the barrel forward. His limbs were beginning to stiffen. He'd never known such cold.

Morning sunlight peeked over the hazy horizon, silhouetting something big. At first, they thought their eyes were playing tricks, but soon they could make out sails.

"WE'RE OV-V-V-VER HERE!" Noa called out, cupping his hands around his purple lips and chattering teeth. "OV-V-VER HERE!"

Vim leaned down to help paddle with his hands, and his eyes suddenly bulged into saucers.

"Noa! They're—they're coming!" he screamed.

"I know they're coming!" said Noa, his spirits lifting as the ship loomed closer in the morning fog.

"Not them, *them!*"

Vim pointed below, but there wasn't enough time to react. Webbed hands shot out of the water and pulled Noa under. He thrashed, reaching for kelp stalks only to have them bend like spaghetti when he grabbed them. The creatures' needle-point fingers pulled him to the seabed and slammed him into the chilled mud. His air escaped in a burst of bubbles and his pendant, freed by a slash in his shirt collar, floated above his face.

Then something odd happened. The creatures *stopped*. Noa felt their bony fingers abandon their grip as they fled into the stalks, their enormous black eyes fixed on the pendant. Noa tried to make his move. They recovered quickly, jerking him down with more force.

"Imposssssssster!" they hissed. "IMPOSSSSSSSTER!"

Noa's head buzzed. It felt as though an invisible hand ground his ribs into his sternum—he needed to breathe! He flailed helplessly, random fleeting images crossing his mind: Lana's poofy dress . . . Alya's lips he had never kissed . . . and, inexplicably, his room; he regretted leaving it in such a mess.

Desperately, he repressed the urge to inhale. He'd read about drowning and the continuous involuntary gulping that would fill his lungs with water. He knew it was only a matter of time before it happened to him too.

Then in one swift motion, Noa's knees were thrust into his chest. He was pulled out of the darkness, past the towering kelp forest, and into the morning sun.

CHAPTER 11

PENDANT PROBLEMS

Noa felt people handling him, untangling him, and then laying him down. His cheek pressed into the hard, wet deck as he gasped and coughed. Nearby, Vim shouted to give him space.

"I'm innocccccccccccccccent," said a familiar, chilling voice. Noa's bloodshot eyes flew open. The boys surrounded a blue man, a fishing net wrapped around its slimy legs.

"What's going on?" Noa coughed and tried to stand. Puddles followed him with each dripping step he took toward the group.

"Stand back!" Dagan snapped at Noa. "You're lucky the twins found the fishnet, or else you'd be dead."

"Give him a rest, Dagan," said Vim. "I would be sleepin' with the fishes if it weren't for him."

Noa stole a surprised glance in Vim's direction. It wasn't a thank you, but it was something.

Shuffling forward, Pan cleared his throat. "We have a problem. Those things tossed our food overboard through the gunports, along with some of our extra swords—"

"—and oddly enough, Aaron's blankets," added his twin, Fig.

Aaron whined in dismay.

"They only stopped when we set off the coconut crackers. Didn't like the sparks."

"We have no food? None?" Noa asked in alarm. Beside him, Bones cracked his knuckles nervously.

Pan stole a guilty sidelong glance at Fig. "There are a *few* extra things the blue men didn't find . . ." Noa couldn't believe it; the twins had been stockpiling dried fruit under their cots again.

Panic ensued from learning their food supplies had depleted. Some wanted the blue man dead, but no one wanted to kill it. Others wanted to throw the creature overboard, only to reconsider when they imagined it coming back with its friends. Eventually, they decided to lock it up and guard it. Bones's carpentry was used to create a cage they would throw in the brig, for double protection. The blue man hissed at this decision.

"When we return home, the law can determine its sentence," said Noa.

Vim turned to Ravie suddenly, towering over her. "Ain't it funny the first time we see a blue man is when you come along?"

Ravie looked taken aback. "D'you think this is my fault?"

"You knew what to do," said Vim, indignant. The others observed the girl.

Ravie adjusted her cap, recognizing the boys' honest confusion. "My mother is a sailor, yes? She came across the blue men once. They are normally polite monsters. They only attack who they put in a trance. But I hit it in the face with my spyglass, yes? So, it didn't turn out well."

"You're saying you've always known about those things?" Noa asked, dumbfounded.

Ravie nodded. "My mother visited my school to talk about it when we were studying History of Conjuring Creatures. You've learned about them too, no?"

"In bedtime stories . . ." said Noa slowly, and a strange pity came over Ravie's face. Only the waves splashing against the hull could be heard as the crew exchanged confused glances, altogether aware this was bigger than them. Either their parents didn't know of mythical creatures either, or they did know and had lied about it. Noa could see these worries building like storm clouds in their eyes.

Whether the villagers knew or not, the real culprit, Noa feared, was the one who would undoubtedly have known the truth and said nothing: Noa's father.

Finding their voices, the crew exploded in outrage.

"Why didn't we learn about mythical creatures in school?"

"Are the grown-ups lying to us?"

No one had answers. The boys could do nothing but disperse to their morning tasks, brooding with contempt for their home. Malloch took his place at the helm. Ravie and Aaron found the only two mops left after the attack and began swabbing the deck, a necessary chore to rid the wood of salt.

Alone near the mast, Noa told Dagan what had happened below the waves.

"When the blue men saw the pendant, they looked afraid." He pulled off his tunic and draped it over the ratline to dry in the wind, then examined the pendant hanging off his bare chest. "I think they confused me for someone else."

Dagan smirked. "Who? A butt-sniffing monkey?"

Noa let out a false laugh. "Sure, laugh now, but I reckon I'm the first to be entranced by a blue man and live to tell the tale. They'll write about this in the history books . . . study it . . . why, they may even rename the Salgueeze Sea after me."

He waited patiently for Dagan to process this information.

"No fair!" cried Dagan moments later. "*I* want to be famous! Last week you said magical creatures were nothing but mer-tales!"

"What can I say?" said Noa, with a contemptible smirk. "I always knew I would be a part of a scientific discovery."

Quick as lightning, Dagan pounced on Noa, and although Dagan had the upper hand in strength, Noa was always better at squeezing out of tight situations. Wiggling free, he rubbed his knuckles into Dagan's scalp, spreading his brother's midnight locks in every direction.

"You're—wrecking—my—hair!" Dagan shrieked, wrenching free. He shoved Noa into a passing Ravie, who flew backward, her mop and bucket clattering to the deck. Flat on her back in the watery mess, Ravie did nothing to complain. Instead, she stared, bug-eyed, at Noa's bare chest.

"Why are you wearing *that*?" she asked, pointing to the pendant.

Noa pulled the girl to her feet. He didn't like the way she was watching him. "I found it."

"Found it? You know what it is, yes?"

Noa and Dagan, who was desperately smoothing his hair back into its usual cowlick, stood up straighter, intrigued.

"A pirate medallion?" asked Noa.

For the second time that night, Ravie looked shocked by the boys' lack of knowledge.

"That's no pirate symbol; it's the symbol of the Death King! That pendant belonged to his most trusted followers. How did you find it? They've all been lost, no?"

Noa felt his mouth fall open. *The Death King?*

"I knew it!" cried Dagan, pointing to the pendant with gleeful surprise. "Didn't I say it belonged to the Death King? Didn't I say?"

Noa tugged on the chain, an undeniable sickness coming over him. Why had he seen this symbol in his father's chamber?

Eyeing the boys warily, Ravie gathered the mop and bucket and turned to leave. "I should go . . . if you need me, I'll be in the galley sorting what's left of our breakfast rations. Captain, Prince Dagan."

"Wait," Noa grabbed her arm. "I never thanked you for saving my life. You were brilliant."

The smile ripening at the corners of Ravie's lips was

unmistakable: the smile of someone who never received compliments. Noa knew it well.

"Perhaps one day you can return the favor."

"Let's hope there'll be no need."

"Weird one she is," said Dagan, watching Ravie go below deck. "Did you notice she wears a necklace too? She wears it backwards. I can see the chain at the back of her neck, but I've never seen her take it off."

"So?"

"So . . . I have a theory. I was on the pooper at the ship's head—"

"—I don't need to know *where* you came up with this theory—"

"All right . . . while I was doing . . . *you* know, I kept thinking . . . she's hiding something. She could be a spy."

"That's ridiculous."

Dagan slapped Noa on the back. "She knows an awful lot, don't you think?" Then he shrugged, looking embarrassed. "Anyway, Malloch and I will take the wheel today."

Noa wandered below deck to check on the others before he retired to sleep. Aaron, Bones, Vim, and Chaston lay in their cots, staring at the ceiling.

"It's fine, Aaron," Noa assured the boy when he tried to explain why they weren't working.

Noa slumped on the cot next to Bones. Aaron looked over sadly, the blankets on his own bed lost to a watery grave. They stared into space as they each remembered the night's events, listening to the creaking ship.

Lying on the bed with his hands behind his head, Bones asked, "Why does the map show a castle?"

Noa explained Dagan's theory that the castle contained the venom Edjlin sought.

"Then who does the castle belong to? It can't be the Death King's. We destroyed his castle in the Battle of the Mines," said Bones.

"The venom ain't supposed to exist either," Vim pointed out. "Isn't that what it said in your book?"

Noa nodded. He wondered if the castle existed, or if it was a trick, like a tapestry of a castle or a castle shield.

Pan and Fig tumbled down the ladder, giggling and whispering as they tried to protect the contents of a bucket. When they saw the others, Pan shielded the bucket behind his back and whispered hoarsely, "Don't let him see!" They kept their eyes on Vim as they skittered up the ladder once again and out of sight. Noa guessed they were planning another prank on Vim, but he didn't bother to speak up. He needed some entertainment tomorrow.

None of the others had noticed the twins. They were still lost in their thoughts. On the cot, Chaston rolled onto this stomach, frowning. "I hope my house is still in one piece. My mum's already busy with my little brothers; she can't rebuild a house too."

Noa knew Edjlin wouldn't destroy the village—he needed the villagers to cooperate—and he told them this.

"Who says they'll cooperate? We didn't," said Vim.

Noa stared at the knots and swirls of the planks above him, thinking of Ondule. He felt a twinge of guilt knowing his home, though it could be taken over, could never be destroyed as their feeble cottages could. How could he show these boys this would all be over soon?

He sat up suddenly, knowing just what to do to build their confidence, and dashed up the ladder. When he returned, he unraveled parchment onto the table, and the boys circled him.

"I've been working on this map from spare parchment I found in Edjlin's desk," he explained. "The map in the captain's quarters is too big to carry to the helm, and I like to compare it with the magical map to see where we're going. See here? That's Hamaruq, may they rot in the sea. That's Martesia, they might as well rot too for what they did, and this is Ondule."

"This is brillylent," said Bones, studying the legend in the corner. "Absolutely brillylent."

"Are those supposed to be electric octopuses?" asked Aaron, pointing to small, eight-legged drawings that better resembled spiders with lightning streaks coming from their heads.

Noa nodded, surprised Aaron even had to ask. He dragged his fingers past Martesia to the open ocean. "We've been sailing north-northeast since Martesia. If my calculations are correct, we are somewhere here. It can't be long before we find this castle."

"There are no more islands in this direction. We're passing the boundaries to the realm," Chaston pointed out. Fixing his ponytail, he glanced up to see if Noa confirmed his suspicions.

"Yes . . . but there must be an island out there, perhaps too small to put on a map. There's no other explanation for the map leading me in that direction."

"Maybe it ain't that it's small," said Vim slowly, pulling away from the chart. "Maybe the island ain't on the maps of Aztrius because it ain't supposed to be found."

Noa ran his hand over the blank spaces representing the ocean, wondering what else awaited him that his father had failed to mention.

CHAPTER 12

THE UNQUALIFIED EXCHANGE

In the days of sailing that followed, new forms of fun distracted the boys from hunger. The food the twins had stockpiled was enough to keep them alive a week more if they were smart about it. The crew's favorite game quickly became "Save the Doop," where two teams battled to rescue a tied-up Aaron who, with bedsheets draped over him and a mop on his head, had involuntarily been chosen as the designated "Doop."

"Ravie, join in!" hollered a drenched Jonath after one game had turned into a water fight. Above them, the crew's makeshift flag flapped on the foremast.

One look at Aaron hanging from the mast by his soggy underpants made up Ravie's mind for her.

"Can't," she said, shuffling back inconspicuously, and the mousy girl dropped below deck just as the twins dumped two buckets of seawater on Jonath's head.

When the sun shone its hottest, Malloch gathered the boys below deck to educate them on the correct terminology for the sails, rigging, and ropes. Rarely did it last, however, before their restlessness resulted in sword-fight training with Dagan or gunfire lessons with Chaston. The blasts rendered them deaf for several hours afterward, which wasn't a problem until Vim mistakenly took Aaron's "I'm hungry" signal for wanting a punch in the stomach.

On the other hand, Noa's swordsmanship had never been so good. If he wasn't staring at the map, he found himself practicing the steps Dagan had taught them. All the while, the boys sailed guided by the magical map, wondering what awaited them at the glowing castle.

It was on the second night that Noa had volunteered to take a shift guarding the blue man, despite the crew's protests that he shouldn't expose himself to the hypnotic creature again.

"Three sharks have been following in the vessel's wake all day—it's a bad omen," said Malloch nervously, blocking Noa's path to the brig. Noa slipped past, careful not to disclose the real reason he wanted to see the blue man.

"I'll only be on watch until Aaron's morning shift," he assured him.

At the sound of Noa entering the brig, the blue creature

retreated to the far corner of its crate and hissed. Its skin looked like the aftermath of a bad sunburn—no longer slimy, flakes of skin peeled at its joints, and its seaweed hair had dried and stiffened.

"It looks terrible," said Noa as Chaston stood up from his post. "Have we given it anything to eat?"

"You can't be serious," said Chaston, his own lips cracking from lack of water. He turned to leave but stopped at the door. "Be careful."

The blue man hissed in response. Noa took his seat and watched it curl into the fetal position. Cloth covered its eyes, its hands and feet were tied, and with each rasping breath, it exposed its black, triangular teeth.

The blue man was as real as Noa's own flesh. He remembered the ceramic bowl Alya had shown him when she'd snuck into the castle—magical creatures *did* exist. He could no longer deny it. He almost wished Alya could see the blue man, to know she had been right all along, but then he reconsidered. He didn't want that thing anywhere near her.

Perhaps, Noa surmised, his father had kept magical creatures a secret for his protection? But that didn't make sense. Not knowing about the creatures almost cost him his life. Titus must have known about the animals if other islands, like Martesia, were teaching about them in school, yet he'd pretended they were only stories for children.

Hatred welled like bile in Noa's belly. How could his father betray the kingdom like this?

"Sssssssssssso deeply you ponder, Your Highnessssss."

Noa leaned away. Could it read his mind?

"You've come for answerssssss," taunted the blue man. It lifted its head, although the cloth still covered its eyes.

Noa cleared his throat. "What can you tell me about my pendant?"

The creature jeered at him. "You are an imposssssssster . . . the necklace issss the Pendant of Privilege!"

"What's that?" Noa asked in one quick breath.

"Ssssssssssorry, Your Highnessss, I cannot help you until you help me. I need the ssssssssea."

It curled up again, waiting. Understanding what the creature needed, Noa hollered for Aaron to fetch him a bucket of water and dumped the seawater onto the beast. Instantly its hands regained their slime, and its seaweed hair slid once more like tentacles across its bony back.

"Ahhhhh . . . " it sighed deeply.

"Now tell me what you know," ordered Noa.

The blue man snickered scathingly, but it obliged. "Pendantsssss were worn by the Death King'sssss clossssssssssest friendssssssss. They were the privileged, the onessss who would help him build the new world."

"New world?"

"Yessssss, a world where the oppressssssed become the oppressorsssss . . . where one kingdom controlsssss both the lands and the ssssssea. The Death King alone wasssss ssssssssstrong enough for thisssss."

"But he failed . . . he has no followers left."

A devilish smile pulled at the blue man's lips.

"How many are there, then?" demanded Noa, rattling the cell.

"Many," it said icily.

Noa rubbed his thumb over the cool metal design. He understood its symbols now: the mountains represented the earth, and the waves represented the ocean. The Death King wanted the world.

When his shift finished, Noa strung the pendant on a hook in the brig. It clinked against the metal lantern with each toss of the sea.

"Let this remind you the Death King is dead," he told the blue man. "No one wears the pendant now."

By breakfast on the fourth day, they were down to a daily four biscuits each. Aaron's hungry eyes followed Noa as he crossed the deck to give him his rations. Crumpled in a heap beside him, Ravie slept. They all slept more these days. Near Ravie, Noa found one of the twins folded over the railing like a shirt draped over a chair.

"Look at all that undrinkable drink," Pan croaked, gazing at the passing sea. He held a homemade fishing rod over the edge. It hadn't brought in a single fish. Their only net had been torn by the blue man. Noa hurried away to retrieve the twins' rations before one of them collapsed.

They were almost out of grog, a mixture of palm beer and water, rationing it to a cup a day. Still, they saw no sign of civilization.

"We're nearly out of the realm boundaries. I thought we

would have reached the castle by now," said Noa that afternoon, comparing the glowing map with the one he'd drawn. Clouds cast shadows over the ocean like splashes of spilled octopus soup.

The brothers lounged around the captain's quarters in their underpants, their sweat-stained clothes hanging from wires above them. The afternoon sun beat down on the ship, and Noa's mouth felt uncomfortably dry.

Picking a book from the shelf, he strode over to the bed.

"That's my spot."

"Seriously?" Dagan sighed and moved to the sofa, while Noa crawled into the still-warm bed.

Ever since he had realized magical creatures existed, he couldn't stop reading about them. He studied how to heal from sea-sprite bites and how to avoid offending a mermaid (asking the weight of her tail or commenting on another maiden's beauty were at the top of the list for provoking mermaid attacks). Noa read about one sailor who told a mermaid she reminded him of his mother and was never seen again.

He flipped to the part called "Categories of Humanoids," where he'd left off earlier, absentmindedly plucking his eyebrows as he read:

Monstrous Humanoids

Those who fall into the above category are humanoids who instill fear in the human species. They act similarly to a human through speech and movement but are not human. The most feared humanoid of the sea is the blue man, a creature dreaded by seafarers of old because of its supposed ability to entrance its victims into willingly drowning. The blue man (more commonly

*known in its plural form "the blue men" because of its tendency
to group) cannot resist gossip and has often been found to tell
stories to its prey. The blue men congregate in the relatively calm
waters of the Salgueeze Sea, lying north of the island Martesia. Due
to its strong clockwise current, the Salgueeze Sea has significant
amounts of kelp and seaweed found in the area and contributes
to the blue men's natural habitat.*

"Why do you read so much?" asked Dagan. He stared longingly at the cover in Noa's hands as if he wished he had the
desire to read too. Noa caught the look just before it disappeared.

"Dunno," said Noa simply, but he sensed Dagan wanted
more. He closed the book in his lap. "Mother taught me to love
it. You and Father had adventures; Mother and I had books."

"You could have had adventures with Father too."

Noah hmphed.

Dagan frowned. "Will you ever forgive him for what happened to her?"

"I . . . have," said Noa, stiffening against the headboard.

Dagan snorted. "Sure. I heard you say you hated him. I don't
think that's fair. It's not his fault she got sick."

"I don't want to talk about it."

"Why? You never want to talk about Mother."

"I said I don't want to talk about it, all right?" Noa snapped.

An uncomfortable silence settled between them, one only
interrupted by the twins strolling in unannounced and handing
Dagan a bundle of kitchen knives. Noa didn't even bother to ask.
He flipped through the pages until he found his spot once again,
only to stare blankly at the infinite black letters on the page.

Thunk.

A knife stuck into the painting above Noa's head. Slamming the book shut, Noa stood up, catching his balance on the tilting floor, and pointed an accusing finger.

"Are you *mad*? You almost killed me!"

Dagan shrugged. "Nah, not even close. D'you want to give it a go?"

Noa shook his head furiously. "NO—I—DO—NOT—WANT—TO—"

"Suit yourself." Dagan seized another knife and threw it as hard as he could. The blade stuck deep in the painting's center.

Noa scrambled away before Dagan could fling another. "What is *wrong* with you?"

"Relax," said Dagan, tossing the knife playfully into the air. "Wilson and I have been practicing. Oh! Oops." He laughed sheepishly. "I thought you were Father for a second."

Few things could have hurt Noa more. "I know how hard it must be to differentiate between the brother who has taken care of you every day since Mother died and the man who sent us away to live among the commoners."

"Come off it. You love the village," said Dagan, flinging another knife. "You know, you've always been like this. You think Father doesn't have time for us, but when did you last make time for him? You're not the only one who misses Mom."

"I didn't say I was."

Noa wondered what Dagan would say if he knew the truth about her death.

The thump of a knife hitting its target pulled him from his thoughts.

"You act like it," said Dagan. "And by the way, people don't like it when you're a bossy butt."

Noa scoffed. "I'm sorry I can't goof off and drink coconut juice all day like you. Some of us have real responsibilities—like becoming king! Not like *you* would understand."

"Oh, yeah?" said Dagan, firing up. "Well, if being next in line for the throne makes you an uptight fart sniffer, then I don't want it anyway!" He marched to the door with his nose so high in the air that he tripped over the rug and clocked his nose on the doorknob.

Blood flowed freely, smearing on his cheeks as he cradled his face in his hands. Noa grabbed several sheets of parchment to stop the bleeding and rushed to Dagan's side, guiding him toward the desk chair.

"You're still a fart sniffer," said Dagan through a mouthful of paper as he sat down.

Noa said nothing to this. He knew his brother was right. "Pinch your nose, Dag. You have to stop the bleeding."

"For your information," said Dagan, taking more parchment from Noa's hand, "Mother loved it when I goofed off."

"I know, Dag." He sighed. "I know."

Twenty minutes later, they sat in silence watching the horizon bob up and down through the window, dried blood on both their hands. A burst of spray signaled a whale nearby. Noa scraped the red from under his fingernails with a knife, and suddenly he had the urge to throw the knife as hard as he could. He did. It landed in a book more than three feet away from the desired target.

"You're doing it wrong, you ninny," said Dagan, taking the paper off for a moment to speak. "Focus on your target. Imagine it's the evil broccoli who kept stroking your eyebrows."

"Dag!" Noa playfully nudged his brother into the desk. "I never should have told you that dream."

Dagan chuckled, unfazed. It took Noa a moment to refocus, but when he did, his knife hit much closer to his target.

"What's this?" asked Noa when he retrieved the knives that landed in the bookshelf.

The Rise and Fall of the Death King

Noa's heart skipped a beat. He dropped the knives and pulled the book off the shelf. Flipping through it, he spotted chapters on the different islands who agreed with the Death King, his methods of torture, his voyages, conspiracies, and then . . .

"Grandfather's in here!" he gasped.

"What does it say?" Dagan peered over Noa's shoulder to read the same page.

Venicius Blackburn, king of Ondule, remained faithful to the Treaty of the Seven Kingdoms until his death. He fought alongside his longtime friend, Galvin Driggonhall, in the Battle of the Mines, along with the armies of Albert Caraway III and Haden Horatio, forging a pact now known as The Four Good Kings. Blackburn was the only king to die in the battle.

Noa looked up. "The Four Good Kings . . . Galvin Driggonhall, that must be Edjlin's father. Albert Caraway is the father of the king of Martesia, and Haden Horatio must be the last king of

Blightip—they supported the Treaty of the Seven Kingdoms that protected the islands from invasion, even when some of the other islands fell away to join the Death King."

"I figured that," said Dagan, "although I'm not sure I understand why it's seven kingdoms when there are only six."

Noa frowned. "The seventh island belonged to the Death King. Only rubble was left after the battle. It's been erased from all maps . . . I'm not even sure where it is, but the Treaty means one kingdom cannot invade or become independent without the agreement of the others. It helps balance power—peace against traitors."

"Some good that did," Dagan scoffed. "We got invaded and no one believed us."

Noa flipped through the pages, biting his lip. "After grandfather died at the hands of the Death King's pirates, Father stopped at nothing to drive out the pirates and restore justice to the realm. He's the biggest enforcer of the Treaty I know."

"Ironic, isn't it?"

Noa chuckled. "I know. Does this book have any more . . . ah, there it is. There's a whole chapter on it." His eyes flashed across the pages while he read. "The battle *did* happen in mines. I always thought that was a metaphor."

Dagan waited for Noa to explain.

"They mined the mountains like us, but this island was volcanic. It says here they were famous for their jewels and traded them throughout all of Aztrius, but the Death King became greedy and tortured his people for more work until The

Four Good Kings stopped him in what we now call the Battle of the Mines."

"Who killed the Death King, then?" asked Dagan, crumpling the bloody parchment in his grip.

"No one. It says he poisoned himself."

A thought came into Noa's mind, and he grabbed *Sea of Kings: A History of Aztrius*. He stopped on the circled paragraph he had read earlier. Eyeing the question mark inked in the margin, he scrunched his brow, wondering how it all fit together.

At the helm, Malloch and Noa steered the ship. The sunset stretched across the clean horizon like pink ribbons on one of Lana's dresses, branding the clouds with its paint and reflecting in shards across the fragmented water, but even the beauty of its blending colors was tainted by the hunger pains gnawing at Noa's insides. He licked his lips, trying to recall the taste of a juicy mango or the crunch of a garden carrot.

Straightening up, he grabbed the spyglass. There was something out there. Focusing his sights on a gray bump in the distance, his heart leapt. He checked the map. The compass arrow pointed directly at it.

"That's where we're going," he told Malloch, a grin widening on his sunburned face. "We're almost there."

An island, a castle, a secret army . . . whatever it was, they were on their way to reaching it. Soon his kingdom would be back in rightful hands. What riches awaited in the map's castle that he could use to bargain with Edjlin? He dreamed of wearing a cape more beautiful than his father's, a glittering sword in his hand and piles of treasure resting at his feet . . .

"Ahhh, Captain! Wake up!"

Noa jerked awake on the floor of the quarterdeck. Nightfall had thrown its cloak over the sky, and Malloch stood above him at the helm pointing to lights twinkling on the black horizon.

"Is it the glowing castle?" Noa asked, rubbing his eyes. They were the only two on deck.

Malloch handed him the spyglass. "It's a ship."

Noa's stomach twisted. It was too dark to see what colors flew on the mast. Was it help or the enemy? He unfurled the map to see if they'd travelled off course, but his heart stopped. The glowing compass was gone. In its place, the traditional map of the realm had reappeared. Plain, boring, and useless.

Where was the glowing compass? Where was the up-side-down castle? Noa's heart began to pound.

"It's probably a fishing boat. . ." he told Malloch, trying to steady the quiver in his voice. Discreetly, he tucked the map into his pocket. "Keep a straight course. . ."

At sunrise, the distant sails were not so distant anymore. The silhouette of a man at the helm stood out against the pink sky, confirming Noa's fears. It was a man with a tricorn hat.

"It's Weston," said Noa, his mouth pursing into a thin line. "How did he find us?" Noa glanced from the pirate ship to the distant gray speck, his spirits sinking. If they continued sailing toward the map's destination, they would collide with the pirates on the open sea. The choice was clear: they had to turn around and run away. With a heavy heart, he gave the command. "All hands on deck! Prepare to come about!"

Tired boys scampered to their posts with confused and worried looks.

"What's going on? Ain't this the wrong way?" asked Vim, looking past his pointy, rat nose to glare into the sunrise.

"We'll come back in the night," said Noa.

The *Evangeline* changed course until Weston's ship lay directly behind them. Wind filled the sails, and they sped over the waves away from the enemy.

"Slosh my bucket! Those are pirates!" cried Ravie, adjusting her cap to watch the approaching ship.

"They're gaining on us," said Malloch, wiping a nervous sweat from his brow. "We've gone the same direction since Martesia. They must have caught up during our detour with the blue men."

Dagan sprinted up the steps, glancing frantically between the two. "What should we do?"

"We won't outrun them," said Malloch fearfully. "Not today."

Noa's face hardened. His fists clenched. It wasn't fair. They were so close. "Make ready the guns," he announced in a firm voice.

Malloch turned, eyes wide. "*What?*"

"We have no choice," said Noa. "If they take the ship, they'll kill us. You saw how they tried to sink us the first day. Our only chance of surviving and reaching that island is to cripple their mast and stop them from sailing altogether."

Dagan pulled Noa to the side. "Those are skilled sailors, skilled *murderers*, and you want us to battle them single-handed?"

"Not single-handed," said Noa, shaking his head. "We'll take down their mast before they come aboard." He gripped Dagan's arm. "I've done the calculations. If you strike the mast at a forty-five-degree angle, you'll get the most power. I've seen your aim, Dag. You hit bullseyes with throwing knives, you can do it with a cannon."

"I don't know how much forty-five degrees is!"

Noa wasn't listening. "Shoot down their mast, and we won't have to fight. Trust me. This will work."

Dagan studied Noa's face as he made up his mind. For once, he seemed apprehensive about something dangerous. Noa, on the other hand, couldn't be surer.

"They're *pirates*," Noa went on. "You've heard the stories; they'll force us to join them or walk the plank, and I swear on Mother's grave I will never join with pirates."

It took a moment for Dagan to gain composure. Then straightening up to face the crew, he bellowed out the dreaded command. "MAKE READY THE GUNS!"

Chaston led the crew to the cannons below deck. Before Noa could fully grasp the situation, Weston's ship trailed in their wake and pulled up broadside, their gunports springing open. Unshaven pirates jeered beside fully loaded cannons as the ships sailed side by side. Standing above his crew, Weston grinned wickedly, adjusting the strap to his eye patch for a better view of the carnage.

"Surrender, lads!" he bellowed. The ships had slowed as crews left the sails to man the guns.

Noa hesitated, his heart thumping in his chest. This would work, right? He unsheathed his sword. "FIRE ALL!"

Weston retaliated without missing a beat. Cannons shot from both ships, blasting wood into the air. Dagan fired and clipped the enemy mast. All they needed was one more good shot, and the mast would topple, rendering the pirates helpless. As the guns reloaded, smaller bangs reverberated around them.

"They're using Boomers!" Malloch screamed, covering his ears.

Weston's crew fired at them with smaller, hand-held weapons. They worked similarly to the cannons, firing little metal balls out the barrel, but they were illegal in Aztrius. It was considered dishonorable to kill a man without giving him a fighting chance. *Typical pirates.*

Dagan's second shot missed. He quickly reloaded. Noa climbed onto the rigging, swatting at the pirates trying to swing aboard. Two splashed into the sea, but one pirate landed on deck. Noa parried the pirate's sword as quick as his feet could carry him. He felt the difference his practice had made ten times over.

BANG!

An explosion sent Noa flying backward. He slid across the floor and fell to the lower deck, landing at the bottom of the ladder with a smack. Pain reverberated up his spine. Another wave of cannon fire exploded from both ships, spraying wood chips like confetti.

In the brig, the wall blew away in an ear-splitting bang,

sending the blue man flying against the bars, smashing its crate, and loosening its bonds. Scrambling to its feet, the creature dove through the open wall into the sea.

Noa staggered toward an animated Chaston, who was firing with Ravie at his side.

"Shoot their mast! They're boarding the ship!"

Chaston hollered back, "We're trying! Look out!"

A pirate kicked Noa in the back, knocking him to the ground. He pointed his sword at the back of Noa's head.

"Surrender, boy. Or I cut ya to the deck."

Rolling over, Noa stared down the blade, sweat dripping into his ears. Behind him, Chaston shouted that the pirates' mast had been hit. Victory!

Noa grinned at the pirate. "I think it's you who needs to—"

The next thing he knew, an explosion blasted him clean across the deck. A bed slammed into his chest, pinning him against the wall. Pain shot through his forearm as the bed frame pressed into his skin, cutting off his circulation. He tried to free himself, but splinters held down his sleeve. Beside him, the pirate lay limp, a splinter in his neck.

Panicking now, Noa screamed, "HELP!" He could see nothing but the mattress. Had Chaston and Ravie been hit by the explosion as well?

"Noa! Spitting sea serpents, where are you?" Dagan followed Noa's cries for help until he found him. "Are you hurt? I'm getting you out."

The boy grunted, his face reddening as he tried to push the bed off his brother, but a cannon had become stuck in the bed itself. It was too heavy. He couldn't do it alone.

Voices echoed from above. Weston's familiar drawl snapped orders at his men, telling them to tie Noa's crew to the mast.

"Leave me," said Noa desperately. "Give Weston the fake map I drew. It might buy us enough time to sail away before he figures it out."

Dagan glanced anxiously above him. He reached inside the cramped space and pulled out the magical map from Noa's pocket, a dangerous look coming over him.

"Not that one, give him the fake map!" Noa repeated.

Boot buckles jingled from the entrance to the lower deck, signaling the pirates were coming below.

Dagan ripped the canvas drapes from the bed.

"I'm sorry about this," he said, and he gagged Noa with the cloth. Noa yelled through the fabric, and somehow over his screams he heard Dagan say, "Weston isn't stupid. He won't believe the fake map, and he doesn't just want the map, he wants *you*. You're the only one who can read it. But he can't have you, or all of this would have been for nothing. Now be quiet and find a different way to save our home."

Noa screamed for Dagan to come back. The gag muffled his cries. He tried in vain to wrench his arms free. He couldn't believe what Dagan was about to do. *The idiot! The . . . the . . .* Tears filled his eyes, spilling onto his cheeks. What had he done? He'd failed his family. This wasn't supposed to happen. Where was the justice? Was losing his mother not enough? Did he have to lose his brother too? Did he have to watch his people crumble under the power of murderers and thieves?

Pirates flooded the lower deck.

"Grab 'em, boys! He's the one we want," Weston hollered.

Hidden by the bed, Noa froze, terrified for his brother. His heart throbbed against his shirt so hard he couldn't breathe.

Dagan cleared his throat. "I am Noa Blackburn, Prince of Ondule. I order you to unhand me at once."

Noa's stomach fell to the floor. *No . . . he didn't . . .*

Weston growled. "Where's that red-haired servant of yers? I want to teach him a lesson."

At this, Noa stopped breathing altogether. He waited for Dagan's next move.

"He's dead," Dagan declared.

There was a long, suspicious pause.

"Search him," came Weston's reply.

Noa could hear the pirates ruffing up Dagan's clothes, and then one of them spoke out. "He's got the map, Cap'n!"

"Where did you get that?" came Weston's cold demand.

"My father gave it to me. Give it back, you squid-faced bed wetter! It's mine!"

Weston laughed menacingly. "You fired at the wrong ship. We can fix our mast faster than you can say 'you fell for my plan.' Aye, if you thought you could outrun me, Prince Noa, yer as daft as Edjlin. The fool still thinks I'm on his side!"

"You're . . . not?"

"No . . . no, I've got me own plans for that map, and yer goin' to lead me to where I want to go. Take him to the ship, boys. He's coming with us."

CHAPTER 13

ADRIFT

Noa felt numb. His brother was gone. Dagan . . . Dagan was gone. With his body pinned and his mouth gagged, the only thing Noa could do was cry. Cry and wait for someone to find him. He replayed Weston's conversation in his head, crushed in guilt yet amazed at his brother's courage.

Soon he heard Ravie wake up somewhere on the lower deck and gasp in pain. He tried calling for her, but his screams were nothing more than muffled grunts. Scrambling to the upper deck, she returned with the crew, explaining what needed to be done about a splinter in Chaston's side.

"Vim, find the medicine box. You three, look in the galley for nacru root. It's used as a tea, yes? My people package it in a rectangular box with a red lid—hurry!"

Chaston yelped. Ravie must have torn out the splinter. Vim

cursed repeatedly, and then, to Noa's surprise, cried. More than one pair of footsteps stomped away, returning with more hope.

"We found the medicine!" yelled one of the twins.

Trapped and helpless, Noa listened as Ravie ground up the root. He hoped years of blowing things up had made Chaston used to injury, but the boy still cried out as Ravie pressed the medicine into his wounds.

"This will numb the pain and stop him from getting an infection," she told the others.

Not long after, Noa heard a thump and realized Ravie had collapsed on the ground. He listened as the girl protested she didn't need attention and that she wanted to be left alone.

When they finally found Noa, his arm had lost all feeling. Pan and Fig leveraged the bed away with a beam, bathing Noa in sunlight which streamed through the cannon holes.

"You're all right!" said Aaron, rushing toward him, a deep cut clotting in his brow. To Noa's relief, circulation tingled back through his arm. Aaron untied the gag and freed Noa from the splinters before throwing his arms around him, tears running down his cheeks.

Noa couldn't even protest. His arms were heavy and awkward. He asked about Chaston, and Aaron pointed to a bed where Chaston slept, his long blond hair flowing over the pillows.

"Ravie said he should be on the mend as long as we keep his wounds clean," said Aaron. "Vim and Jonath are cleaning up on deck."

"Where's Bones?" Noa asked. In the hour he had been trapped behind the bed, he had not heard Bones's voice, nor any mention of him. Aaron looked away, gulping in air as a new set of tears poured down. A sickening feeling welled inside Noa.

No, not Bones. Please, not Bones . . .

"Bones is gone," Vim said.

Noa hadn't seen Vim climb down. He tried sitting up. Dizziness overcame him in a wave. Blood pulsed painfully back into his arm. It gave him a headache, but he needed to look at Vim. He needed to know the truth.

"How . . ." He gulped the lump in his throat. "How did it happen?"

Coming closer, Vim rubbed his puffy eyes with the back of his hand. Dried blood stuck to his neck from a gash by his ear.

"He's not dead. Bones joined the pirates."

The words slammed into Noa like a tidal wave. *"What?"*

"We think he did it to protect Dagan."

Noa blinked away his shock. Both his brother and his best friend's fates rested with ruthless pirates. He stared at his lap, lost for words, and felt their eyes on him.

With a sick feeling in his stomach, Noa told them what Dagan had done and that Weston had the map. The twins slumped onto the ground in defeat. Vim's face turned chalk white.

"If Weston has what he came for, he'll never give up Dagan and Bones," said Aaron, shaking his head.

"No . . . no, we'll find them," said Noa, finding his voice. "We'll take them back. We'll get help from another island—"

"There's more, Noa," interrupted Fig.

"It's bad," said his twin, Pan.

"Cannon fire blasted the hull. It flooded the bilge. We can

stop it, but that's not the worst part." Fig exhaled deeply. "The mast keeled over when they boarded the ship. We don't have a way to repair it."

Noa studied the twins, fearing he already knew the answer. "What does that mean?"

The twins spoke in solemn unison.

"We can't sail the ship."

Wood littered the upper deck. The railings were blown off in one spot, and in the middle of everything, the enormous mast had fallen against the wheel like a wounded soldier in battle.

Noa headed to the captain's quarters to survey the damage from inside but couldn't open the door.

"Ravie's locked herself in," explained Aaron.

Noa pounded on the door. "Open up, Ravie."

"Leave me alone."

By nightfall, Ravie had still not come out of the captain's quarters. Noa looked through the keyhole. Streaks of blue moonlight revealed the red-stained bandages around Ravie's thigh as she lay in bed, shivering despite looking flushed and sweaty.

The boys tried to break down the door, but Ravie had pushed the desk in front of it to stop anyone from entering.

"Why won't Ravie come out?" he asked Aaron around the table below deck. Orange lamplight glowed inside the room, illuminating the boys' sullen faces. With little food to eat and no way to sail, they could do nothing but talk. They barely noticed the ship drifting with the currents.

Aaron didn't look Noa in the eye. "She's embarrassed of being a burden. She used all the medicine on Chaston. She wants to die alone."

Noa's heart clenched. "She said that?"

"She didn't need to," said Aaron gravely.

The next day, Noa tried again to coax Ravie out of the room, but his duties to the rest of the crew made it difficult to linger. They spent hours rotating shifts on pumping the bilge, while others searched the debris for scraps of food, medicine, or blankets to brace the chilled winds that entered through holes in the hull. That night, the group collapsed in the lower deck, murmuring among themselves.

"You know what's interesting? Every time something bad happens, Ravie is in the middle of it," said Jonath, picking at his sunburned arms. Chaston sat up in the bed beside him, looking much better than the day before.

Noa swallowed his tiny portion of grog, but his mouth still felt dry. "What do you mean?"

"The electric octopus? The blue men? Weston's invasion? They all happened once Ravie came aboard."

"She saved us from all of those things!" Aaron protested.

Noa found himself objecting.

"Wait . . . I think he's onto something," he said, stroking his chin. The boys' peeling, sunken faces waited for him to go on. Dagan had warned that Ravie could not be trusted. He should have listened. Perhaps it wasn't entirely Noa's fault the pirates had won . . .

"Let's look at the facts. Pirates worked for the Death King.

Ravie knew the rumors about the Death King, she knew my pendant was the Death King's symbol, and she knew all about the blue men. Those creatures are on the Death King's side. They stopped fighting me once they saw the pendant."

The boys openly shuddered. The night before, they had discovered that the blue man had escaped through a cannon hole in the brig. Truthfully, they were all glad to be rid of the creature, though every moment they suspected it would return from the waves for revenge.

"You ain't thinkin' Ravie's one of the Death King's followers?" asked Vim, half laughing.

Noa gave a noncommittal shrug. Then he remembered what Dagan had told him days ago. "She's wearing a necklace too . . . has anyone seen it? It could be the Death King's pendant . . . if she's a pirate working for Weston, it makes sense why she has a pendant but doesn't show us. Most pirates still believe in the Death King's principles."

Uneasy silence followed, with only the creaking ship to break the tension. In the floor below, the rising water sloshed around with no one attending the bilge pump. Noa couldn't believe he'd put this all together. It was as if those ideas had been at the back of his mind and the exhaustion and anger of the last two days had pushed them out.

He wiped his palms on his trousers, waiting for someone to speak.

"She's too young," said Pan finally.

"Ravie said her mother is a sailor; she could be a pirate too," said Noa.

"She ain't workin' for Weston. Weston left her for dead," Vim pointed out.

Jonath cut in. "That's true, but Weston could have *used* Ravie to find us and steal the map, then betrayed her afterward. He's a pirate, after all."

Noa nodded, more confident about his accusation. Fig reminded them pirates had piercings and tattoos, something Ravie lacked, but Jonath had an idea about that too.

"It would be interesting if that's why Ravie's locked herself up," said Jonath, sitting up in bed. "She doesn't want us to bandage her, or we'll see her pirate tattoo."

Aaron stood up angrily. "This isn't fair. Ravie's done nothing but help us. She saved our lives!" He shook his finger at Noa. "You're blaming her because you don't want to admit it's *your* fault. It was *your* idea to fight back, and look where it's gotten us! Pirate or not, Ravie's our friend. We can't abandon her. I'm breaking down that door."

Aaron staggered weakly toward the ladder and climbed out of sight, spreading guilt in his wake.

No one said anything. No one even moved. Not until clanks and thuds from the main deck brought them rushing up to see what was the matter. Standing in front of the captain's quarters, Aaron wiped his brow and lifted a sword up for another blow at the wooden door. Chips splintered out as the blade dug in.

"Let me," said Jonath, looking remorseful for his accusations as he reached for the sword.

Sighing, Noa grabbed a sword of his own and helped too. *What was wrong with him?* he wondered as he threw his back into chopping down the door. Aaron was right. Ravie had saved him from the blue men. Pirate or not, he owed her his life.

The swords broke through, taking chunks of wood with them. It was enough to reach in and unlock the door, then shove the desk aside so they could enter.

Ravie looked worse than Noa had imagined. Her clothes were stiff with old sweat, but she was no longer sweating. A very bad sign.

"Get her some grog. She's dehydrated," Noa instructed. Jonath left immediately to fetch it. Aaron knelt by her bed.

"Ravie? Can you hear me?" he whispered, squeezing her arm. She groggily turned her head.

"You . . . broke . . . the . . . door?" she said in a raspy voice. "I told you not to . . ."

"You're one of us, Ravie," said Aaron. "We'll make you better."

Not long after Jonath returned with grog, she fell asleep again, exhausted and warm to the touch. Aaron, Jonath, Malloch, Chaston, Vim, and Noa were gathered in the tiny room, watching the dying girl sleep . . . staring at the chain that had slipped out from the neckline of her tunic.

They just wanted to know.

Noa bent down and gently, gently lifted the silver chain off her neck. Indeed, there was something hanging at the base of it. Noa recognized it instantly from his studies of foreign kingdoms, but it wasn't a pirate symbol. It wasn't the Death King's symbol either.

"It's an insignia," said Noa, holding up the ring attached to the chain. "Like a sort of badge."

A purple gem was held in place by silver octopus legs. The others sighed in relief, not understanding the jewelry's significance. As Noa gently put the necklace back over her head with the ring attached, he wondered how in the realm she had gotten it.

Thirst overpowered Noa's senses. He stared at the vast blue, letting his mouth hang open, dry and sticky. Malloch glanced warily at Noa beside him. They'd tried everything—steering the ship without the main mast, elongating the intact sails . . . they had even searched for oars. None of it made a difference.

Noa spent hours staring at the ocean that morning, painfully recalling the events of the attack. The map had changed right before Weston's ship caught up, but he couldn't understand why. Did the map know they would be attacked? Had the map changed allegiance? Could Weston now read the map?

They'd given the last of the grog to Ravie, and the crew randomly drifted into hallucinations. Noa rubbed his temples where a headache pulsed, half listening to Aaron tell stories to Ravie as he lay on the floor beside her bed in the captain's quarters while she murmured through her nightmares. Earlier, she had complained about purple monkeys sucking on her toes.

Escaping the heat of midday, the boys sprawled lifelessly on their beds below deck.

"We're not going to make it," said Malloch, licking his puffy, chapped lips.

Noa's silence was as good as an agreement.

"I was going to open a pastry shop one day, right beside my father's bakery. It was my dream," said Jonath.

Malloch grunted. "I thought I wanted to be a sailor like my father. Should have thought that one through."

"Not me," said Chaston, pushing long, greasy hair away from his face. "I wanted to make black powder when I grew up. My little brother was going to do it with me. We'd blow up rock for the quarry."

"Making house bombs on the side, I expect?" asked Malloch.

"Naturally," replied Chaston.

Noa listened. He had never known the freedom of which they spoke. His destiny was set the moment he was born—a prince, a future king. There was no alternative. Although now it seemed he might not live to see that future come to pass.

Vim rolled onto his back, staring at the ceiling. "Last thing I said to my pap was I didn't want to be seen with him at the princess's celebration. I ain't never gonna have the chance to apologize now."

Noa's eyes fell to the floor, recalling the choice words he'd spoken to his own father. He couldn't bear looking at the boys around him any longer, their exhausted bodies murmuring their last goodbyes. They had almost made it to the map's destination, and now they were inches away from death. He had failed the kingdom, his friends, his family. He had failed Alya, who had entrusted him with her little brother, and he'd failed Dagan and Bones . . . he had failed them all.

When Noa and Malloch crawled above deck sometime later, something dark marred the endless blue sky above them. The airy, feathered animal soared toward them, beating its wings without a sound, and landed on the railing at the bow. Noa gazed at the bird ravenously, watching it fix its feathers. He felt Malloch's hungry eyes upon the animal as well.

Carefully, they stepped toward it.

The bird cocked its head out from fixing its wing and took flight over the sea. Noa's heart sank as he watched it fly away, but the bird's destination sat on the horizon. Noa grasped the meaning of the hazy gray line instantly.

It was an island.

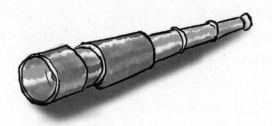

CHAPTER 14

MISCHIEF IN THE MANGROVES

The sight of land should have made Noa happy, but instead, he watched it approach anxiously, discussing with the others what they might find there. Or who. They were past the boundaries of the realm; no islands were charted this far out. Could this be where pirates berthed their ships?

It was late afternoon, and the wind carried smells of soil after rain. It blew over Noa, lifting the tips of his auburn hair as the white foam of water meeting land distinguished itself against the blue. By sunset, the boys found themselves pressed against the railings, transfixed by the lush hills and tree-covered mountains which glowed orange in the dimming light. A reef surrounded the island as far as they could see, and mangroves replaced the sandy beaches Noa knew from home.

There were no signs of civilization.

"Water," someone croaked.

"Food," whispered another.

Stumbling to the captain's quarters, Noa fell at the bedside. "Hold on, Ravie, just a little longer."

Noa's legs buckled from the force of the anchor hooking onto the sand. They had drifted near a break in the reef, a sign of fresh water flowing into the sea, as corals could only grow in salt water. Regaining his balance, Noa gathered the crew together to execute a trip ashore.

It would waste time to go out for supplies and leave Ravie on the ship, so they brought her along. They needed food and water, and most importantly, a medicinal plant they believed would heal Ravie's infected wounds, something Pan and Fig described as a blue flower with red berries. The twins' mischievous lives had landed them in the Health House countless times but had also brought them to understand which plants were used for healing, most recently when Fig dropped a pastry knife on his foot in Jonath's family bakery. If this island had the flower, they needed to find it fast.

Jonath, whose years of kneading bread dough made him the strongest of the group, retrieved Ravie from the captain's quarters. She looked worse than ever. Her mousy hair stuck to her forehead beneath her cap, her eyes were bloodshot and barely open, and her mouth was a puffed, cracked line. Jonath carried her over his shoulder and lowered himself down the ship's ladder to the sea.

With all lifeboats destroyed, the boys were forced to wade into the water carrying their belongings above their heads. Darkness overtook the sky. They waded into the mangrove forest, stepping over hundreds of roots rising from the water, Vim assisting a limping Chaston and Ravie hanging over Jonath's shoulder like a life-size doll.

Freshwater droplets speckled the leaves from a recent rain shower. The boys sucked them off before sluggishly moving on. Swinging a lantern to scare away the darkness, Vim lit their path to shore. Though helpful, the glow attracted unwelcome mosquitoes.

"Are there sh-sharks in here?" asked Aaron through his chattering, purple lips. The water rose higher on him than anyone else, and he glanced restlessly into the shadows.

"Heaps," said Fig matter-of-factly.

"Snakes too," added Pan, slapping a mosquito on his cheek. They laughed as Aaron scurried closer to the safety of the light.

At the back of the group, Noa heard something that made him stop dead in his tracks.

"What was that?" he asked Malloch, looking around. His arms prickled with mosquitoes, and he blindly smacked them off.

"What was *what*?"

The lamplight faded as the others moved on without them. Noa squinted into the mangrove shadows and listened. Malloch did the same. The retreating tide gurgled and splashed against the mangrove roots. Crackling crabs scuttled unseen across the roots.

Then they heard it. Someone with a high-pitched voice was singing.

Beware, lost sailor, who tries to swim
Under the trees where lights glow dim
Aqua young with teeth to bite
Come swiftly for your legs tonight

Vim sloshed through the water toward them carrying the lamp, followed by the twins.

"It ain't a bleedin' stroll in the garden, you two! Catch up!"

Then Pan screamed. "Something bit me!"

Noa's heart stopped. Sea snakes. One bite from a sea snake would turn from pain into paralysis in a matter of hours. There was no cure. Pan would be dead by morning light.

Pan reached into the water and pulled out what bit him—but it wasn't a snake. A bald child no bigger than Pan's hand struggled to free itself from his grip. Noa stared. The creature looked like the wingless fairies he'd read about as a child. Pan squeezed her torso, and she squealed for escape.

"What *is* that thing?" asked Vim, backing away in disgust.

Malloch gawked in disbelief. "Ahhh . . . that . . . that is a sea sprite!"

The sea sprite's yellow eyes were wide with terror. Her green skin had wavy white lines across it. She pounded her fists on Pan's hand, then sunk her teeth into his finger.

"Ouch!" He dropped the sprite, cradling his bloody hand.

"Shine the light over there," Noa instructed, pointing to

where the sea sprite had disappeared. A swell of water barreled toward them. Beneath it, sea sprites swam at them at top speed, their sharp teeth bared. "What in the king's name—RUN!"

Sloshing through the marsh, they ran as fast as they could. Fig tripped, falling into the water, and came up hollering as three sea sprites clung to his arm by their teeth.

"What's going on?" demanded Jonath, when they'd caught up with him and Aaron, an injured Chaston, and a limp Ravie.

"SEA SPRITES!" they shouted.

Sprites leaped from the water, biting each chance they saw a juicy piece of skin. Aaron endured the worst of the attack. When Noa caught a glimpse of him in between struggles, five sprites were hanging off his bottom.

A fresh bite stung Noa's thigh. Prying the sea sprite from his pants, he threw it against a tree. In front of him, a swarm of sea sprites pulled Malloch's sack off his shoulders and ripped it apart, their lantern eyes lit with excitement.

Noa smacked away the oncoming sprites and grabbed Malloch's arm, pulling him to shore. They reached the safety of the muddy banks and collapsed beneath the trees. The others followed. Any sea sprites left scurried away, apparently not keen on leaving the water.

Noa didn't know who said it, but someone shouted they'd found fresh water, and the group stampeded to the bubbling spring, dunking their faces and slurping it up like dogs. The fresh, icy water flowed in like liquid heaven. It streamed into Noa's stomach, extinguishing the fiery hunger pangs and renewing his mouth with a new layer of saliva.

When he'd drunk so much he'd burst, he leaned against a tree, rubbing the tender bite marks. If he had once wanted the mer-tales of his childhood to exist, he wished he could take it back now. He hated magical creatures. The less he saw of them, the better.

It was Jonath who reminded them why they were there.

"A blue flower with red berries?" he asked, leaning Ravie's limp body against a rock.

The identical brothers nodded. Noa ordered everyone to pair up and search. Boys wobbled to their feet and lumped together. Aaron rushed to Jonath's side, clearly comforted by his height and least amount of bite marks, but in a matter of twenty feet, Aaron had strolled into a spider web, tripped over a root, rolled onto a fire ant hill, and lodged his foot in the jaws of an enormous fly-eating plant. Jonath made Aaron stay behind to watch Ravie and dashed off into the trees before he could protest.

"It must be here somewhere," said Noa, pushing jungle leaves aside. Much to his annoyance, he'd been left with Vim. However, the fresh, cold water had awakened Noa in a way he hadn't known since Weston's attack. Alert and in much better spirits than before, he noticed Vim's change in behavior. He hadn't once blamed Noa in the hour they'd trudged through the forest, and he hadn't disagreed when Noa gave suggestions on where they should go next. He was almost, dare Noa think it, pleasant.

When they returned to camp, a flower with red berries was

the only thing missing from the pile of supplies. Noa and Vim had found purple berries that Noa recognized as safe from one of his books. The twins brought ruby melons, but after one splattered on the ground and its juice melted the surrounding soil, they threw them out. Jonath and Chaston dumped an armful of foul-smelling green fruit and coconuts into a pile. They ate what they could, force-feeding Ravie to give her energy, and made their beds buried in the cool mud.

Lying under the stars, Noa and Malloch discussed their options.

"You and I both know the *Evangeline* is beyond repair," whispered Malloch gravely. "Even if we still had Bones's skill with woodwork, it would take weeks to cut enough lumber to patch the holes, and don't even get me started on the mast."

"There's always another way. We can make a raft."

"We'd drown!" said Malloch.

"Then we'll find a bird and send a letter—"

"We're wanted for piracy. Who would help us?"

"I don't know, all right? But I can't give up—they've got my brother!" Noa had flipped onto his stomach, glaring at Malloch, his nostrils flaring.

Malloch sighed deeply. "I know."

Noa returned his gaze to the stars. He watched the dots appear as the night grew darker, specks of light sprinkled throughout the raw sky. He counted five shooting stars before he fell asleep, unaware of the pair of eyes watching them from the trees.

Voices awoke him. Exhausted, Noa tried to fall back asleep before his eyes adjusted to the morning sun.

"Ravie's gone!"

Noa sat up, wide awake. "What?"

"I saw someone in the trees," said Vim, pointing to the jungle. "I left to see who it was, and when I came back, Ravie wasn't here!"

Aaron's face pinched tight. "What did you do to her?"

"I didn't touch her! She's really gone."

"She couldn't have walked out of here."

"Maybe she did," said Jonath, shrugging.

"*What?*" asked Aaron.

The baker's boy shrugged again. "Maybe she was faking."

Noa considered this for a moment, then recalled Ravie's feverish state and shook his head. "She wasn't faking."

The twins began searching the camp's perimeter. Vim folded his arms and sat down, daring someone to challenge him again.

"What do you mean you saw *someone,* Vim?" asked Noa.

"I know I ain't had a wink of sleep, but I swear someone was there, probably one of you fools walkin' in your sleep."

A twig snapped in the jungle, and the boys glanced around nervously.

Noa lifted Vim to his feet. "There are clearly beasts in the forest," said Noa, gathering the boys together. "Stay together. We'll search for Ravie as a group."

He reached for the map in his pocket by instinct, dropping his hand by his side when he remembered with crushing anguish

218

that it was gone. He would have to move forward without something telling him where to go.

"I'm sorry about Ravie," Noa whispered to Aaron when they'd stopped for a water break.

Aaron slurped the stream water in his cupped palms, then wiped his mouth with the back of his hand. "Ravie was my best friend on the ship. You're all so much older than I am . . . but she's my age, and she doesn't make fun of me like everyone else." He shrugged, turning pink. "I wanted to bring her to Ondule and show her Capture the Conch. Then I wouldn't be the only new one joining the team next season."

Noa patted him on the back. "We'll find her."

A twig snapped, and Aaron bolted upright, eyes wide as he searched the trees. "Ravie?"

Before Noa could stop him, Aaron had jumped to his feet and sprinted after the sound.

"Aaron, wait! You don't know what's out there!"

Quickly, the group finished drinking and ran after the boy. They maneuvered through the bushy undergrowth and jumped over creek beds until they found themselves crashing over each other in a clearing.

"Get off me!" someone bellowed from the bottom of the pile, entangled in a mess of legs.

One by one they freed themselves. Noa didn't need to ask why the group had stopped so suddenly. All eyes were on the cliff several feet away. It shot one hundred feet down into the ocean below.

"Ahhh . . . what in the king's name are those?" asked Malloch.

They turned around, instantly frozen by the sight. Furry, hostile-looking creatures had closed in around them, holding spears.

Noa had never seen anything like the creatures. Stout, with short limbs and a long tail, each one looked like a cross between a rodent and a jaguar, except it stood on two legs. The animals held their spears with monkey-like hands. Noa almost would have thought them cute if it weren't for the unnerving, human-like intelligence behind their eyes.

"We mean you no harm," said Noa cautiously, holding his open hands in front of him. "We're just looking for our friend. What's your name?" The others bunched together. Creatures nervously flicked their tails. The nearest animal's large ears lay flat against its head, but it watched closely as Noa pointed to himself. "My name is Noa. Can you say that? No—ah."

The creature lifted its spear to Noa's chest, silencing him. Standing on its hind legs, it barely reached Noa's knees.

"Thoo bar bou?" it asked.

Noa gulped. What did it say?

"Thoo bar bala biz biz?"

Clueless, Noa glanced from furry face to furry face, trying to make sense of their language. His eyes landed on a creature wearing a familiar object on its head . . .

"Isn't that Ravie's cap?" he gasped.

Like lighting the wick of a bomb, Aaron's nerves blew up at this new information. "They took Ravie! They took Ravie!" He stomped bravely forward, pointing an accusing finger. "Give her back, you giant rats, or I'll—"

Aaron crumbled to the ground, unconscious, an orange feather dart stuck in his neck. The furry creatures lifted bamboo sticks to their mouths and fired at the others. Noa felt the dart sting his skin just before he slumped to the ground.

CHAPTER 15

NEW FRIENDS

Peeling sunburns . . . slivers . . . conversations about puberty . . . Noa added one more to his list of unpleasant experiences when he awoke dripping in sweat inside a wheeled cage.

"Where am I?" he mumbled before his head flopped to the side. It felt like someone had stuffed a rock inside his skull. Aaron, Malloch, and Chaston were squished inside the cage with him, each of their wrists tied to the bars like his own, but they were not yet awake. The furry creatures pulled the enclosure through the jungle. It jostled and creaked as it rolled through the thick, humid undergrowth. Noa needed to gulp air just to breathe.

The deeper they ventured into the jungle, the bigger things got. Trees soared as high as the clouds, practically blocking the sky with their luscious leaves.

It seemed like hours had passed before the creatures finally stopped inside their village. The whiskered jaguar-rodents came in all sizes here. Babies clung to their mothers' fur, staring at the visitors.

Behind them, an enormous ladder hung in between the gap of trees. In the highest branches, houses with banana-leaf roofs rested comfortably, and suspension bridges connected the homes together. Buckets of water ascended in a pulley system, no doubt the village's water source.

As the creatures wheeled the cage in the direction of rising smoke, Noa pleaded. "Let us out!"

A furry creature reached through the bars and flicked Noa in the face to shut him up.

"Bobo bak," it told him.

Noa, Aaron, Malloch, and Chaston were carried to a clearing with a heaving bonfire in the middle. It appeared roasted kids were on the menu tonight.

The cage dropped to the ground with a thud. Another cage holding Vim, Jonath, and the twins landed beside them. Vim glanced at Noa with wide, terrified eyes. The furry creatures crawled around the cages, peering in and murmuring to one another in their strange language. They started thrusting their hands through the bars and stealing from the boys' pockets, then tossing away the things they didn't like. Handkerchief? Toss. One pargent coin? Toss. Stale nut covered in lint? Keep.

An old creature strutted into the clearing, waving his cane in a jovial manner while he munched an apple. Not a creature, a *man*. A human! The creatures bowed to him as he neared.

"Help!" Noa called to the man. "Get us out of here!"

His shouting awoke the other boys. Although groggy, they sat up taller and peered out of the bars to see the new village.

The old man approached. Lines creased his face, and freckles sprinkled the bridge of his dark nose.

"Who are you?" he asked Noa, tilting his head to the side.

"Let us go!"

"Are you pirates?"

Noa shook his head.

"Tell me your name."

Noa tried to hide the quiver in his voice. "Noa Blackburn."

The old man smiled like he had just discovered the answer to a riddle. He tossed his apple to the side and spoke to the creatures in their language. Then to Noa's surprise, the animals opened the cage, pulled him out, and cut his bonds. He fell to the ground and began massaging his wrists.

"Come with me, Mr. Blackburn. There is much to discuss," said the man.

Noa didn't move. "I'm not leaving my friends."

"Your friends will not be harmed. Laklak will take care of them."

Beside him, the creature's ears perked up at the mention of his name.

"You expect me to trust them after they tied us up?"

The old man thought for a moment. "Yes," he said simply, "and if you come with me, I will tell you why."

Noa didn't like it. He followed the old man into a giant woven basket, and under the creak of the pulleys, it jerked into the air.

He stared warily at the jungle floor moving further away, his head still pounding from the drugged dart. Beside him, the old man sat comfortably with his hands clasped together on his cane, smiling at a green parrot passing by.

It took all Noa's strength not to faint when they reached the skyscraping top. The trees grew more than twice as high as the castle cliff on Ondule, and Noa followed the old man down the many wooden walkways linking the trees together.

"Welcome to my home," said the old man when they reached a moss-covered hut. An overpowering smell of herbs wafted through the door as they entered. *Herbs*. Had this man traded with Martesia? Noa hoped the news he was branded a pirate hadn't reached this island yet, although the hostile welcome party stifled this hope quite quickly.

"Sit down. Mint?" the old man asked, holding up a twig of green leaves.

Noa shook his head, still massaging his wrists. The man popped a leaf into his mouth like candy, chewing and smiling simultaneously.

Collections of the most absurd and random objects decorated the hut. Bottles filled with purple and green liquids sat on the shelves next to a treasure chest, crocodile pelts were strewn across the floor, and a wooden rocking chair sat in the corner next to a bucket of shells.

"You must be thirsty," he said, pouring Noa a cup of purple liquid. Noa accepted it but didn't drink.

"Are you going to kill me?"

"Kill you? I never kill anyone in my own home—very bad luck."

It wasn't until he winked that Noa realized he was joking.

"Why did those creatures drug us?"

"A precaution. You are the first outsiders the village has seen in many years. Most people don't make it past the sea sprites, and those that do . . . well, the thimblewims do not take kindly to strangers."

"Thimblewims?"

"Yes, yes, very loyal creatures. Smart too. Luckily for me, they had a rather nasty snake problem when I got shipwrecked here with my granddaughter. I helped them build houses in the trees to escape predators and floods. In turn, I live here in peace. Go on, drink. We'll return to your friends soon."

Noa didn't know what to say. Hungrily, he examined the sloshing liquid in his cup. It smelled as sweet as syrup. Cautiously, he took a sip. An explosion of berries poured down his throat, and he gulped the rest down.

"I take it you want more?" the man chuckled, refilling Noa's glass. "It's my own creation, you know. I'm quite proud of it. I'm currently working on a pineapple-and-sea-sponge mixture if you would like to have that as well, although last time I tried it, it tasted vaguely similar to soggy shoes. Mint?"

Noa shook his head again, and the man leaned back in his chair, chewing happily on the leaves. Noa noticed a name etched into the handle of the cup.

"Dakki Hallowbit . . ." It sounded familiar. "Is that your name?"

"You may call me Dakki."

"Okay, Dakki," Noa stammered. "Why am I here?"

"You landed on my island, Mr. Blackburn, so it seems you are better fit to answer that question."

Noa considered the old man. "We're stranded. I was following a map my father gave me."

Dakki's green eyes twinkled. "Splendid. I was wondering when he would give it to you."

Noa stared. "Sorry?"

"I trust you know how it works?"

"Who *are* you? How do you know so much?"

Dakki tapped his cane impatiently on the ground. "Your father and I were friends once, long ago. It was I who gave your father that map. I have been watching closely for the day when someone would use it again. Only those who are given the map willingly by its previous owner can use it for its true purpose."

Noa's eyes widened. That explained why Dagan couldn't see it. He didn't allow himself to dwell on the thought of his brother with the pirates. "What's the map's true purpose?"

Dakki refilled Noa's glass and set a basket of roasted nuts on the floor between them. "The map does not consider where you want to go, only where you are *meant* to go."

"The glowing compass turned back into a regular map. Does that mean I was no longer meant to follow it?" asked Noa, reaching for a handful of nuts.

"You are the Map Keeper now, Mr. Blackburn. You are always meant to follow it. However, the map does not work if the Map Keeper has the wrong intentions." Noa scratched his head, munching thoughtfully. "Oh yes, it's quite temperamental. Pardon me asking, but have you ever wanted the map to lead you somewhere for your personal gain?"

Noa shook his head. Then it rang true. Right before the glowing compass disappeared, he had dreamed of the riches he might find in the castle. Wanting his father and island to praise him, he had lost sight of the real reason he followed the map.

He scuffed his shoe against the floor. "How do I find out why I'm meant to go to this castle?"

"Ah, that's what it shows you. Your purpose there is for you to discover. Please, tell me, where is my map?"

Noa bowed his head and told him about Weston's attack.

"Oh my," said Dakki solemnly. "Tell me about this castle then. How did it look?"

"Like my castle," said Noa, fidgeting with his fingers. "Stone build with a wall around the village . . . but I think the map is broken. It draws the castle upside down."

A grim look crossed Dakki's face. He replaced it with his familiar wrinkly smile. "We will speak of it later. I have something to show you."

He led Noa out the door and over the boardwalks. Colorful birds twittered above their heads. Noa recognized some from a book he'd read at Salaso's Scrolls and wished he had the charts to tell which species he was looking at.

"Why haven't I heard of this island before, Dakki?"

"There are many things you still must learn, but it is not for me to tell them all."

"Did my father get that from you too? Secret keeping?" Noa

snorted. He crossed another suspension bridge and tried to avoid looking down.

"Your father understood no one is ready for everything at once," said Dakki without a trace of offense. "When one knows the end at the beginning, he unknowingly fails to work for this end. You will learn the reason for the map, Mr. Blackburn." Dakki stopped at a small hut. "I do apologize for holding you captive earlier. We can't be too careful, what with more black sails on the horizon each coming year, but please accept our hospitality as an apology. The thimblewims will see to it you and your friends are bathed before the banquet tonight—it will be held in your honor. For now, I believe someone is waiting for you."

Noa blushed. He had completely forgotten he'd slept in the mud last night. He assumed his smell wasn't inviting either. And a banquet held in his honor? This meeting with Dakki had turned out far better than he could have hoped.

Together they stepped inside the hut.

"Ravie?" Noa gasped.

"Your Highness!"

Noa rushed to her bedside. Ravie's hair and face shone with cleanliness, no longer sweaty from a fever, and she sat up in bed, hugging her blanket.

"We thought you were dead!" Noa examined her recently infected leg. Banana leaves wrapped around the deepest part of the cut, but Noa could see the edges were already scabbing over.

Dakki smiled at the reunited pair. "When the thimblewims found your camp, they could tell she was a young one of my kind and near death. They brought her to me immediately, then went back to find you."

"I'm glad you're all right," said Noa, giving her a long-awaited hug. He could see the chain of her necklace poking out in the back, and as they separated, she pulled up her collar self-consciously.

It probably wasn't the time to talk about it, but he had so many questions for her that he decided to ask the one he wanted to know the most.

"Ravie," he whispered. "I saw the ring, the insignia—" Ravie froze. Her eyes were wide, and she instinctively reached for the necklace beneath her shirt. "It belongs to the person with the highest rank in the Martesian army, General Narthol. Why do you have it?"

Ravie said nothing.

"Is that why you hid on our ship? Because you stole it?"

Ravie sighed and leaned back on the bed. "It's a long story."

"A story for another time, I'm afraid," Dakki interjected, striding across the room. "Mr. Blackburn must wash up before he eats, and you, young lady, need to rest. You may feel good now, but you have a long way to go before you are fully well again."

Not wanting to push his luck, Noa agreed to drop the subject for now. As he made his way to the door, Ravie piped up.

"I didn't steal it."

Noa looked at her questioningly.

"I got the idea to hide on your ship from a book I read once," she explained. "*Hazardous Heroics*. Captain Herring's niece wanted to join his treasure hunt, but he said she had to finish school, so she—"

"—switched places with his cabin boy and joined the crew," said Noa, finishing her sentence. "Those are my favorite books."

"Mine too."

When Noa slipped outside, he couldn't hide his smile.

Mud pooled at Noa's feet like brown soup. It was no small task to rinse the grime off his hair and body, but at last he sat freshly bathed in the banquet hut, ready to eat. A large banana leaf with fruit and boiled pork sat in front of each child, along with piles of roasted cockroaches and maggots.

"We thought they wanted to poke our eyes out with needles," said Malloch, examining a roasted maggot. "Then I realized they were sewing us new clothes. Ahhh, the pants are itchy though." He bit the grub and spit it out. "Yecch! Disgusting!" Wiping his fingers on his new brown shirt, its fabric made by the thimblewims using tree bark, he helped himself to more mango.

Noa gnawed a chunk of coconut, his mind elsewhere. He barely noticed the twins parading beside him and cupping coconuts over their chests.

"Why haven't we heard of this island before?" asked Jonath, massaging the calluses on his fingers from years of kneading dough. Behind him, tiny thimblewims were sneaking around the adults, their tails flicking side to side, trying to glimpse the mysterious visitors.

Noa frowned. "Why haven't we heard of sea sprites? Or the

blue men? The only book they're in is *The Completed Edition: Mer-Tales of Aztrius!*"

Jonath went on hopefully. "I don't know, but at least they saved Ravie. When can we see her again?"

"Tomorrow."

Aaron scowled, rubbing his sore neck. "They may have saved Ravie, but they shouldn't have poked us with those sleepy needles. That wasn't nice." He turned to Malloch. "Are you going to eat these?"

Malloch gratefully pushed his roasted maggots away.

"Take it slow, Aaron," warned Jonath.

"Ya, it ain't gonna be nice when you overeat and blow biscuits," added Vim.

Noa stared at the pile of pork strips on his leaf. It didn't seem fair they had a feast tonight while Bones and Dagan might not eat at all. How long would Weston keep them alive? From the stories Noa read, pirates never held on to a prisoner for long unless they had a good reason. Vim appeared to know his thoughts.

"It ain't helpin' them if you starve yourself," he said. "You need your strength."

Reluctantly, Noa nibbled a pork strip and gave in. For once, he agreed with Vim. He vowed the next chance he laid eyes on Weston, he'd be ready for him.

After sunset, Dakki announced it was time to retire for sleep. Noa followed the tired thimblewims outside into the night, and his mouth dropped—the village *glowed*. Roofs and railings glimmered with bright-green moss that lit the boardwalks. Glowing tree frogs croaked in the branches. Stars appeared in the sky like speckles on a kingbird's egg, peeking through the luminous leaves. Noa wished Lana could see it.

Dakki bent down to pick up a youngster who had strayed from his mother.

"Remember the snake, young one, remember the snake," he whispered to the furry child.

Wobbling down the boardwalks with the creatures, Dakki returned soon after with a girl dressed in the same barkcloth as him. She looked slightly older than Noa and carried a spear in one hand and a basket of fish on her hip. She was the first human Noa had seen besides Dakki, and she looked eager to meet him.

"Mr. Blackburn, this is my granddaughter, Zuri."

"Hello, Mr. Blackburn!" said the girl. "Had I known you would come, I would not have gone hunting today." Dropping her things on the floor, she grabbed him eagerly by the forearm and pulled him in for a headbutt.

"Ouch," said Noa, rubbing his forehead.

Dakki chuckled. "That is how the thimblewims greet their friends. Perhaps you can teach Zuri the ways of your culture."

"Pleased to meet you, Zuri. Call me Noa." Noa held out his hand to shake. Confused, Zuri took his hand and headbutted him again.

"I want to know all about your island. Tell me what it looks like, and what your house looks like, and what kind of animals live there, and what games you play . . ."

As Zuri asked question after question, Noa was distracted

by something he'd heard Dakki say earlier to a thimblewim. Finally, when Dakki left for more pudding, Noa got the courage to ask Zuri what it meant. "What does 'remember the snake' mean?" he asked.

Zuri wrinkled her nose. "Oh, that. It's a story about a baby who was eaten by a giant snake. The thimblewims tell it to their children to keep them from wandering off."

Noa straightened up, intrigued. "This snake . . . it doesn't have venom, does it?" Noa hesitated. "Er—magical venom?"

Zuri squinted at him curiously. "If it did, I would know," she said, lifting her barkcloth pants to reveal a snakebite on her leg. The fang marks stretched across her calf like the wings of a spotted butterfly, and one look had Noa's stomach squirming. "It bites only to keep you still. Then it coils around you and squeezes you to death."

Noa gulped. "Squeezes?"

"Mm-hmm."

"Lovely," Noa mumbled, feeling suddenly unwell. It felt impolite to ask more questions, and he was grateful when she remembered her duty to dry the fish before bed.

"We'll talk again soon," she assured him, and she set the basket on her hip and disappeared down the boardwalk.

That night the boys slept in hammocks strung in the banquet hall, pungent fumes of roasted maggot lingering in the walls. Noa rocked his hammock side to side, staring at the ceiling. He thought of Ravie. He thought of the strange island he had spent the last day in, and how it didn't exist on any map. At the beginning of the banquet, Noa had warned Dakki not to believe any news from Martesia, only to discover Dakki never traded with the other islands. The spices he carried, along with all their food and supplies, were produced on the island.

Soon Noa's thoughts went to his family, Alya, and home. He wondered if the glowing castle was on a secret island too, carrying a weapon to defeat Edjlin's army.

Tossing and turning in his hammock, he stayed up longer than he should have, imagining Weston begging forgiveness as Dagan made him walk the plank. Noa had saved pork strips for Dagan and Bones and left them wrapped in a banana leaf under his bed in case they made it to the island tonight. The smallest hint of sunrise illuminated the crack beneath the door when Noa finally closed his eyes.

CHAPTER 16

HIDDEN RELATIONS

Noa slept soundly in his hammock until midday. Rolling out of bed, he examined the package of pork strips beneath him only to find them coated in ants. He scowled and threw the meat out the window.

Villagers bustled around the boardwalks, carrying out their daily chores. He passed a group of thimblewims weaving coconut baskets, their dark eyes focused beneath tufts of jaguar-print fur, and soon after, he found the boys soaring between trees in a giant swing.

Jonath explained his glee as he harnessed himself into the vine. "The thimblewims have agreed to help us repair the ship! All they want in exchange is to have free reign to study the workmanship and learn how it sails. We've been waiting for you to wake up to tell you!" With that, he jumped off the platform, hooting and hollering as he swung like a pendulum across the jungle floor.

Noa's heart leaped with excitement. They could rescue Dagan and Bones!

"Mr. Blackburn, lovely morning, isn't it?" said Dakki, waving his cane when Noa jumped into the elevator basket. "Try this—I find it is especially good for the mornings."

He plopped into the basket beside Noa and handed him the animal-skin canteen hanging over his shoulder. Noa's face puckered with the taste of the sour lime drink.

"Is it true the thimblewims can help us repair our ship?" asked Noa, returning the canteen as the basket descended to the jungle floor. The drink's taste lingered, tingling his taste buds.

"Ah yes, the thimblewims are skilled in the way of wooden architecture, wouldn't you agree?" He gazed proudly above him at the treetop village, folding his hands over the knob on his cane. "We can begin repairs tomorrow. Take Zuri to your ship today and tell her what needs fixing."

"Oh! I could probably remember . . ."

"Nonsense! It will be good for her to spend time with someone other than her old grandfather."

In the jungle, Zuri walked as close as she could to Noa, overloading him with more questions about his home and the rest of the realm.

"Messages in bottles is your *mail*?" she repeated when he told her about this island quirk. "So . . . what's mail?"

The questions continued as they passed what looked like a miniature orchard: orange orbs dangling from the branches, bananas ripening in bunches, and golden pears ready to fall to the ground. It surprised Noa how orderly their crops were, but Zuri had just realized he lived in a castle and wanted to know more about this strange building, so he didn't bother asking about it.

They hiked down the mountain. All around him, birds twittered their calls, insects hissed, and palm fronds rustled from scattering lizards. When the ground leveled, swamp water soaked up to their ankles. Brackish water, Noa assumed, since he could hear the ocean nearby but trees still surrounded them.

They took a short break. Lifting a rotten log above her head, Zuri let it smash against a nearby tree. It cracked open, revealing a worm the size of a small snake. Noa recognized it as a common shipworm, a mollusk he'd studied when researching Ondulian whelk, which chewed through wood causing many ships to sink. Zuri pulled the worm from the wood and dropped it in her mouth like a long noodle.

Not a moment too soon, they reached a hidden beach away from the mangroves. Zuri stared curiously at the *Evangeline* sunken in the sand. The tide had retreated, and coral reefs stuck out dangerously close to the vessel on either side.

Noa strutted onto the wet sand, leaving Zuri fascinated on the beach. Pushing off the corals, he slid through the gunport, then doubled back. A shiny object hung from the hull by a long string. He hadn't noticed it before, and he brought the metal closer, as far as the chain allowed.

He couldn't believe it. It was Alya's dolphin whistle. *Is that how the dolphin found us?* he wondered. He tugged on the string, but it wouldn't come off. Alya had tied it tightly to the ship's ladder.

When he dropped the device, it rested where the waterline would be if the tide were not down. The running water from the ship's speed must have been enough to create the whistle effect. He shook his head in amazement at Alya's genius. She must have attached it just before the guard pulled her into the sea.

Inside the ship, wood littered the floor around empty beds. A hollow ache gnawed at Noa's insides. He'd actually missed this place. Zuri followed him inside, peering cautiously around her.

Examining the destruction, Zuri calculated the repairs.

"This will require one log . . ." she mumbled as she passed through the ship. "I think we could use bamboo to fix that . . ."

When they reached the mast, lying on the deck like a snapped twig, she ran her hands solemnly over the thick pillar. Before long, they were finished.

"Can I stay to look around?"

Noa gladly let her. His mouth had gone dry from explaining everything from the deadeyes to the anchor. Stealing a moment of silence in the captain's quarters, Noa slumped behind the desk.

Dents in the wall revealed where Dagan had taught Noa to throw knives. Noa stared sadly at them as he thought of home . . . Lana watching him play Capture the Conch from the rocks, Dagan bursting through the surface with a conch in hand . . . he wished he could return to that simpler time.

Before returning outside, Noa tidied up the room for the thimblewims who would see it tomorrow, picking up the pieces of framing he had used to pierce the octopus in Martesia and tossing them out the window. The portrait inside the frame had rolled itself up, and as Noa carried it to the desk, he noticed writing on the back.

Eric Driggonhall
Our beautiful boy
Loved beyond measure.

Noa stared, dumbstruck. He unraveled the painting to look at the blond boy with one blue and one brown eye. The boy in the painting was Edjlin's son.

Eeriness crept in like the painting could see inside his very soul. After all, if magical creatures existed, then why not ghosts? He rushed to the bookshelf, yanked open *Sea of Kings: A History of Aztrius*, and flipped to the paragraph circled in black ink. Why hadn't he made the connection before? Noa scanned the section about the venom's supernatural properties.

It is believed Hallowbit depleted the entire venom's magical properties, as it was never recovered.

Mind racing, he tossed the book inside his Capture the Conch sack and bolted outside.

———————————

"Ahhh, King Edjlin wants to bring his son back from the *dead*?" Malloch asked for the fifth time.

All of Noa's crew were lounging in hammocks inside their hut, listening to Noa speak.

"Yes, and he thought the map would lead him to it!" Edjlin's efforts to revive his son had destroyed everything Noa held dear. It wasn't Noa's fault pirates held his brother captive; it was Edjlin's.

"Why does it matter what Edjlin wanted?" asked Pan.

"Yeah, Weston has the map now," added Fig.

"It matters because we don't know *why* Weston wants it. What if he's trying to build a pirate army? What if he wants to resurrect all the pirates my father killed?"

The crew stared at the ceiling as they swung in their hammocks, contemplating this chilling thought. Noa had the strange suspicion that if Dagan were here, he would find the idea of an undead pirate army rather thrilling.

That night at dinner, Noa sat cross-legged with the book he'd taken from the ship, reading the same circled paragraph over and over.

"Aren't you hungry?" asked Aaron between mouthfuls of hot pudding. He passed Noa a basket of the same thick, slimy worms Zuri had eaten raw and set it on Noa's book.

Noa looked up, suddenly aware of his growling stomach. He picked up the slimy mollusk, which felt like a booger in his fingers, then dropped it back in and passed the basket onward. Glancing one last time at the circled paragraph, he reached for a chunk of pineapple from his banana leaf and watched Aaron fill his bottomless void.

"You haven't said much since you told us about Edjlin," Aaron told Noa between mouthfuls. "Are you thinking about the undead pirate army?"

"I've got a lot on my mind. Did you see Ravie today?"

Aaron nodded, his cheeks full of food.

Noa cocked his head. "And?"

"And she looks much better."

Noa knit his brow as he munched his pineapple. He had been too nervous to confront her about the necklace again, but secretly he had hoped she would say something to Aaron. After all, Aaron had said they were best friends.

Next to him, Pan and Fig were secretly slipping extra kiwis and canistels up their sleeves for a midnight snack. On Noa's other side, Jonath, Chaston, and Vim listened to Malloch rave about the thimblewims' and Zuri's woodworking abilities.

"One day! Can you believe it? They built this hut in *one* day. We'll have this ship fixed in no time."

Vim dipped his pineapple chunk into his pudding. "It ain't gonna be longer than the next new moon, as long as we help 'em understand the ship better. We sure need to, what with them afraid of the sea and all."

Noa's stomach did a nervous flip. The new moon was in four days. Four more days before they could return to the sea and begin their rescue. He hadn't the slightest clue *how* they would rescue Dagan and Bones, but it didn't matter how—soon they would no longer be useless.

"How do you know how quickly they can fix it?" asked Noa.

"Babki told us. You know, the old man?"

"His name is Dakki." Suddenly, Noa bolted upright. Not just Dakki, Dakki *Hallowbit*. He knew he recognized the name from somewhere.

Noa excused himself and found Dakki minutes later chatting with a thimblewim whose gray hairs peeked through the rosette pattern of its fur.

"Dakki! You have the same last name as Gravner Hallowbit!" said Noa, pointing to the old man. "I saw it written on the mug you gave me—and Gravner Hallowbit is the Death King."

Dakki spoke in a strange language to the thimblewim beside him, then answered Noa in a hushed voice. "Not the sort of talk I'd like to have at supper please, Mr. Blackburn."

Noa didn't listen. "How are you related? Were you his father?"

"Oh my, do I look that young to you? I must get out in the sun again, I see," he said, grabbing a half-coconut and sipping its sweet milk. Tactfully, the thimblewim exited to allow Noa and Dakki to speak in private. "We are not related, but I know Gravner, yes," said Dakki when they were alone. "Many years have passed since we've spoken."

"*Knew* him," Noa corrected. "He died. He accidentally poisoned himself."

"Oh yes, of course . . . poisoned himself, yes, but I do wonder if it was an accident."

Noa furrowed his brow.

Dakki looked solemn. "Gravner found an opportunity to cheat death, and he took it at the expense of his own life."

"What does that mean?"

Dakki avoided his gaze, distracted by a fly that had fallen into his coconut drink. He picked it out by its wings and carefully placed it on his palm to dry, whispering encouraging words to help it recover. Behind him, Noa noticed the twins struggling to explain to a large, unhappy thimblewim why kiwi juice was leaking from their armpits.

"Dakki, you know the history of Aztrius I've been sheltered from," said Noa, trying to steer the conversation back to the Death King. "Tell me what you know—it may help me find my brother."

Dakki was silent. Then he handed Noa a twig of mint leaves and announced he was going to bed. "There is too much to tell. We must rest, Mr. Blackburn. Tomorrow is a big day. I bid you goodnight."

Noa stared at Dakki wobbling away. *What are you hiding, old man?*

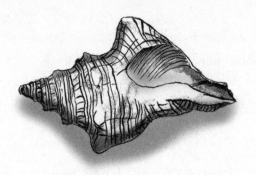

CHAPTER 17

SIRENA SHARES
HER SECRETS

Almost every thimblewim awoke at sunrise the next morning
with Noa and his crew, eager to see the ship. A scab was
all that remained of Chaston's side wound after the past two
days of natural medicine, and he trudged through the forest
with the others, carrying bundles of wood on his back. With
Chaston's recovery, Vim had finally relaxed and returned to his
usual, critical self, though to everyone's relief, he had focused
his insults on the bug-infested jungle instead.

Hours blurred together as they repaired the ship. Initially, it
took forever to corral the furry creatures into separate tasks, as
they all examined the ship in awestruck wonder. Still recovering,
Ravie stayed in the village, but several of the older thimblewims

who had been taking care of her tagged along to harvest the snaky mollusks at low tide. On the eve of the fourth day, they restored the mast, surrounding it with four logs to keep it steady. Noa cheered with the others. The ship would sail again.

"You still haven't spoken with Dakki?" said Ravie reproachfully inside her hut. Noa shook his head and sunk into his shirt. He had tried, but the old man would slip into a crowd and disappear. Now their time in the village was running out.

"You still haven't told me where you got that ring," he retaliated.

Ravie scowled. "Not fair."

Noa raised his brow.

"Your Highness, talking to Dakki is more important," she continued, pointing her half-eaten banana at him. "Dakki gave your father the map, no? He knows more about it than he's letting on."

Noa scratched his head, still thinking about the ring. "I don't understand. I've seen you sail through a storm, fight blue men, fight pirates, and even try to take care of your own wounds. Telling me who you really are can't be worse than that."

Caught off guard, she scoffed, then fidgeted with the blanket she sat on. "Maybe not . . ." She studied his face. "You already know, don't you?"

Noa shrugged. "Maybe. That's not the point."

She returned to her banana with a dismissive glance. "Talk with Dakki before it's too late."

"Come on, Ravie . . ." Noa petitioned. "What are you afraid of?"

"I'm not afraid . . ." Ravie sighed deeply. "Fine. My mother is General Narthol. There, I said it."

Nervous warmth filled Noa's chest. His suspicions had been right, and with an ally like the general's daughter, perhaps they could fix the mess they'd left behind in Martesia. But first, he needed to know where she stood.

"Did you run away, or were you sent to us?"

"I ran away."

Intrigued, Noa couldn't help but ask why.

"It doesn't matter. I'm not going back."

At that moment, the string-shelled door jingled, and Zuri skipped in from the dark to inform Noa that Dakki wanted to see him. Ravie squeezed her banana so hard it shot out of its peel into Noa's face.

"This is your chance!" Ravie squealed, hardly containing her excitement.

Reluctantly abandoning his talk with Ravie, Noa followed Zuri down the glowing boardwalks into the symphony of croaking frogs and cicadas.

"Come in, Mr. Blackburn," said Dakki, pacing anxiously beside his chair when Noa arrived. The familiar smell of mint lingered in the air, clinging to the bottles and baskets which cluttered the walls.

"Do you know what this is?" he asked Noa, holding up a white conch with brown spots.

"A shell?"

"Not just any shell, Mr. Blackburn. This is a Sirena, used by the merpeople. Extremely rare, you know."

"*Merpeople*? Spitting sea serpents, this is taking some getting used to."

"Your father kept many things from you, I see. Whether for good or bad, I cannot say, but it is because of your father I brought you here tonight. Mr. Blackburn, I need you to do something for me."

"What is it?" asked Noa hesitantly.

"I want you to imagine your father. Close your eyes."

Noa closed his eyes.

"Can you see him?"

Noa gave a thumbs-up sign.

"Good. Take the shell—gently—now listen."

Noa pressed the shell to his ear. Immediately he heard voices speaking within, but they were too faint to understand.

"How is this possible?" he asked, lowering the conch in disbelief. "Can they hear me too? Hello? Hello?"

"No, the Sirena allows you to hear conversations with the person you are thinking of, so long as they are currently taking place. It only works in one direction, but it's easy to see the appeal, I presume. With it, you can spy on your enemies. Ancient stories speak of men fighting over Sirenas, even killing their friends over misunderstood conversations, until all but three shells were lost or destroyed. Your father holds one of the last Sirenas, as do I, and it is your father who you hear inside."

"My father?" Noa asked, returning the shell to his ear in earnest. The muffled conversation left him grasping for answers. "If my father has a Sirena, is that how he knew Edjlin would attack? He overheard Edjlin let the pirates into the castle? Only . . . why didn't he hear it sooner?"

"The *man* chooses the conversation to overhear, not the shell," explained Dakki as he wobbled to the nearest shelf and pulled down a bottle of blue liquid. "Your father had no reason to spy on his friend and therefore did not foresee his fate until the last moment." Noa vaguely remembered touching a shell while he stumbled through his father's chambers. Titus must have just heard the conversation right before Noa snuck in.

"Did the merpeople make more Sirenas?"

Dakki shook his head. "The merpeople use them to speak to one another, but we humans can only hear. Only a handful of magical items exist in our realm, you see, to combat the evil that sweeps our lands with each new generation. Most have been lost. The merpeople saw the destruction the Sirenas brought to humans and vowed never to create another. Now please, Mr. Blackburn, the longer we wait, the more conversation we may miss."

He pushed the bottle to Noa. "*This* will help you hear better. Sirenas have never been strong above water, just like our voices are muffled below the water, you see? My drink will help you hear almost everything. There may be a few words hard to understand, but you can usually guess. Not bad for hearing a conversation several day's journey away." He popped off the cork and lifted it closer to Noa's mouth. "Do not worry, Mr. Blackburn, it hardly has any risks."

"What kind of risks?" Noa asked, leaning away. The drink

looked like a goopy, mashed jellyfish. He couldn't imagine putting it into his mouth.

"Minor, of course. Nausea, hallucinations . . . occasionally you can pass out for a day or two. Now drink. You cannot delay any longer."

The conversation echoed softly from the shell like a ticking clock. Hesitantly, he took the drink and chugged it. It slid down his throat like a slug. Gagging, he looked to Dakki for more instruction.

"Imagine your father," urged Dakki.

Noa closed his eyes, fighting back the need to throw up. He couldn't rid his tongue of the slimy texture. He pictured his father's broad shoulders slumped over his desk and his bushy black hair running into his beard. Nothing changed in the muffled voices for nearly a minute as the drink settled into Noa's stomach. Then Edjlin's voice amplified in his ear.

"The dreams tortured me, Titus. Every night I saw the venom locked inside. I had to snack!"

Noa thought for a moment and realized Edjlin must have said *act*, not snack. He hoped he would understand the rest of the conversation.

"But Weston is a pig mat, Edjlin." *Did he mean "pirate"?* "How could you not foresee his betrayal? You should have come to me first."

"Would you have done it for me? Weston swore an oath he'd find the venom if I freed him from Justice Isle."

"A pirate's oath is good for nothing," Titus interrupted. "You know what those monsters have done. If my bums come to harm, the sea forbid it, it rests upon your shoulders."

In the silence that followed, Noa recognized his father had said "sons," not bums. At least, that's what he hoped.

Finally, Edjlin said in a dull, defeated voice, "At least you learned from my milk cakes and kept your sons at home."

Titus sighed. "No . . . I should not have sheltered them as I did. They're braving the fly cheese without any experience."

"The Martesian ships have not found them?"

"They're still searching."

"Titus . . . there is still time. I want you to enjoy the venom. Please . . . do it for me."

"You *dare* ask me to—?" said Titus, firing up, but Edjlin cut in.

"Think of your boys! Boa and Wagon could have a better life."

Noa could almost picture Edjlin, with his blond beard, leaning anxiously toward his father. Someone snapped their fingers, and doors creaked open. It sounded like they were in the throne room.

"If Weston gets the venom . . ." said Titus after a moment or two, "we can talk."

Strange dizziness overcame Noa. The sounds of the conversation were muffled again until they slowly disappeared altogether. He tried to open his eyes, but they wouldn't open, like a dream he couldn't escape.

The scene changed.

Ripples of ocean crests appeared. Noa flew over the white-caps until he reached a flat, charred island. Barren and deserted, the only signs of life were a few pathetic plants.

In a blink, he floated beneath the sea. In front of him, the island rested *upside down*, reaching incredible depths to the ocean bottom. Forests hung on the mountainside beneath the waves, and in the distance, a large stone castle sat upside down on the rock.

Noa's vision blurred, but he swam closer to the castle. Air sticks like the ones found on his own island stuck out of the ground in clusters. A flag on the village wall swayed in the current, a symbol sewn into its soaked fabric. Then the world blurred black.

CHAPTER 18

THE GUARDIAN

66**Y**ou're quite right, Zuri, he does look like he'll vomit."

"Could be just his face."

"Mint, Noa?"

Noa rubbed his eyes. The old man's outline came into focus. Then the quirky hut regained clarity. Noa's fingers tightened around something hard and spiky.

The shell.

"The venom!" he yelled, bolting upright.

"Calm down, my boy, you've only just awoken," said Dakki, pushing Noa gently back to the ground. "You've been asleep for some time. Magic has its price, and I'm afraid you are not used to the effects of the Sirena. Zuri, will you share your juice with Mr. Blackburn? He will be thirsty, if I recall."

Zuri reluctantly passed her freshly cut coconut to Noa, who

guzzled the drink immediately. Wiping the milk from his upper lip, Noa switched his attention to the old man.

Dakki leaned forward. "Tell me what you heard, and I will tell you what it means."

Noa told him. It all seemed unreal, like a vivid dream, and he didn't know how to feel about it. Martesian ships were searching for them at this very moment on the open ocean. What was worse, Edjlin was successfully convincing his father to get the venom and use it. The prospect of his father using the venom for himself caused Noa to stare numbly at his interlocking fingers.

"Something else happened," he said when Dakki returned the spiny shell to the shelf. "I had a dream. I saw an island flipped completely upside down in the sea."

At this, Dakki froze.

"You had a vision, Mr. Blackburn. I often have experienced similar visions under the influence of my potions. What you drank focused your senses so precisely on hearing that your other senses acted defensively. In this vision, you wouldn't have heard anything, only saw, felt, smelled, or tasted, correct?"

Noa nodded slowly, remembering the silence amid the stink of seaweed and the goosebumps that had tingled his arms. "Is it a real place?"

Dakki answered in a grave voice. "I believe you know the answer to that question, Mr. Blackburn."

Noa's heart quickened. "It's where the Death King lived. I saw his symbol on a flag."

Dakki nodded and collapsed into a chair. "It's calling to you, Mr. Blackburn."

"Calling to me?"

"I do not pretend to know everything about magic, but magic is power, and there is power in destiny. *Your* destiny."

Dakki rubbed his tired eyes and asked for a drink. Zuri popped the cork off a green mixture and handed it to Dakki, and the old man sipped it for only a moment before his cheeks bloated as if to hold back vomit. It had been the soggy shoe mixture.

"I've meant to label my bottles," he apologized weakly.

When at last Dakki had drunk something to bring back his energy (sapodilla and pineapple with coconut water), he slowly sat up to brace himself against the pleading look in front of him.

"Help me, Dakki," Noa begged. "Everywhere I see mention of this venom. Tell me what you know. My brother's life depends on it."

"He deserves to know, Papik," said Zuri, folding her arms in agreement.

Dakki sighed. "They call him the Death King now, but I will always remember him as my young Gravner Hallowbit. You were right, Mr. Blackburn, I did know him—very well, for this island was not always my home. Gravner was the prince of the island Sulo, and I was his guardian. The king hired me from my home island, Blightip, to tutor the prince at an early age. I taught him mathematics, oceanography, and unfortunately, it was I who taught him about magic."

Dakki glanced at Noa and Zuri in shame.

"Many years ago, Aztrius had peace. Islands traded with one another; everyone prospered. Sulo's crowned resource was a hollow rock which created cement. When Sulo's ruler, King Hallowbit, found jewels in the rock, everything changed. They stopped trading their crowned resource and made mines to extract the jewels. The king traded the jewels to Blightip but felt cheated when he discovered their worth in the realm. Blinded by his pride, he stole them back. Blightip retaliated by stopping trade of their lumber. The king tried to sell his jewels to other islands at a higher price with little success.

"Villagers were forced to use resources from their own island to make up for the loss in trade, cutting down trees and overfishing, all the while working in the mines to provide jewels for the king's own enjoyment. Gravner watched his father's greed grow. They fought, and to teach Gravner a lesson, the king sent Gravner to labor in the mines too. I didn't see my young prince for many days . . . until one night I found my bottles missing and the king dead."

"You're saying he mixed the drinks to poison the king?" asked Zuri, stunned.

Dakki nodded. "Gravner took the throne. He wanted to be the leader his father never was. Quickly, he realized the island's resources had been ruined under his father's rule. He sought help from other islands, but because they had heard of the suffering people, they were only willing to help if Gravner stopped mining altogether. Gravner argued the mine was all the island had left to bargain for trade, and then he started to believe the other islands wanted him to fail. He was convinced they wanted him to be useless so they could overtake his throne. Soon he was working his people the same way his father had, trying to prove to the realm he didn't need their help. Villagers slaved away until they began to die off. It was then he received the name "Death King" by his own people. It was also then he learned of the venom. Realizing his island was a lost cause, he went looking for this alternative way to have power.

"We were alone. It wasn't long before the mine dust leaked into the groundwater, poisoning the livestock and plants. We ate rats to survive because the fish had gone too. I'll never forget the first time I found a child lying in the street, useless money still in her cold hands."

Noa swallowed the lump in his throat. He had heard stories of the Death King, but not like this.

"I tried to stop him, Mr. Blackburn. I called the other kingdoms for help. Gravner traveled between islands, gaining followers by promising immortality and a place in his new, greater kingdom. He was no respecter of persons. Anyone, or *anything*, who showed loyalty to him was promised a place in his kingdom. But first, they had to get rid of the opposition. That's when the war broke out."

"The Battle of the Mines?" asked Noa.

"Yes, and many lives were lost. I escaped with help from your father and came to this place."

Noa was impressed. He hadn't known his father had helped Dakki escape.

"What happened?" asked Zuri. Judging by her expression, she had never heard any of this before. "Did the Death King die?"

Noa glanced at Dakki inquisitively. "A book I read said he poisoned himself, but you don't believe that, do you?"

Dakki smiled weakly. "I have my doubts. It appears King Edjlin questioned it too."

Zuri frowned. "Why have you never told me this?"

Dakki looked out the window as he said, "Some memories are better left alone."

"I've always trusted you to tell me everything, Papik, but—"

"Then *trust* me," he said, turning back to her. "You are not in this room by accident, Zuri. I know you desire to see the realm. You must realize that knowledge opens doors, including doors we wish we'd never seen inside. The Death King is a terrible yet essential part of our history. I wanted to make sure you were ready for it."

Zuri's face flushed pink, but she didn't argue again.

"Why is the castle on my map upside down?" asked Noa nervously, already fearing the answer.

"The upside-down castle on your map and the upside-down island in your vision are no mistake. It is the great island Sulo. After the Battle of the Mines, the island was overturned to bury the horrors committed there."

Noa's mouth dropped. "Overturned? How?"

"There are two kinds of magic, Mr. Blackburn. Organic Magic, which comes naturally to certain ocean beings such as mermaids and sea sprites, and Made Magic, which is what those on land can replicate. My potions are Made Magic. Your map is Organic Magic because it came from a merfriend of mine long ago, the only one of its kind. The Death King was the first to ever combine Made Magic with Organic Magic when he created the venom drink, and it was also a combination of these two magics that hid what he left behind."

"And I'm . . . I'm meant to go there?" Noa stuttered, gobsmacked.

"If that is what the map says, then yes," said Dakki. "Sulo cannot be found with a normal map. It lost its connection to the ocean floor and drifts forever more with the currents, away from the realm."

Noa ran his fingers through his hair, taking it in. The night wind howled through the trees outside the hut, almost as loud as the ideas buzzing in his head. The Death King, mystical creatures, magic . . . a whole world had been hidden from him.

"You'd best return to your hut, Mr. Blackburn. I fear a storm is coming."

Raindrops thundered on the rooftop of the boys' hut. Noa had awoken the entire crew to explain what he'd heard in the Sirena—even Ravie had come, limping down the boardwalks—and they had talked well into the next day.

"That's where the map leads—to Sulo, the Death King's island!"

Jonath shrugged. "What does it matter where it directs you? They fixed the ship. King Titus has control of the kingdom again. We should return home!"

"Ahhh, but what about Dagan and Bones?" asked Malloch. Lightning lit the side of his face from the open window, followed by rumbling thunder. Jonath had no answer.

Behind them, Vim lay in his hammock, staring at the ceiling with a dazed look over his face. Ravie sat in the hammock next to him, her feet hanging over the side. She gazed around the room, chewing on her lip.

"What's your plan, Noa?" she asked.

Noa tugged on his tunic, massaging the fabric between his fingers. "Weston is still after the venom. If we find it first, we can make a trade—the venom for the freedom of Dagan and Bones."

Noa waited for the reaction, but the boys' faces were unreadable.

Chaston stopped gnawing on the twig in his mouth long enough to say, "You want to bargain with a pirate?"

"What other choice do we have?"

"He won't be fair, Captain," Malloch warned. "He'll cheat us and keep the venom without freeing them."

Vim stood up, the hammock hitting him on the back of his thighs as he got out. He looked Noa square in the face.

"What you're askin' for ain't possible. Think about it. We can't find Sulo without the map. In case you ain't aware, Weston has it. Even if we did find Sulo, it's still overturned. We would need to get inside a flooded castle beneath the ocean. And let's say we do make it. Let's imagine, just for one moment, that we don't all drown on our way to this castle—how do we find the venom? It ain't gonna be sittin' on a pedestal. It could be any-where—a cupboard, a chest, a bag—and that's *if* it is in the castle.

"Let's face it. We ain't got a fish's chance in the fryin' pan. Chaston nearly died the last time we saw those pirates, same with Ravie. I ain't riskin' my life too by followin' your suicidal plan!" Vim breathed heavily as silence fell over the room. "The *Evangeline* is ready to sail today. Let's just go home. Have your father send an army out for Dagan when we return."

Dagan would never abandon Noa, that Noa knew for sure.

"We can't give up," said Noa numbly, unconvinced by his trembling voice. "By the time we go home and out again, Dagan and Bones could be dead."

"But Vim's right," said Pan. "It's impossible."

"We almost died last time we saw the pirates," agreed Fig, scuffing his shoe against the wood floor. Another rumble of thunder boomed overhead. "Plus, the Martesians want to lock us away for piracy —"

"You can fix that, right Ravie? There must be *some* benefits to being the daughter of the general."

He realized his mistake immediately, but it was too late. Glancing at Ravie, he silently urged her to confess the truth, but she flushed like she'd just swallowed a hot pepper. Vim's eyes narrowed with suspicion.

"Hold on," he said, staring at Ravie's incriminating look. "You're a general's daughter? General Narthol?"

Ravie shrank into her shirt as she confirmed the truth. At once, Vim grabbed her by the collar and pulled her off the hammock. "Dagan was right! You're a spy!"

Aaron stood up, gawking in disbelief.

"You're hurting me!" she cried, struggling to free herself.

"Leave her alone!" said Noa, breaking them apart.

Vim dropped Ravie to the floor and rounded on Noa. "You

knew about this. How long have ya known?" The crew's astonished faces darted between the trio.

"Does it matter?"

"How. Long."

Noa scratched his head. "Since our first day here."

Vim shook his head in disbelief. "What kind of game are you playing at? The entire Martesian island wants us for piracy, and her mother is *leading* them! You didn't think we deserved to know this? You ask us to risk our lives, but you ain't willin' to be honest with us. The king kept secrets; I should have known you would too."

Noa stood his ground. "She's on our side—"

"I ain't interested," said Vim. He left the hut into the pouring rain. Noa watched painfully as each boy followed.

"Aaron, stop," Ravie called out.

Aaron paused at the door, but he didn't look behind him as he disappeared into the rain.

Ravie slid down the wall and put her head in her hands. Noa kicked the wall and slumped onto the floor beside her. "I'm sorry, Ravie. I didn't mean to say your secret."

"I've ruined everything," she mumbled, not taking her eyes off the floor.

"They're mad at me."

Ravie leaned against his shoulder. She reminded him of Lana. He wished he had been there to comfort Lana during the invasion. Of course, Bonnie would have comforted her, but Lana was his responsibility—she was his only sister.

Some time passed, and then suddenly Ravie sat up. "Your Highness, I have an idea."

Noa raised a questioning brow.

"Come . . . come with me." She jumped to her feet and pulled him into the early-morning rain. "We should have thought of it sooner!"

"Slow down, Mr. Blackburn! Are you sure this is what you want?" asked Dakki when the drenched pair had reached his hut and explained their plan. Noa pulled the enormous shell from the shelf.

"Positive," he said. "The map doesn't work for Weston. He's probably lost in the middle of the ocean. This is how we find him—he's bound to speak his bearings at some point."

Noa pressed the Sirena to his ear and squeezed his eyes shut, drowning out Dakki's other questions. To hear Weston, he must picture him in his mind—the pirate's tricorn hat, his red overcoat, the scars meandering across his face, the patch covering his eye . . .

Noa heard a sleepy snort, and then smacking lips. It was quiet for several minutes. Then he heard Weston laugh manically and whisper, "Sell the snail before it poops." Then the pirate started to snore.

Noa couldn't believe it. He was listening to Weston talk in his sleep.

He waited for several minutes more, listening to Weston's steady snores, before he decided to imagine someone else. He'd seen another pirate on deck with Weston, and now he imagined the fat, dirty man. Miraculously, he heard his voice.

"Eleven," said the pirate.

"Nah," said another. "Too many."

"I swear on me mother," the pirate insisted.

"You can fit *eleven* limes into yer mouth?"

"Aye, those little baby ones."

"What about buttons?"

"Forty."

"You can fit *forty* buttons into yer mouth?"

Noa had enough of this nonsense. He strained his brain to think of the one person he longed to hear, and soon Dagan's voice echoed in his ear.

"We need water!"

A metal door clanked shut.

"Shut up! Yer causin' enough trouble with the Cap'n, making us change course an' all. You'll get yer rations when *he's* done his job."

"Please," said Dagan's shaky voice. Noa melted in guilt. "Hasn't he fixed the ship enough?"

"I'll be fine," said Bones. "Don't worry about me."

"Aye, he'll be all right. He's a carpenter. Yer the bleedin' blaggard who can't read the map. You'd better hope we find that brother o' yers soon, or you'll be sleepin' with the fishes by nightfall tomorrow."

Noa squinted harder, trying to picture Dagan's black hair and almond-shaped eyes, but the voices were fading.

Noa awoke with a start.

"You've slept for some time, Mr. Blackburn. It's nearly evening now. Oh yes," Dakki went on when Noa rubbed his eyes and frowned. "You have not yet mastered the strength of magic."

Noa couldn't believe it. He had no recollection of the hours between listening to the Sirena and waking up. The power of magic was stronger than anything he'd ever known. He couldn't imagine how the Death King had handled a stronger form of it.

Dread filled the pit of his stomach as he told them Dagan was running out of time.

"They know I'm alive," said Noa gravely. "They said they changed course, so I think they're coming back to find me." Dakki listened as he finished tying labels to his bottled concoctions. Then he handed Noa a bottle of coconut-bananaberry juice to drink.

"What do you propose we do?" Dakki asked.

Noa gulped the sweet nectar and set the bottle down. "I need Weston to find me. I need them to come."

"That can be arranged . . ." said Dakki, stroking his chin. "Smoke signals will alert any ships nearby of life on this island, and if they are returning in this direction, they may see it. We can lure him to the island. Zuri and I, as well as the thimblewims, have trained for years to withstand the poison of the tree-dwelling centipede. It is the poison used in the darts, which I'm sure you remember . . . if the pirates come ashore, we have many means of stopping them."

Noa shook his head. "I need to go on his ship."

Dakki patted Noa's knee. "No need. The thimblewims and I are highly capable of defending this place—"

"No, it's not that!" Noa stood up, breathing hard. "Weston knows how to enter the upside-down island, or he wouldn't attempt to reach it. The venom is evil . . . it corrupts good men like Edjlin and my father . . . I need to go on Weston's ship and find the venom. I'm going to destroy it myself. Weston won't harm me," he added when Ravie opened her mouth to object. "He needs me to read the map for him. I won't let him harm the crew either, or I won't cooperate."

The easiness of this plan surprised him. He wasn't sure how it had come to him, but he knew as he said the words that he must go through with it.

Ravie shook her head. "He's a pirate, yes? He'll *make* you cooperate."

"I'll give Weston the impression we've given up, then set terms and gain his trust," said Noa, pacing the room. "Once I have the venom, I won't give it to him until he sets us all free . . . but I won't give him the real venom at all. I'll switch it with . . . with this!" He picked up the cloudy yellow drink Dakki had given him. "I'll pour the real venom into the sea and replace it with banana-whatever-you-call-it juice before Weston knows the difference."

Ravie's gaze darted back and forth as she went over the plan in her mind. Dakki had begun to smile.

"I will concoct enough juice for your needs, then. Although I believe you have one other reason for wanting to join this pirate,

266

Mr. Blackburn, do you not?" he asked. "The map says you are meant to go to Sulo. You want to know why."

Noa clenched his jaw. "I *have* to know why. It's the only thing that doesn't make sense."

Dakki folded his arms and nodded. "You will know soon, Mr. Blackburn, though I fear you will not like what you find."

CHAPTER 19

RETURN TO THE SEA

Noa let the fat, warm raindrops splash his face. Though he'd missed an entire day, he felt strangely productive, like he'd spent his time asleep concocting the plan. Dagan and Bones would return to him if he just waited for Weston to come. And with the pirate's help, he would reach the venom too. At last, the stars were beginning to align in his favor.

Gentle thunder rolled in the distance, drowning out Dakki as he bid them goodnight. Noa carried Ravie on his back down the slippery boardwalks, skidding and sliding over the treetop walkways. Raindrops streamed off the leaves and onto their heads. On the forest floor beneath them, the water had flooded dangerously high, but they were too far above it to care.

It was unnerving how Dakki knew things about Noa before Noa did. Indeed, Noa's first thought was to save Dagan and Bones from Weston's ship and then to reach the venom. Did he also want to find Sulo for himself? To know his destiny there, as Dakki had claimed? Perhaps his purpose *was* to reach the venom and destroy it.

Shaking off the rain, Noa entered the hut, letting Ravie slide off his back and limp to the nearest hammock. Wiping his eyes, Noa reached for a snack from the nearest fruit bowl, but it was empty. He looked up. The hammocks hung from the ceiling, motionless and vacant.

Uneasiness settled in his stomach.

"They should be back, yes?" said Ravie, tugging nervously at the short hair beneath her cap.

Noa opened the door and peered outside through the downpour. No one was in sight. Where was his crew?

———————

Floodwater reached Noa's waist when he toppled out of the elevator basket and sloshed through the jungle. Never had he seen so much rain from one storm. He practically swam through the jungle foliage, the treetop village above him keeping the thimblewims safe and dry.

It wasn't long before he and Ravie found the crew wading through the murky water. Most carried baskets of food above their heads.

"Wait!" Noa called, splashing toward them. Boys turned,

eyeing the pair. "Where are you going? Don't leave! Weston is coming. We're going to tell him where we are!"

"WHAT?" said the crew in unified shock.

"We'll use smoke signals to alert them. I can explain everything. Just please, don't leave without us."

"We're not leaving," said Chaston, scratching his side wound subconsciously. His soaked ponytail looked like a blond snake over his shoulder. "We've been stocking the ship. This is our last trip before we all set sail tomorrow."

With this good news, Noa couldn't stop himself from telling them his new plan. The boys shifted uncomfortably in the water as they listened, leaning their baskets against the flooded trees to give their arms a rest.

"Well?" Noa asked earnestly, after he had finished.

"Let me see if I heard you correctly," said Chaston, after a long pause. "In your first plan, you wanted to outsail Weston and find the venom first. Now, you want to join him and find the venom together?"

"He needs me to read the map and I need him to show me where the venom is hidden. Since he's already looking for us, we can use smoke signals to tell him where we are—"

"—but why do you want the venom? I thought we wanted Dagan and Bones."

"We'll use the venom as leverage. I won't give the venom to him until everyone, including Dagan and Bones, is safe on our ship."

Aaron's trembling voice squeaked from a nearby tree. "We can't give Weston the venom! He'll never die!"

"Weren't you listening to the plan?" said Noa, starting to grow impatient. "I'll *pretend* to give it to him. What he's really getting is Dakki's coconut-banana-berry juice!"

Chaston squeezed out the water from his ponytail and shook his head. "Listen to yourself. This isn't a mer-tale. Sulo has been upside down for years. The venom is lost to the sea."

Malloch came forward, lugging a basket of mangoes. "Ahh, Chaston's right. It won't work. If we go with Weston, we're food for the sharks."

Noa couldn't believe it. "We're giving up?"

Malloch slapped the water. "It's bad luck, this storm. No good will come if we return to the pirates. We can't expect to leave Weston's ship unscathed." The boys around him nodded their agreement. "We want to go home. If the Martesians find us, we'll turn ourselves in. I'd rather sit in a prison cell than face those horrid pirates again."

"Noa ain't gonna do that," said Vim, wiping rain from his beady eyes. "It's his brother out there. You wouldn't leave your family behind, would ya?"

Noa's face lit up. "You'll stay then?"

"No," said Vim. "It ain't my brother. I'm not goin' anywhere near those pirates."

At this, Ravie broke her silence, her face a heated, drenched mess. "This is how you treat the princes of Ondule? You ignore what they say or leave them for dead? That's treason, no?" She turned to Noa. "You are the leader. *Order* them to follow your plan. *Order* them to stay!"

Noa's heart pounded. He looked at Malloch, whose freckled

nose shone with rainwater, and to Aaron, whose hair stuck to his forehead in wet triangles. They watched him through the rain . . . waiting . . . waiting . . .

Malloch placed his hand tenderly on Noa's shoulder. "You can't save everyone, Noa."

Noa shook him off. "Yes, I can. Go. Find help. I'm turning myself in to Weston and ending this once and for all."

The relief flooding through the group was undeniable. With Noa's permission, they could go home at last. They had the provisions they needed, and with the pirates arriving at any time, they decided to set sail straightaway. They each said their goodbyes and wished Noa good luck. Aaron stayed back the longest.

"Be careful," he said, giving Noa a hug. Pulling away, he motioned for Ravie to come.

She crossed her arms and didn't move.

"Go with them, Ravie," Noa ordered.

"You don't have power over a Martesian," she said flatly. "I'm staying with you."

Her eyes met Aaron's. She gave him a hug, then slowly took off her necklace and held it in her hands.

"This ring belongs to me," she said, holding it in her fingers. Raindrops bounced off the purple stone and octopus band. "It's a duplicate of my mother's, yes? If you do see a Martesian ship, signal them to come and give them this ring. Tell them I sent you. They'll help."

Biting her lip, she watched him catch up to the group with the ring in his hand and disappear into the jungle.

Noa trudged through the brown water in a daze. "You didn't have to stay."

"I don't want you to be alone," she said, following behind him. "Will the plan still work with the two of us?"

"I don't know," Noa admitted.

They had reached a hanging ladder which scaled to the treetop village and began to climb. When they touched the top, Zuri came out of a nearby hut and ran toward them to pull them out of the rain.

"I'm sorry your friends left," Zuri sympathized, bringing Noa and Ravie dry clothes. They faced opposite walls so they could each change in privacy.

"It's better this way," he lied, rolling down his heavy, wet pants and replacing them with new ones made of barkcloth. Pulling the dry shirt over his head, Noa stared at the wall in front of him. He had planned to trick Weston by giving him fake venom and destroying the real venom and then sail away on his own ship. Now he wasn't sure how he would ever return home. He doubted the pirates would give him a lift. "I'm changed," he announced.

"I am too," replied Ravie, and Noa and the girls turned around to face each other once more.

"Are you afraid your friends will die at sea?" Zuri asked when Ravie had left them to rest in a swinging hammock.

Noa looked at his cold, wet feet. She took that as a yes.

"It wouldn't be your fault if they did. They could have died here too," she said, flashing her snake-bitten leg in his direction.

Feeling like this was an invitation, he asked, "What happened?"

Zuri sighed. "Three moons ago, it rained, flooding the jungle like today. All I saw was the flick of its tail, and then its fangs sank into my leg."

Noa winced, imagining the pain. "How did you escape?"

"The thimblewims heard me scream. They bit the end of the snake's tail and it let me go . . . but you know something?" she asked, leaning back as if to laugh at herself. "While it was squeezing me to death, all I thought was I won't get to cook the squirrel I caught. *That's it.* I've lived my whole life on this island, and all I have left to show for it is a dead squirrel?"

Noa hesitated, wondering if he should plunge into the unruly sea that was Zuri's mind. He thought he knew where she was going with this, but he decided to let her finish.

"I was only a baby when my parents sent me with Papik to have a better life while they stayed in Sulo to fight. I can't help thinking if they were still alive, what would they say? I've never done anything important. Maybe . . ." she continued hopefully, "if I came with you . . . I could have my chance to make them proud?"

And there it was. Noa sighed as he shook his head.

"You don't know what you're saying. It's dangerous."

Dakki had been kind to Noa and his friends; taking Zuri, his only family, onto a pirate ship was about as likely as the ocean drying up. Noa couldn't risk not bringing her back. Zuri saw it differently.

"I can help get your brother back," she said. "I can use the sleeping darts—"

"I'm sure you could, Zuri, but it's—"

"Don't say it's dangerous again. I know danger. I have lived in a dangerous jungle my whole life. Haven't you ever wanted to do something that truly mattered?"

Noa felt shame rising in his gut. Could he deny Zuri the chance to live out her dream?

He rubbed his tired eyes. "Fine." Zuri's eyes, however, had lit up like fire. "If Dakki says you can come, you can come."

Zuri squealed with joy, gave Noa a hug, and dashed off to find Dakki. She soon returned drenched and ecstatic to tell Ravie the good news. As the girls talked, Noa slipped outside and ambled down the luminescent boardwalks, the smell of soil after rain hovering in the air.

It wasn't long before he found Dakki sitting on a bench alone, gazing thoughtfully at a suspension bridge which hung like a glowing necklace between the trees. A tree frog croaked calmly in Dakki's hands.

"I wondered when I introduced you to Zuri if she would follow you off this place," Dakki said when Noa sat beside him.

Noa scooted to the edge of the wet bench, his pants now sticking uncomfortably to his bottom, and prepared for a lecture. Instead, Dakki said, "I'm proud of you for seeing that she needs this."

That wasn't what Noa expected.

"But may I speak frankly, Mr. Blackburn? These wrinkles didn't come at birth, you know. Time has revealed much to an old man like me." He stopped petting the frog and squeezed

Noa's hand. "Even the easiest paths are hard when we go them alone, and you have by no means chosen an easy path."

Noa remembered his friends with a twinge in his stomach.

Dakki silently returned the frog to a nearby branch. "Why did you follow the map?"

Noa told him his father's instructions.

"That's a boy's answer, Mr. Blackburn. Why did you *really* choose to follow the map?"

Noa looked away, twisting his fingers around the bottom of his shirt. Why *had* he chosen to follow the map? Necessity, obedience . . . but there was something more.

"I followed it because I'm not like my father." He spoke slowly and deliberately as the right words formed in his head. "My father deserts people when they need him most, and I wanted to show my people that I was different. I followed the map to save my home."

"Do you feel he deserted you, Mr. Blackburn?"

"I *know* he deserted me." Noa scuffed his shoe on the boardwalk, staring at a cluster of fireflies nearby. "You don't understand. He gave up on Mother when he found out she was dying, then he gave up on us too: Dagan and Lana . . . and me. He didn't see us or speak to us for three months after she died. Not even Lana could reach him. Then one day he came back and acted the complete opposite, suffocating us with rules and chaperones as if that could make up for his absence. He never was good at understanding us. How could I ever see him the same after that? He's a coward for abandoning us. Even more, he's a coward for feeding the kingdom lies about the realm."

Dakki gazed at the glimmering branches, his hands clasped on his cane. "I've often thought the hardest part of discovering who you are is accepting what you find," he said. "You are the boy I see in front of me because of your father's hurtful actions, and the sooner you can accept this as a blessing instead of a curse, the sooner you will know happiness.

"Take me, for example. Hallowbit is not my last name. Gravner gave me the cup you saw after a fight with his father. He wished I could be his new father, you see. He was only a boy then, but family is who we are, Mr. Blackburn. If you cannot accept your family, with all their faults and virtues, you are destined to a life of anguish."

Noa remembered something his mother used to say about loving your family, and it made him sad . . .

"So, I should forgive him?" he scoffed. "Let my father love me or leave me whenever he wants?"

Dakki put his hand on Noa's. "Forgiving someone does not mean letting them rule over you. It is the opposite. Forgiveness gives us power to rise above those who look down on us, because we no longer feel beneath them."

"I'm not sure I understand."

"You will, Mr. Blackburn. Gravner could never accept his family, and we have all seen what it did to him, but you will not fall prey to this same fate. I know you have it in you to forgive your father . . . and yourself . . . for what happened so many years ago."

Something stirred in Noa. Did Dakki know the truth of what happened to his mother? Had he heard something in the Sirena?

The two sat quietly. A group of furry thimblewims strutted past, babbling in their squeaky language. Upon seeing the pair, they grew silent. One thimblewim with a particularly large cowlick in its fur glared at Noa, and Noa shifted awkwardly on the bench.

"News travels fast. They aren't too happy about Zuri leaving," explained Dakki, when the creatures filed off to their appropriate huts. "Alas, I'm off to bed. I wish you luck," he said, regaining balance with his cane. Warmth filled Noa's chest as he realized how much he would miss Dakki. "If you'll excuse me, a cup of tea is calling my name."

For the first time since the crew had left, Noa smiled. "Let me guess: mint?"

Dakki gave him a look of utter confusion. "My dear boy, *chamomile*. Always chamomile in the evening."

The old man wobbled away. Noa stared at his lap long after Dakki had gone.

———————————

That night, Ravie snuck into Noa's hut with a midnight snack. They swung in hammocks side by side, Ravie biting into a pink fruit. Noa passed the extra fruit she'd brought him between his hands like a ball, brewing in his thoughts.

It was after some time lying in the darkness, neither one of them able to fall asleep as they thought of tomorrow, that Noa asked for her story.

"You want to know why I left?" She yawned and rubbed her eyes. "I suppose I can tell you now . . . I've been an only child my whole life, and then Mother says she's having a baby—without even asking me! I thought she was too old to do that, no?

"My parents said I would like him, but I don't. All he does is cry and make the house smell. It's Gill this, Gill that. No one has time for me anymore. I ran away to teach them a lesson, but when I came back, they didn't even know I was gone. That's when I really ran away. I saw your ship and hopped on."

Noa rolled over in his hammock to look at her. "Dagan acted the same way when Lana was born. He was so jealous."

"I'm not jealous!"

"My nursemaid Bonnie says it's normal to feel left out when a new baby comes. She used to make Dagan kiss Lana every night until he stopped trying to sell her to the servants."

"Really?" Ravie asked, sounding hopeful.

Noa nodded. "You can't choose your family, but you can choose to love them. My mother used to say that when Dagan and I got in a fight. Then she'd make us hug. We hated it, but . . . well, I suppose it's why we stick together now."

"She sounds nice."

"She was. . ." Noa gazed into Ravie's warm smile, lost in memories of when he was young.

"All right, is there something in my teeth?" asked Ravie, frowning.

Noa blushed. There were in fact several chunks of fruit in her teeth, and he hadn't realized how long he'd been absent-mindedly staring at them without mentioning it. She scowled and turned away to pick them out with her finger.

"Just when I thought I could trust you," she joked, but it

stirred the uncomfortable feeling in Noa's belly. *Trust.* Noa felt the sickness in his stomach intensify.

He swallowed hard. "Can I tell you something too?"

"I have snot in my nose?" Noa didn't have an answer, so she turned around, rocking her hammock. "What's wrong?"

"I, um . . ." His hands shook. He gripped his pants to keep them steady. "Dakki was talking about forgiving people . . . about forgiving myself . . . and it's just . . . I thought if maybe I said it out loud, it would help? I don't know what will happen with Weston and . . . well . . . I may not have another chance."

Ravie was quiet, watching him and waiting. "It's all right, Your Highness," she whispered, reaching out to take his hand.

He swallowed. It was time.

"On our island, children aren't allowed to leave until they come of age," said Noa, deciding to tell her everything, though he couldn't look her in the eyes. "My father said it was for our safety, so when he told me he wanted to take Mother sailing for their anniversary, I didn't understand. I told them not to go. I reminded them it was dangerous. But they left." He swallowed again, hating that he had to relive this. "Their ship was attacked by pirates. The pirates were sick with a disease none of us had seen before, and my mother caught the fever soon after. She died two weeks later."

Ravie lowered her eyes. "I am sorry, Your Highness. That must have been very hard for—"

"You don't understand," Noa interrupted, pulling away from her. His eyes filled with tears. "I found a cure, Ravie." He could hardly say it as he choked on the words. "I read every book we had, and I found one. But I was so . . . I was so mad at my father . . . I was so mad that he did this to her, that I didn't tell anyone. I wanted him to feel guilty for just one more day. It was his fault they were on a ship in the first place. He should have listened to me when I told him not to go. I just wanted to see him suffer for a little longer . . ."

Ravie gaped in stunned silence. Noa squeezed his pants so hard he felt his nails in his palms.

"I let her down, Ravie." At this, Noa broke into sobs. "I didn't know how serious it was, I promise. I didn't think she would die."

Ravie was quiet beside him as he cried, seeming at a loss for words. Noa felt like an erupted volcano gushing hot, sticky lava with no end. Every day since his mother died, he had kept this secret inside him, and it had been screaming to get out. Hearing himself say it out loud felt so . . . final. It was done. And he had to live with that mistake forever.

Softly in the darkness, Ravie started to sing.

"Little pea in a pod. It's a beautiful day.

The carrots and potatoes are asking to play.

Farmer's in the kitchen with a boiling pot.

Stay away or you'll be hot, hot, hot."

Noa's tears waned as he watched her with red, puffy eyes.

"Little pea in a pod. It's a beautiful day.

The carrots and potatoes are asking to play.

Farmer's in the kitchen with a boiling pot.

Stay away or you'll be chopped, chopped, chopped."

"Why are you singing that?" he asked, wiping his nose with his shirt collar.

"It helps my baby brother when he cries. I thought it would help you."

Noa rubbed his eyes and breathed deep, needed breaths. They listened to rustling leaves outside, the tree moss brightening the room through the window with a green glow.

"Are you sorry you told me?"

He thought for a moment and shook his head.

"I don't think you killed your mother, Your Highness. She was sick. You're not a doctor."

"I could have fixed her," he said flatly.

"Perhaps . . ." She lay in her hammock beside him, watching the shadows on the ceiling. "But you have been wrong before, Your Highness. It was a new disease, yes? How could you know if it would fix her? You read a book, and there is no telling if what you found in it would help her or not. Perhaps . . . perhaps it's time to stop punishing yourself."

Noa was silent for a long time, except for the occasional sniffle.

"Thank you," he whispered at last.

She nodded in the darkness, and her reassurance was something he never knew he needed. For the first time in years, a weight lifted off his shoulders. Crisp air entered his lungs. He heard the chirping insects outside and watched the luminescent glow cast shadows on Ravie's face. He felt alive.

"Malloch was right . . . I can't save everyone. But Dagan and Bones are not everyone. They are two people—two people who I am not going to let die. I can't change what happened, but I can change what happens now." He dropped out of the hammock and made his way to the window. Fireflies danced between the branches, pirouetting through the rustling leaves. "Hold on, Dag," he whispered, staring into the night. "I'm coming."

The next morning, Noa returned to the hut, surprisingly alert for not having slept. His Capture the Conch sack bulged from the special materials he had collected from Dakki. Striding across the room, he woke the sleeping girl on the floor.

"Already?" Ravie moaned, rubbing the sleep from her eyes.

Bland pudding awaited them on the banana leaves. They sat with the few thimblewims who had not yet left to tend the crops or hunt in the jungle. When they were ready to leave, Noa thanked Dakki and the thimblewims for everything they had done.

The old man clasped his liver-spotted hands around Noa's. "You are always welcome here, Mr. Blackburn." He hugged Ravie next and pressed a bundle of mint leaves into her hand. "For the trip," he whispered, winking. While Dakki and Zuri said their goodbyes, Noa and Ravie climbed into the elevator basket and waited. Soon the three of them were lowering to the ground. Noa watched the furry people shrink in the treetops. They were on their own once again.

CHAPTER 20

THE UNEXPECTED INVITE

"Welcome aboard, the *real* Noa Blackburn," said Weston greasily. The ship bobbed in the salty waves off the coast. Noa, Ravie, and Zuri had trekked through the jungle the entire morning and waited on the beach for the pirates to find them, the bonfire's rising smoke blackening the sky above them.

At last on the ship, Noa did his best to avoid falling over. His stomach fluttered in the presence of the scowling crew. Climbing up from the rowboat, Ravie and Zuri joined him on deck. Zuri stared at the pirate's scars with a mixture of horror and curiosity.

Weston returned the interest. "Yer not from Ondule."

"She joined us from Martesia," Noa explained, without missing a beat. According to Dakki, no one knew he or the thimblewims existed, and he was determined to keep it that way.

Weston's eyes flicked to the island. "Did she now? I don't remember seeing her when I attacked yer ship," he said with a smirk.

"You clearly didn't see me either, or you wouldn't be in this mess," Noa clapped back.

Weston's smirk disappeared.

Arms crossed, Noa held the pirate's gaze. "You will treat us with respect. If not, I will refuse to read the map, and you will never have what you're after."

"Name your terms," said Weston with a dismissive wave.

"My crewmates and myself will not be harmed—" Several pirates laughed. Noa ignored them, keeping his face firm despite the clammy palms he was stuffing into his armpits, and cleared his throat. "We will receive food and water for the journey. I also wish that we remain together."

Weston fixed his eye patch. "Anythin' else, lad?"

Noa glanced at Ravie, thinking back to what they had rehearsed. "Yes, we keep our things."

Weston edged closer, eyeing Noa's sack as he neared. "I'm afraid I can't do that, lad. As protection against me crew, I've got to search you for weaponry and the like. I'll be keeping yer things with me."

"Search us," Noa challenged, pulling the Capture the Conch sack off his shoulders and handing it to Weston willingly. "We haven't brought weapons. These objects are the only things we have to remember our home."

Weston gave a sidelong glance to his crew and dumped the sack upside down, spilling its contents onto the deck.

"Let's see what we got here," grumbled Weston, pushing aside the specs to pick up a bottle of liquid. "Sneaking palm beer, are you? A bit young for such a strong drink." He popped the cork to take a swig but stopped when the bottle reached his lips, his face contorting in disgust. "Murder a mermaid! What is this? It smells like Two Toes's feet!"

"That's my medicine," said Ravie. "It's for my leg."

Weston returned the bottle and grabbed the spyglass, extending it to look at the horizon. He shut it without interest, picked up the specs and weight belt, and threw them back in the pile carelessly. Then he stood up, kicking the items around with his feet, and shrugged.

"Nothing but a pile o' rubbish!" He laughed mockingly, and the crew behind him joined in. Noa recognized one of the pirates. He was the man he'd seen secretly meeting with Edjlin during Noa's Capture the Conch game. "Go on and take it."

Noa hurried forward, picking up the items and stuffing them back in his sack.

"Hold on, lad."

Weston's sword left its sheath and pricked Noa's neck. The pirate stared down the blade, watching Noa with a look of uneasy puzzlement.

"Yer a smart lad for coming without a fuss, but I'm warning you, if yer planning any bilge against me, I'll spill yer innards and throw 'em to the fish. S'not natural for royalty to go volunteerin' aboard a pirate's ship."

Noa had expected this. He motioned for Zuri to roll up her pants and reveal the gnarly python's bite. She had added red berry juice for a fresher look.

"Worse things are living in the jungle than on this ship," Noa explained. "We'll take our chances."

Weston's eyes widened at the sight of the wound. Then he snarled. His humor had run out, it seemed. He pulled a piece of yellow parchment from the inside of his coat and thrust it into Noa's hands.

"Show us where to go, boy."

The map glowed to life with Noa's touch. The upside-down castle drew itself magically in the middle while a compass in the right corner pointed to Sulo.

"Directly east," said Noa heavily.

Weston's eye glinted with pleasure, and he hollered for someone to take them to the brig. Noa glimpsed the lush island one last time before the crew pushed him aft and below deck.

———————————

"Bones! Dagan—you're hurt!" Noa barely had time to see the bruise spreading over Dagan's puffy eye before his brother slammed into him. The stench of sweat and human waste engulfed Noa's senses as Dagan held him. Bones clapped Ravie on the shoulder, trying to hide a tear that slipped down his dirt-smudged cheeks.

Stifling hot, the brig held the five of them. Crammed inside the cell, Noa cursed himself for failing to negotiate better sleeping quarters while he had the chance.

"I thought you were dead," Dagan admitted, releasing him. His face was dripping, a fate Noa already felt beading on his forehead. "I didn't know they'd destroyed the *Evangeline* until Weston took us aboard. How did you reach an island?"

Noa explained how the currents brought them to the island, then dramatically rehearsed the events with the sea sprites. A guard stopped picking his ear long enough to shout at them to keep it down, but Noa had already lowered his voice to tell them about Zuri.

At first, Dagan regarded Zuri with suspicious bewilderment, only to relax as he learned more about her life, satisfied she could be trusted. Bones couldn't believe she had lived with the thimblewims for so long, and Dagan reintroduced himself flirtatiously, slicking his unwashed hair back before shaking her hand.

"Where are the others?" whispered Bones, cracking his knuckles anxiously. "Did they escape? Are they infilterating the crew in the night?"

"*Infiltrating*," Noa corrected.

"You know what I mean! Well?" Bones glanced uncertainly around the cell.

Noa couldn't look him in the eye as he told him the truth. "They sailed home," he said quietly.

The ship creaked and groaned against the sea in the stillness that followed. Noa thought of the crew for the umpteenth time, wondering if they'd managed to spot a Martesian ship. He didn't dare imagine they'd come back. It was better to believe the facts: they were indeed on their own.

"Cheer up," Ravie piped in, bringing them back. "We have more to explain, yes? Better discuss it now, so we're ready when the time comes."

The others reluctantly agreed, and with that, Noa crammed between Dagan and Bones on the hard floor and began to whisper the plan.

Hours passed quicker than expected, as Weston routinely demanded that Noa check their route. With his hands through the bars, Noa would hold the map until its blue glow showed him which direction they must sail. Then the pirates would yank it from his grasp and push him back into the dank cage. The only one who ever left the cell was Bones. His carpentry skills were still needed to repair the ship from the damage Noa's crew had caused.

Inside the cell, the group took turns sitting or standing. With each change of the guards, Noa realized the dumbest crew members had been assigned watch duty. Weston clearly didn't see them as a threat behind bars. That was how Noa liked it.

"I never thanked you for taking my place," whispered Noa on the second night. He scooted closer to Dagan on the floor to let Zuri roll over in her sleep. Under the glow of orange lamplight, Ravie slept in a ball near the gate with Bones draped over her legs, her mouth open and drooling. "I'm not saying it was smart to tell Weston you were me, but it was brave. You're a good brother."

Dagan shrugged. "Well . . . you're my best friend."

Not for the first time, Noa was amazed by the kind of brother he had. If Noa was a complete prat, Dagan would forgive him, even if Noa would not have offered his brother the same mercy. It was pride Noa wished he didn't carry, but he couldn't help it.

Not knowing how to respond, he ruffled his brother's hair, then in disgust wiped off the residue of Dagan's greasy head. "Yuck. Don't forget to wash your hair before you go back to all the girls at home."

Dagan shifted uneasily against the bars.

"I can only imagine how many shirts they'll ruin when we return," said Noa, wiping the perspiration from his upper lip. "Bonnie may have to ban you from going into the village—"

"Don't you mean *if* we go back?"

Noa watched his brother in the dim light. "The plan will work," he assured him.

Dagan tilted his head indecisively and stared at the ground. Noa nudged him with his shoulder until he looked up, made a face, and sighed.

"Only one girl on the island fancies me, and she's—" Dagan grimaced. "She's nine."

"Nine!"

"Well, you started it! You saw the bottle messages in my mailbox and assumed they were from different girls instead of one."

"But . . . there are always girls crowding you," said Noa, confused.

"I snatched a bun from a kid once—one of Lana's friends, I thought—and hid it behind me," Dagan explained, sighing heavily. "I told her to come get it—as a game, you know—and she looked me over and ripped my shirt down the middle. How could I know the kid would become obsessed with me and keep playing the game with her friends? All right, I will bait them now and again to make the other girls jealous," admitted Dagan in response to Noa's skeptical look.

Noa couldn't hold it in; he burst into laughter, instantly feeling Dagan's warm hand press over his mouth.

"It's not funny!" he hissed. "She's starting to scare me. She sent me a letter and signed it 'Mrs. Dagan Blackburn'!"

Noa laughed harder under Dagan's hand, then Dagan busted into a fit. They tried not to wake the others and just sat there in the middle of the filthy cell, shaking silently with their hands over their mouths.

"Do you want to know something even funnier?" asked Dagan when the ship's rocking ultimately calmed them down. Noa yawned and squinted in the dark.

"She already has a ring?"

Dagan chuckled. "I've been staring at these bars for over a week. I couldn't help but wonder how much I wanted one thing to pass the time . . . a book."

Noa cocked his head to the side, then threw his arm around his brother. "We'll make it home, Dag. Many years of frightening love letters await."

The next day, Noa had an unexpected invitation.

"You'll be dining with the Cap'n tonight, boy, and you'll be on your best behavior," said the pirate Two Toes, more as a command than a request. The cell door clanked open. Two Toes poked him in the back with his blade all the way to the main deck. Noa welcomed the fresh air with relief as he viewed the bottomless blue that had replaced the turquoise reefs.

"Ah, the man of the hour," said Weston when Noa entered the captain's quarters. "Come, sit. Eat."

Noa sat at the nearest chair while Two Toes stood guard beside him. Fried fish, hard cheeses, and roasted potatoes wafted their delicious smells toward him.

"You must be hungry," said Weston before taking a swig from his goblet and clunking it down. A pendant around his neck glittered in the candlelight. Noa hoped his own pendant had sunk to the bottom of the sea.

Noa glanced at Two Toes with uneasy puzzlement. To poison Noa now would be useless, unless Weston no longer needed his directions. In that case, were they near the map's destination? Two Toes glared back at him. He'd replaced his sword in its sheath but threateningly gripped the handle.

"The Cap'n says to eat," he said, kicking Noa's chair and pinning him against the table. Noa gasped and reached for a chunk of bread and a slice of cheese. It was probably safe to eat, and oh how Noa wanted to devour it. He gulped down the food faster than Bonnie would have deemed appropriate manners.

Weston watched him as he took another swig of palm beer and wiped his mouth with the back of his hand.

"I s'pose you're wondering why I brought you here, Prince Noa?" Noa chewed his food but did not attempt to answer. "Lad, I thought it would be good and proper to say you did not disappoint. You followed the map better than I'd expected, that be true."

Noa reached for another bun and bit eagerly into its soft crust a smile ripening at the corners of his full mouth. Weston would encounter more than he expected once Noa executed his plan to destroy the venom and take over the ship.

"I imagine we'll reach the island tomorrow," Weston went on, absentmindedly twisting a ring on his finger as he spoke. "At last, this is coming to an end. It wasn't easy convincing Edjlin to do my biddin' and retrieve the map."

"Edjlin should have known better," said Noa through a mouthful.

"Edjlin is a poor excuse for a king. Never have I seen someone with a weakness so deep as Edjlin's for his son. Pathetic. Rule number one of being a pirate: don't get attached."

"It doesn't matter what Edjlin wants. Only I can use the map—"

"Because yer father gave it to you willingly, as I hoped he would do when he realized Edjlin was after it," said Weston, his gaze fixed on Noa.

Noa stopped. The food sat on his tongue like a weighted ball, and he gulped it down in one uncomfortable lump. "You *knew* I'd end up with the map?"

"Aye, I wanted you to follow it."

Noa's spine prickled. "Why me?"

Weston's good eye twinkled with excitement as he continued:

"I placed the *Evangeline* farther away from the bay so you would take it. I *let* you win the ship. When you sailed to Martesia for help, I ensured yer only option was to follow that blasted map. King Edjlin wouldn't dirty his hands—he thought too highly of yer father, you see—but I'm not afraid to show King Titus who's in charge. Royalty always think they have the upper hand, but as it is, some leaves be fated to fall."

Noa couldn't believe what he was hearing. He'd been a pawn in Weston's game. "Why try to kill me then?" Weston raised his brow questioningly. "When we first met, you would have run your sword through me if not for the arrow that struck your arm."

"I wasn't trying to kill you, lad! I had to play the part. I cut the rigging to set loose the sails. Don't you see? I led you here, and you couldn't have managed without all the books I gave you."

Noa stared.

"*Sailing Fundamentals for Landlubbers*? *The Seventy Stupidest Things to Try with Saltpeter*? You read them, didn't ya?" he asked, admiring his stubble in the reflection of his spoon. "Just as he said you would . . ."

"Who's he? Edjlin?" Noa ground his teeth in disbelief. Was the pirate speaking the truth? "You attacked our ship!"

"Aye, that be all a bit o' show. You wouldn't stand a fish's chance in the fryin' pan if I put up a fair fight." Weston's expression turned serious, and for a split second, Noa saw a hint of fear. "My instructions were to bring the Map Keeper aboard and disarm the others. I knew you would have enough food and water to last several days, plenty of time for the ship to reach an island or a nearby ship. You are a prince! And a lad.

I may be a pirate, but murdering youngsters is too messy for the likes of me."

Noa's lips pursed in suppressed fury. *All a bit of show*?

"You monster!" Noa yelled. Weston laughed (or growled—it was difficult to tell the two apart), but Noa's anger only grew. "The blue men took our food and water. You wrecked our ship! We nearly died! You even let Edjlin believe he could see his dead son again. You're no better than the scum that coats the bottom of this ship."

Weston didn't laugh again. He stared Noa down, massaging his bandaged arm which still hadn't healed since the arrow in Ondule.

"Strong words from a lad who lost his ship to . . . mutiny, was it?"

Noa stood up, pushing his chair back several feet. He wanted to jump over the table and wring Weston's neck. Two Toes's blade whipped out and pressed against his chest, and Noa was forced to sit down.

"Why am I still here?" he asked through gritted teeth. "Why not order me to give you the map and find Sulo yourself?"

Weston tugged thoughtfully on his earring. Then he leaned forward across the wooden table until Noa could smell the alcohol on his breath. "The map leads each to different fates, but your fate is Sulo."

"*Why?*"

"That," said Weston, leaning back in his chair, "I shall tell you."

Noa's anger melted. At last, he would have answers.

Weston refilled his goblet with wine as he spoke. "I've been to Sulo before . . . it was a long time ago, and the island left its mark . . ." He gestured to the scars on his face. "This time will be different. Let me explain how this works, lad. I need you to open a chest which lies in the heart of the castle. You will willingly open the chest because you need the riches inside to rebuild your kingdom from its recent—" He smirked. "—fiery upsets. If you open the chest, I will set you and your friends free. Do we have an accord?"

Noa's eyes narrowed. Of course, he had considered the money they would need to rebuild his father's fleet and how this would affect the way of life for his people. They would have to lower the price of their crowned resource, Alston stone, and sell twice as much to afford wood from Blightip to rebuild the ships. Anyone able would work in the mountainous mines. Bones's family toy shop would close, as would Larry's Hermit Haven and any other nonessential shop. The Capture the Conch games would be no more. The thought of solving this by simply obtaining the Death King's lost treasures was tempting, but Noa needed to stick to the plan: destroy the venom.

"The venom is in the chest you seek?"

Weston's one good eye twinkled. "Aye, you're a smart lad, and a smart lad is what I need for a puzzling chest. It's too tricky to open me'self. The venom is in the chest, and it's the only treasure I'll be takin'. I swear on a mermaid's tail, you can take the rest." He lifted his goblet to toast. "This is your fate, lad. You are meant to follow the map to retrieve Sulo's treasure and ensure your island's survival. Take as much as you can carry."

"I have your word?"

Weston nodded. Wine leaked down his unshaven face as he gulped down his glass, staining his shirt blood red.

"LAND HO!"

Noa heard the shouts above deck from his cramped position in the cell. His stomach twisted as he imagined the shriveled black island from his dream.

"This will work, yes?" Ravie whispered, gripping her spyglass. With her back to the guard, who was entertaining himself by rolling his boogers into balls, she unscrewed the refracting lens from her spyglass. Inside the hollow barrel were tiny feathered darts.

Noa closed the lid for her and hissed, "Not yet. The plan will work." It had to work. They would surely be put to death if caught. Still, he needed to ensure they had options.

"If I don't return," he hissed to Dagan, pulling him aside and passing him a tiny bottle of green liquid, "do Plan B. No matter what happens to me, you must make it out. You'll be a better king than I ever dreamed, and I'm sorry I ever thought courage could be measured by how many books you've read."

The endless purr of passing water died away as the ship slowed, accompanied by the creaks of changed rigging above. Then it stopped altogether. Noa waited in the cell, rocked gently by the swells. His eyes met the others. They each knew what was coming.

Two guards appeared at the door, barking Noa's name, and

hustled him away from the brig, prodding him up the ladder to the main deck. The wind chilled his skin. It was colder here.

Guards led him to the mast to prepare for the journey to Sulo, the underwater city. Noa rolled up his pants and pulled off his shoes, then placed his Capture the Conch specs over his eyes and the weight belt around his waist. Although Noa had expected they would swim to the upside-down castle, the idea filled him with questions. How deep could they go? He remembered from his vision that air sticks grew on the island, but he didn't know what would happen if they ran out.

Exiting the captain's quarters, Weston emerged in a tunic and trousers held up by suspenders, looking much younger without his overcoat and tricorn hat. Noa was surprised to see a pair of specs on his head as well, fancier than Noa's and made of glass, strapped around his eye patch. Two Toes came after, another pair of specs on his head.

Noa felt himself deflate. Weston hadn't said anything about Two Toes coming along.

Rough hands shoved Noa down the plank. The deep blue ocean foamed and splashed against the hull beneath him as he inched forward onto the board's wobbly surface. As he looked down, doubt crept in. Could he really trick the pirate and destroy the venom? Or was this a suicide mission after all?

Climbing up the rails, Weston turned around to address the crew.

"The lad comes up with me, or he doesn't come up at all."

The pirates growled their understanding. Satisfied, Weston dove off the side. Two Toes followed Noa onto the board. His weight shook the board so much that Noa fell off the end into the water, smacking the waves on his side.

The shock was like falling into liquid ice. He choked on the salty water and took to the surface immediately. Two Toes jumped in after him and came up pointing a dagger at Noa's face. Noa got the picture. He pressed the specs against his eyes to ensure a tight seal, then swam down, amazed at the water's clarity. Losing his specs would be disastrous. The salt would burn his eyes and blur his vision, making it impossible to find his way to the surface from the darkness below. He prayed they would stay on as he followed Weston toward the black mass in the distance, swimming fast to warm his limbs and popping his ears as he descended.

Island features came into focus. Slimy tree stumps that once were a forest hung upside down on the island, and bamboo air sticks stuck out from the ground like quills. The muffled waves above died as he swam below the tree stumps after Weston, Two Toes taking up the rear. It felt like entering a flooded cave . . . a cave with no bottom.

Noa took the freshly cut air sticks from Weston with numb hands. He bit down and filled his lungs with new air. Instantly relieved, he grasped the miniature bottle of coconut-banana-berry juice Dakki had given him and pushed it deeper into his pocket. Without the yellow liquid, he could not make a convincing switch with the venom. Noa promised himself he would not lose it to the sea.

Swimming fast, they only paused to breathe their air sticks. Light had faded almost completely. How they would see in the darkening water, Noa didn't know. Until they came upon the castle.

Sulo's castle stunned him. Although surrounded by black water, the castle itself radiated light like a candle in the dark. Fish, eels, jellyfish, squid, and a multitude of luminous creatures glided around the stone fortress like blue stars streaking across a night sky. In their light, Noa glimpsed bamboo air sticks growing down the castle walls.

Weston impaled a glowing jellyfish with an empty air stick, then motioned for Noa and Two Toes to follow him into the castle. Goosebumps prickled every inch of Noa's body. He breathed air from another stick and, after ensuring he had enough air sticks for a return journey, followed Weston through an enormous entryway. Where two doors had long since rotted away, an upside-down message above the entry read: *Sulo: Kingdom of the Rich.*

The jellyfish's glow lit the flooded halls. Passing crumbling suits of armor with slime-coated bones piled inside, they finally reached stairs spiraling into a dark pit above. It was the way to the throne room. Like Noa's castle, the throne room had been built into the ground, with only the dungeons and cellar beneath it. For an upside-down Sulo, it was the room closest to the surface. They swam up. Noa's ears popped, fizzing as they released their pressure. Soon he found himself gasping for breath in rotten-smelling air.

CHAPTER 21

A SEALED CHEST

Noa crawled onto the stone landing, trembling, his fingers ghostly white. Two Toes came after him, gasping for breath. The jellyfish's blue glow lit the foyer. It had a low ceiling, and slime coated the walls and dripped over the upside-down sconces where torches were once lit.

Noa's heart quickened. "Where's the chest?"

"Shut yer hole," barked Two Toes, although Noa could see he was wondering the same.

Weston tossed the jellyfish into a glass vase, and it landed onto its bell-shaped hood, followed by its tentacles. Noa had once read that a jellyfish had no heart or brain and probably couldn't feel pain, but its splat as it hit the bottom still made him cringe. Filling the vase with water, Weston used the glowing jelly like a lamp.

Two Toes shoved Noa forward. Noa's numb feet didn't feel like his own, but rather like he had slipped into someone else's skin. The floor did nothing to help. Its frozen, slimy state reminded him exactly how deep he rested beneath the sea. He shuddered to think how one good blow against these walls could crumble the castle, leaving him to drown beneath a pile of rock.

Only when Noa stood at his side did Weston answer his question about the chest.

"The treasure be in here, lad," he said, gesturing to the wall. But it wasn't a wall, Noa realized, it was a metal door sliced into circular sections like rings on a tree.

Weston pressed a hidden button on the first ring, and an opening revealed itself on the second. A message was carved into the metal on the door's third and final ring. Noa tipped his head to the side to read the upside-down words.

Upon Pivotal Means Shall One Enter

Noa stared at the tiny opening, waiting for something to happen. *Upon Pivotal Means . . .* what did it mean? Weston stood calmly to the side, pulling his pendant from his neck and rotating it in his fingers.

Didn't "pivotal" also mean *"to turn"?* Then Noa knew. The pendant was a key.

Weston thrust the pendant into the opening and twisted it in the lock. A clank of metal against stone echoed across the walls. Door rings rotated. They formed a single upside-down image: the Pendant of Privilege, the symbol belonging to the Death King's followers and those who believed they had the right to take control of the realm.

The door swung open to a dark room.

"High seas," mumbled Two Toes in awe.

"You first," said Weston. He yanked Noa by the collar and thrust him into the darkness.

Noa's feet buckled beneath him, and he slid down the bowl-shaped wall on his back. Weston joined him soon after with the light, and Two Toes came after him. The door slammed shut behind them, sealing them inside.

"This way," Weston instructed.

Two Toes prodded Noa with his dagger. "Move along, boy."

Shuffling into the darkness, Noa devised a theory on how air was trapped inside the castle, something he imagined he might explain by pushing a glass cup directly over water. He wondered if magic also played a role in preserving this underwater tomb, though if it had, it was waning. He could only see a few feet in front of him by the jellyfish's glow, but he heard the distant echo of dripping water.

The room went on forever. They sidestepped smashed armchairs and chunks of wood, occasionally climbing over an archway or tiptoeing around a chandelier. What baffled Noa the most were the books. Everywhere he stepped, moldy books squished and crunched beneath his feet.

He sensed they were close when Weston slowed down and began illuminating the walls. Noa's heart skipped a beat. Shelves, ladders, another landing with intricate gold railings . . . this wasn't a throne room like Noa's castle—it was a library, the biggest library Noa had ever seen.

"There it be," said Weston.

Noa looked. An enormous rectangular box sat in the middle of the room, half covered in books. It looked more like a coffin than a chest. A trapdoor in the floor (which was now the ceiling) rested above the chest, dripping water on top of them. Noa prayed the trapdoor would hold. If it broke, water would flood the room and drown them inside.

Casually he felt his pocket for the bottle of coconut-bananaberry juice, ready to make the switch with the venom when the time was right. Then he inched closer to the chest to read the writing etched into the stone.

Letters under hand carved into stone

Place where you may but place alone

If worthy be yours to undertake

The waves which crash, these contents make

Speak only words gifted at birth

Lest it stay inside 'til ends of the earth

Noa scratched his chin, mumbling the words under his breath as he reread the description. It was just like a mystery novel. He could do this.

"If I solve the riddle and open the chest, I'm free?"

"Aye, as I promised. Yer friends as well."

"The riches inside are mine to keep?"

"Save for the venom, yes. Now open it, lad." He set the

glowing vase on the stone to help Noa see. Two Toes watched greedily from the side, wiping his dirty hands on his beer belly.

Moments later, Noa snapped his fingers.

"'Letters under hand' means the riddle itself. It's telling me to place one hand on the writing and say the 'words gifted at birth,' or rather, my name."

"I knew you could do it. Go on then, lad."

Noa didn't like the look in Weston's eye. It was too easy. *That* was the puzzle too difficult for the pirate to solve? Was it booby-trapped? He folded his arms. "You open it. I've told you how."

Weston agreed and placed one hand on the chest. He said, "Weston." Nothing happened. He tried to push the enormous chest off its lid, for it was face down, but couldn't.

"Is Weston your full name?" Noa asked.

"Nah, not the Cap'n," chimed Two Toes, moving closer so as not to be left out. "He named his'self, see?"

"Shut up, Two Toes."

Noa thought this odd. He studied the chest carefully, glancing back to see what the pirates would do. Weston waited. Two Toes glanced anxiously from his master to the chest.

Finally, Noa resigned and placed his hand on the writing.

"Noa Blackburn," he declared to the stone box.

The chest split down the middle, then crumbled away, erupting in a cloud of dust. Powder descended onto their eyelashes as the contents of the chest spilled over their feet: gold and silver coins, jewels, pearl necklaces, a sword encrusted with a coral handle, beautiful fabrics still in pristine condition . . . and a black statue.

Noa pounced on the treasure, digging his hands into the coins and stuffing as much as he could into his pockets. He needed to find the venom first to make the switch. Two Toes rushed forward to the treasure too, but Weston held him back. The captain didn't even bat an eye at the riches. Instead, he bowed and forced Two Toes to do the same.

Noa scoffed. *They bow to treasure but not to a prince?* Then Noa stopped, staring in horror at the statue lying amidst the wealth. It was coming to life. The statue's hands changed from black rock to pale flesh. The man's oily hair unstiffened and fell like bleached worms behind him, dark robes covered his frail body, and he lay on the ground, his chest rising with new breath.

Noa stumbled over books and jewels to back himself against the shelves. The statue-turned-man opened his eyes, and Weston groveled at his feet.

"My liege, yer freedom."

Noa's eyes flicked to the vial gripped in the man's hand and felt the weight of his mistake like the castle itself had crushed him. This was no ordinary chest, no ordinary man . . . he had raised the Death King from the dead.

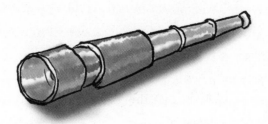

CHAPTER 22

THE PIRATE AND THE PRINCE

"Help me up, you fool." The Death King spoke in a raspy, wheezing voice. Weston lifted the Death King to his feet, and immediately the king pushed him away with his bony hand. His bloodshot eyes met Noa's, and Noa barely stopped himself from screaming.

The Death King's face almost belonged to a middle-aged man, save for his sunken cheeks, so caved in they resembled bowls, and his skin. It was missing in places, revealing tendons and purple veins branching across it, and white as the underbelly of a fish.

The Death King focused on Noa. "I knew you would come. Welcome to my ranks, son of Titus."

Noa blinked with astonishment, frozen in place. How did he know him? The Death King took a step forward, and Noa snapped back to reality.

"Keep away!"

"Come now, come now, don't be afraid," the Death King cooed. "Only the blood of one who has sealed my tomb could open it again. *You* have your father's blood. You were chosen for this. The map led you here to help me regain my power."

"You're lying!"

Is that why Weston couldn't open the tomb? Beside the one-eyed pirate, Two Toes looked as terrified as Noa felt.

"I came for the treasure . . . I need it for my home—" Noa stopped himself, clenching his fist to keep his hands from shaking.

"And you came to destroy my venom?" said the Death King with a look of pity. He held up the vial, tipping it playfully and watching the liquid dip from top to bottom. It was all a game to him. "Come now, son of Titus, you don't understand its power. A single prick of this venom kills in seconds. Only I know how to produce the potion which wields its poison, bringing life instead of death."

"My liege," said Weston, bowing again. "We promise to rule beside ya with honor."

The Death King's cackling laugh cut him off. "Your place shall be in my palace, yes, though if you suggest ruling at my side ever again, I shall leave you as helpless as I found you."

Weston looked like he'd been slapped. "But our agreement,

my liege. I brought you the boy in exchange for a place at yer side—"

"You shall not argue with me again," said the Death King, raising his voice. He coughed horribly, wheezing. "Prepare our exit. Take the fat one with you. I wish to speak with the boy alone."

Noa understood preparing the exit to mean finding something to lift them back up to the door. Naturally, it was close to the ceiling and would need ladders or an enormous pile of books to reach.

Looking stunned and mortified, Weston turned on his heel and disappeared into the darkness with Two Toes scurrying behind, leaving Noa and the Death King in the faint blue glow.

The Death King watched Noa gaze after Weston. "Weston would crumble under the burden of nobility. You are stronger. You are wiser."

"You don't know me." Noa's lips were numb with fear as he spoke.

Dipping his hand into the treasure, the Death King pulled out a handful of silver coins. "Trapped in this tomb, I was caught between life and death," he said, flipping coins between his bony fingers. "I could not live, for I had no air, no food, but I could not die, for I had consumed the venom and given my blood immortality. I was alive only in my mind, and with my powers, I entered the minds of others."

The Death King lifted a coin to his temple. "I watched Titus through his thoughts, his dreams, willing him to come back for me. I almost had him too. After your mother died, I sensed his weakness and plagued him with dreams. He hid in his chambers to stop himself from ordering his men or his children to come to my aid, unwilling to confide in someone about what beset him. It was wonderful to watch. He thought he was going mad." The Death King coughed again. *Heeeeee, heeeeee, heeeeee.* "It took months, but in the end, he blocked me out." The Death King's face contorted into a scowl at the memory, only to break into a wicked grin a moment later. "Ahh, but Edjlin was weak. It was easy to convince him."

The Death King studied Noa, tossing a coin into the air as he examined Noa's trembling knees and flaring nostrils. Noa stared back, his mind racing. All this time, he'd believed his father had abandoned them after his mother died, but if the Death King spoke the truth, Titus had hidden away to protect them from himself. Lying about the realm, sending them to the village school, creating Capture the Conch . . . these were distractions his father created to stop Noa and Dagan from falling prey to the same power Titus had to overcome . . . the power of the sickly man that stood before him now.

Dropping the silver treasure, the Death King stepped forward, crunching a book spine beneath his feet. "Everything changed, son of Titus, when you found the pendant. You hungered for answers. I saw it. I read your thoughts. I *studied* you."

A chill crept up Noa's spine.

"I know you read book after book to prove you have the knowledge to protect the ones you love. You hope that never again will you be too late . . . a feeling I know all too well," the Death King added, making a sweeping gesture to his library around him. "It was then I knew you were the one. I instructed

Weston to bring you instead. He doubted you would make it, but I knew the map would lead you here. The Map Keeper must have honorable intentions, and you couldn't resist the chance to prove yourself to your kingdom."

Only feet away now, the Death King's venomous gaze bore into Noa, gluing him to the spot.

"Titus is not fit to rule. He failed long ago . . . if only he had listened to your counsel, your mother would still be alive. It's his fault she's dead. You need not prove you are better than him to alleviate the guilt you feel for her passing; you are better already." He let his hand fall paternally on Noa's shoulder. "You are the worthy ruler of Ondule. I see the revenge in your eyes as strong as it is in me. Let me help you take the throne."

Noa shook him off and stepped away. "You're wrong. I don't want revenge."

The Death King shook his head, clicking his tongue sympathetically. "Your mother deserved better, you know she did. . . . Lana deserves better too. Let me help."

Something inside Noa snapped. *Lana.* He shouldn't know her name. He held his gaze, burning with hatred toward the decrepit creature.

"Help me like you helped Weston?" he spat.

"He is a pirate, a scoundrel—although I do not expect much else when it was I who raised him in this sunken prison, trapped and knowing nothing but what I told him. I quickly realized he could be the means to my freedom, and he was. He brought me *you*."

Noa stared at the ghostly man. His heart pumped louder

and faster in his chest with each second he put the pieces to-gether in his mind. Shaking his head in disbelief, he recalled the story the blue man told him about the boy fighting in battle, the painting of the boy on the ship with different-colored eyes, Weston naming himself . . .

"Weston is Eric," he whispered under his breath. Then he lifted a shaking finger and pointed into the darkness where Weston had departed. "Weston is Eric Driggonhall—he's Edjlin's son!"

The Death King smiled, stretching visible tendons beneath the see-through skin.

"The eye patch he wears doesn't cover a missing eye, it covers his different-colored eyes," Noa went on, remembering the painting. The Death King nodded. Then Noa had a strange thought. "Does he know?"

The king laughed. "Do you suppose I would risk losing my closest ally?"

So Weston had no idea who he truly was.

Someone stirred in the shadows. The Death King's attention turned to Two Toes, who had been listening nearby.

"Come," he ordered. "Kneel." Trembling, Two Toes scooted closer into the light. The Death King leaned down, breathing his raspy, foul breath over the wide-eyed pirate. "You didn't hear our conversation now, did you?"

"I swear to you, I heard nothing," he said, though his shaking voice betrayed him. "Just on my way back to tell ya the exit is ready, is all." He looked like he might wet his pants.

"Excellent," said the Death King, strolling to the broken chest and retrieving a coral-encrusted sword that lay in the rubble. He picked it up and swung it playfully in the air as he returned to Two Toes's side. "It would have been a tragedy for you to learn Weston is born of noble blood. Oh, silly me. I spoiled the secret."

Two Toes gulped, his bug eyes fixed on the living corpse above him.

With a quick jab, the sword plunged into Two Toes and out again, and the pirate crumbled to the floor.

Tossing the sword to the side, the Death King yawned. Footsteps approached, and Weston entered the circle of light where stood Noa, the Death King, and a dying Two Toes.

"What happened?" cried Weston, rushing to the pirate's side. "You did this?

"Isn't that what you wanted? I thought you brought him along to dispose of him."

Weston cradled the balding man's head in his lap. "He was me first mate!"

"I will find you another."

In his dying breaths, Two Toes took hold of Weston's collar. "Yer—the—lost —" he gasped, clutching his bleeding chest. "Son—of—"

Slip. The Death King had moved so quickly, it took Noa a moment to realize what he'd done. Two Toes fell limp, a new hole in his chest. Weston looked up, his face full of a thousand fires.

"What have ya *done*?"

"The man was suffering. I merely put him out of his misery."

"He was tryin' to tell me something . . ."

The Death King coughed. "Nonsense talk, most likely. Have you made arrangements for our departure?"

Noa couldn't watch any longer. "YOU'RE EDJLIN'S LOST SON!" he shouted.

Weston's confused gaze traveled to Noa and back to the Death King. "Is it true?"

The Death King rolled his eyes and gave up pretending. "Come now, Weston, of course, it's true. Only one as shortsighted as you would fail to notice the connection in the presence of his own father. If Edjlin hadn't been injured, he would have sealed me up along with the other kings, and I could have used *you* to open my tomb." He coughed again, wheezing like a rag clogged his throat. "Alas, you have proven your worth."

"But . . . my liege . . ." Weston stammered. "You told me my family abandoned me on this island, that they scarred me face in banishment."

The Death King barely bothered to look at Weston as he spoke. "Is that what I said? Those scars are the remnants of falling stone when the island overturned. Don't be wroth, Weston. I have taken care of you as I promised."

Weston laid Two Toes to rest in the rubble. Balling his hands into angry fists, he glared at the undead king. Dripping water echoed around the hall, disturbing the silence.

"Have I not allowed you freedom to join the pirates who tried to plunder here? To sail the seas on my behalf?" the Death King continued.

Weston nodded, bowing slightly. He seemed to be regaining some of his composure, despite looking visibly shaken.

"There, there, I knew you would come around."

The Death King turned to Noa and announced, "Son of Titus, leave this hall with me, or you shall not leave at all. Make your choice."

He dropped the venom into the pocket of his robe, and Noa screamed inside. He had to have it!

"What good is the venom to you if you're already immortal?" Noa demanded.

The Death King cocked his head, pushing aside greasy white hair. "The venom's properties are not permanent."

Noa stepped closer. "What do you mean?"

"It teases me with immortality," replied the Death King, his eyes narrowing suspiciously. Noa frowned as if he didn't understand. "You fool. It extends my life rather than giving it to me forever. I must use it again."

Noa inched closer innocently. He was only a few strides away from the Death King and the venom sitting in his pocket. If he could just reach it . . .

Then something happened.

Freezing water spilled onto their heads, drenching them both and sweeping them off their feet. The trapdoor was open, pouring seawater into the room like a faucet. Barrels and skeletons that had been trapped in the passageway followed, dropping to the ground and smashing into pieces.

Salty ocean carried Noa away into the darkness. On the other end of the hall, the Death King held on to a ladder, seething in the blue glow as the jellyfish jar lodged into a bookshelf beside him.

Above them on the library landing, Weston hollered, still gripping the lever that had opened the trapdoor.

"Mutiny! MU-TIN-Y!" he cried, his voice high and hysterical. "Me whole life was a murderin' lie!" The Death King coughed hoarsely, trying to stay afloat in the flooding room. "You taught me to lie, to cheat, to steal, and it sent me to jail—they could have put me in the gallows save for my young age," said Weston, climbing down the ladder to the watery floor. "For what ya did to me, for what ya did to Two Toes, yer goin' to rot in here until the venom in your veins works no more!"

Neither the Death King nor Weston had noticed Noa reappear from the shadows. Noa waded through the gushing water toward the pair. He'd seen this maneuver done in a *Hazardous Heroics* book once, and he hoped it would work . . .

"Hey!" he called. "Catch!"

They turned. Noa held up the vial of venom for them to see, then threw it as high as he could into the air. The Death King didn't have time to think. He dove to catch it. While he did, Noa dashed forward and dipped his hand into the Death King's robe to retrieve the *real* venom. As soon as his hand closed around the glass vial, the Death King's hand closed on his wrist.

"Do you *think* I'm a *fool*?" hissed the Death King, twisting Noa's arm behind his back.

"Let me go!"

This was *not* how it happened in the book. The Death King laughed wickedly and pushed Noa face-first into the bookshelf. He was surprisingly strong.

"I'm disappointed in you, Son of Titus," he seethed, pinning

Noa to the wall. "Give me back the venom, and I won't slaughter that lovely sister of yours when I take control of your kingdom."

The shelf cut into Noa's cheek. He squeezed the venom in his hand. "Rot in the sea," he cursed, trying to twist out of the Death King's bony grip. The man's fingers were like iron rods tightening deep into his flesh.

And then, with a shattering blast, the Death King collapsed, pulling Noa down with him. Noa yanked free, still clutching the venom. Weston stood above them both, broken glass still in his hand. Curling up in the water, the Death King held his skull in pain, then reached for the dagger on Weston's belt . . .

Noa felt a punch in his leg. He got up and tumbled into the rising water. His leg started to burn, and as he tried to stand up, he fell again. Why did it hurt so much? Near him, Weston attacked the Death King, making him drop the knife in the water, and they wrestled into the shelves. Noa needed to get away. Using the ladder to pull himself up, he started climbing to the second landing, the burning in his leg growing stronger until he collapsed at the top.

The decoy coconut-bananaberry juice had worked after all. He held the venom in front of his face, but it was too dark to see even that.

Water filled in fast. The continual rush as it poured in from the ceiling bombarded his ears, every moment threatening to drown him inside the grimy room. He felt his forehead to pull his specs over his eyes, but the specs were gone. His heart raced in his chest as he tried to imagine swimming out of the castle without a proper way to see. The burning in his leg now felt like a hot poker searing through his flesh.

Eerie blue light from the jellyfish grew brighter as the water rose. Where were Weston and the Death King?

Rasping breath moved up the ladder.

Noa dragged himself in absolute agony to a pile of books and hid behind it. Part of him wanted to pass out just to make the pain stop, but he knew he couldn't. He was safer here on the library balcony. All he could do was wait. Wait for the water to rise. Wait for the Death King to find him.

No one in all his books had ever been where Noa was today. Their journeys were made of ink on parchment; his was happening now. And though he had no proof it would work, his gut told him he couldn't keep the venom. He felt for a book and flipped through the pages in the dark, a motion so familiar he acted on muscle memory, then placed the venom inside. Using his boot as a glove, he smashed the shoe as hard as he could on the closed book. The vial inside its pages shattered in a deadly crunch.

He had done it. He had destroyed the venom.

The pain took over then. Gasping, he lay down and wanted to cry. Warm blood oozed from his leg, filling the air with a metallic odor. Had he been stabbed? Venom sizzled in the book near his head.

All at once, sour flesh bombarded his senses. To Noa's horror, so did a rotting hand around his neck.

"THIEF!" the Death King shrieked, squeezing the air from Noa's throat.

Noa cried out but couldn't make a sound. He couldn't *breathe*! His head felt like it would explode. Blue light illuminated the Death King's face, and Noa would have gasped if he was able. The man's rotting, pale skin was inches from his own, his yellow teeth bared.

Thinking fast, Noa stretched his fingers toward the sizzling, venom-soaked book beside him and jammed the book into the Death King's eye. A surge of raw energy burst through him, radiating from the book and pulling his strength with it. Heat surged from the book into his fingertips and gushed up his hand, charring and blistering his skin.

Noa screamed in pain. The Death King shrieked too. Falling to the ground, the king twitched and convulsed.

Dropping the book, Noa cradled his throbbing hand. He watched the Death King's body in the bioluminescent light swell to twice its usual size, as though the venom had turned his blood to jelly in his veins. Then his inflated body collapsed on itself in sizzling boils and burns. He shriveled like a dried prune and fell over the landing, disappearing beneath the water. The venom's residue dissipated in oily swirls until there was nothing left but seawater.

Noa could feel his heartbeat pulsing through his singed veins. He stared at the rising water, expecting the crippled, pale man to resurface, but he never did.

An arm lifted Noa around the torso, heaving him above the flood.

"He's dead," Weston told Noa.

When had Weston arrived?

Water seeped over the landing and flooded the shelves on the second floor, washing away books and soaking their legs. Books thickened the water like fruit inside pudding. A chair bumped into Noa's back. Noa's head pounded so hard he felt dizzy. He felt *sleepy*. It was difficult to keep his eyes open, but the freezing water compelled him to stay awake. What was happening to him? He knew he would die if he didn't find the door quickly and swim out, but his eyelids drooped over his eyes like weights.

"Stay with me, lad. The fastest escape be through the trapdoor above."

The blue glow lit Weston's scarred, patchless face, the specs pulled over his eyes to protect them from the salty sting. Somewhere around them, the glowing jellyfish floated, its venomous tentacles drifting dangerously near.

Water bubbled up to Noa's neck. His arm felt numb. *Stay awake!* To escape through the trapdoor, he must wait for the room to flood completely or he'd be pushed out. If the layout resembled his own castle's trapdoor, they would then enter an underground tunnel and exit at the back of the castle, hopefully near air sticks.

Weston kept them above water by holding on to the shelves. Noa forced his eyelids open, afraid he would fall asleep if he blinked. He could touch the ceiling now, but he felt himself fading, slumping into the pirate's hold.

"Wake up, lad!" hollered Weston, jamming an air stick into Noa's mouth. Noa didn't feel a thing.

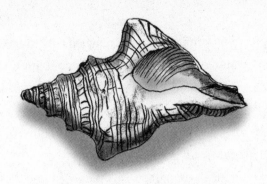

CHAPTER 23

A NEW CAPTAIN

Heaven's light beamed onto him, brightening the darkness behind his eyelids. He didn't want to move. He didn't want to do anything but lie still, soaking in the bliss of the afterlife. Death felt good.

Noa was vaguely aware of the sounds around him, a repetitive swooshing followed by drips and gurgles. Slowly he regained his senses, noticing the soft crunch of sand behind his head and its warmth under his body, the distant caw of a seabird, the clicks and snips of crabs darting about to find food. He always assumed heaven would be a beach, and his fingers reached for the book he knew must accompany him in this paradise.

Instead, his palms pressed into the grit.

Grunting, he opened his eyes. Sunlight pricked his vision, blinding him and filling his eyes with tears. As Noa rolled over

321

to shield his face, his tender, raw hand touched the ground, and he let out an involuntary yelp. He pulled his hand to his chest and pressed his cheek into the hot sand until the pain subsided.

"Enjoy yer nap, lad?"

Noa slowly turned to face the pirate. "Don't . . . kill . . . me . . ." he mumbled groggily, still cradling his hand.

"I told ya murdering youngsters isn't me style," said Weston, leaning forward on the black sand. He'd made a small firepit and was roasting a fish over the orange flames. Gesturing to Noa's hand, he said, "That's a wound of magic, that is. I expect it's why you've been sleepin' since yesterday. Try not to touch it."

Noa remembered how exhausted Dakki's magic potion had made him. He examined his raw, burned hand, then noticed his pants had been torn above the knee and tied around his calf.

"Aye, he stabbed you," said Weston, following Noa's gaze to the bloody bandage. "Just a nick. Yer a strong lad, I'll give you that. Not too many pirates can run away after being stabbed in the leg."

Noa rubbed his bandage with his good hand, at a complete loss for what to say. Weston, the pirate who had invaded his home, destroyed his ship, kidnapped his brother, and made him release the Death King, had just saved his life?

"You hungry?" Weston asked, pulling the stick out of the fire.

And now he was offering him food!

"Er, what happened? Is the Death King really dead?"

Weston nodded as he sucked a piece of charred fish off his fingers.

"Amazing . . . and you're Edjlin's son," said Noa, after a moment or two. "Why wear an eye patch if you don't need to?"

Weston laughed. "I can shoot a pigeon one hundred feet away with only one eye. How many lads you know who can do that?"

Noa nodded politely, sensing Weston was embarrassed.

"I never liked me eyes," he said slowly, talking to his fish more than to Noa. "Didn't want to be remembered by an imperfection."

Noa didn't think they were an imperfection. He'd never seen eyes so unique. "We must tell King Edjlin you're alive. We have to bring you home—"

The pirate held up his hand and shook his head. "I may be a pirate, but I don't turn my back on me first mate, and I don't like anyone that does. It don't sit well with me what Edjlin did to yer father."

So that was it. Weston was Edjlin's son, but the pirate wanted no part in a royal life. Noa thought he understood, but he couldn't help seeing the irony of Weston's judgment against his father when he had spent *his* days murdering and plundering.

"Then, where will you go?" asked Noa, accepting a fish on a stick for himself. The white, flaky meat tasted like heaven to his starving stomach.

Weston merely shrugged.

Hours passed as they waited for the pirates to find them. When the sun started to set, someone shouted, "Over here!"

And then it happened too fast. Hearing the *fwump* of approaching feet in the sand, Noa craned his neck to look around.

He heard, "Spitting sea serpents, he's alive!" and someone ran into him, squeezing him against their foul-smelling shirt.

Noa cried out in agony, pulling his arm away.

"Sink my ship, Noa, what happened to your hand?"

Squinting in the sunset, Noa focused on his brother's face, gripping the wrist of his throbbing hand. Then he glanced around for Weston, but the pirate was gone.

Noa wrinkled his nose. "What happened to *you*? You smell like vomit."

Dagan looked like he didn't know if he should laugh or cry. "That's because of Plan B. Noa, *it worked*. I drank the potion you gave me—dis-gust-ing stuff—and just like you said would happen, I got sick all over the cell! The guard didn't even need to open the door. As soon as he came close to see if I was all right, Zuri shot him in the neck and stole the keys. We used the rest of the sleeping darts that were hidden inside Ravie's spyglass to finish off the crew. The pirates dropped like logs, and only a few of them put up a fight." He pulled off his smelly shirt and threw it behind him on the black sand, almost hitting Bones in the face. "And you stink like dead fish."

"Plan B worked?" Noa repeated in awe. "We have the pirate ship?"

"Even better," said Bones, grinning. "We burned it to the ground. The smoke signal is how the *Evangeline* and a Martesian rescue ship found us—they're here to take us home!"

At this point, Dagan looked around him, suddenly wary. "Are you alone? I thought I saw someone with you . . . where are Weston and Two Toes?"

Distracted by Weston's white shirt peeking out from behind a nearby boulder, Noa considered revealing the pirate's hiding spot. But things were different now. The man, the lost prince, had just saved his life. "They didn't make it."

This came as a huge relief to Dagan and Bones, and they wasted no time in helping Noa return to the ship.

Noa listened for the better part of an hour as Dagan and Bones rehearsed what happened, each with Noa's arm around their shoulders to help him walk. King Edjlin himself had written to Martesia admitting to the invasion and begging for a rescue ship to find Noa and the boys. Malloch, Aaron, Vim, and the others had flagged down a Martesian ship and shown them Ravie's octopus ring, and as soon as the Martesians understood Ravie's predicament, they sent three more ships in separate directions to find her. Smoke rose on the horizon, and they made headway toward it, finding Dagan, Ravie, Bones, and Zuri relaxing on the rocky island with an entire crew of unconscious pirates at their feet. Now both the Martesians and Noa's friends were searching Sulo, hoping to find Noa alive.

In turn, Noa explained what happened below the waves.

"Fry me a flounder, you mean Weston had normal eyes?" said Dagan once Noa had finished. "I didn't know you could wear an eye patch if you still had both eyes! All these years I could have worn one . . ."

"You'll be all right, Noa," said Bones, mistaking Noa's silence for fatigue. "The Martesians will take care of you. They will sail us home."

Noa stumbled over the barren landscape. The idea of seeing

the crew again made him painfully nervous. Did he want to face them?

They reached the coast. Lifeboats sat on the rocks. Sailors and boys scoured the beaches for the pirate and the prince. Behind them, two ships were moored in the sea.

"He's alive! Noa is alive!"

People crowded them. Malloch, Aaron, Jonath, the twins, Zuri, Chaston, and Vim were at the front of a pack of relieved Martesians. No one dared break the circle and touch him.

Ravie stood with General Narthol, smiling and cradling her baby brother in her arms. A familiar octopus ring sat on her finger.

Noa cleared his throat, and the crew instantly burst into a stampede of apologies.

"Ahhh, we thought we were doing the right thing by finding help—"

"The pirates would have killed us!"

"You know what's interesting is you said we could leave, remember? We obeyed orders!"

"Don't apologize," said Noa, finally able to get a word into the conversation. He cradled his burned, throbbing hand as he spoke, shielding it from the beating sun. "If you had come with me to Weston's ship, things could have been much different. We wouldn't have the Martesians here to help us go home."

The boys exchanged relieved looks.

Noa breathed deeply, smelling the seaweed water splashing onto the black rocks. A seabird screeched from a nearby rock, stretching its wings before taking flight into the cloudless sky above. Seeing the crew's faces made it easy to forgive them, but he couldn't ask the others to do the same.

"These are the people you should apologize to." Noa pointed to Dagan, Bones, and Ravie.

"It's all right, Your Highness," said Ravie, leaning comfortably against her mother's chest. She kissed the baby's head and bounced him gently as she spoke. "Everyone deserves a second chance."

Bones and Dagan agreed. "They came back."

It was all Noa needed to hear.

When they gathered to the longboats, Noa found the Martesian captain to make one final announcement.

"Captain, as a last apology, my crew has generously offered to handle all chores aboard the ship, starting today with swabbing the deck. Isn't that right, boys?"

The boys' astonishment was quickly masked by an overenthusiastic desire to help. In no time, longboats carried them all to the ship, leaving the blackened landmass behind them.

"We're going home," said Dagan, squeezing Noa's shoulder. For the first time since the invasion, Noa believed it.

———

They spotted Ondule within days, cutting the journey in half by the sailors' experienced hands. The Martesians believed Weston had drowned. Noa had a sneaking suspicion he was hiding in a cave somewhere, waiting for a chance to start again. The rest of the pirates were brought to Justice Isle to await trial.

Noa was glad he didn't have to see the condemnation awaiting them there.

Nerves grew as Ondule neared. They dropped anchor in the bay beneath the demolished lighthouse and castle, charred docks and shipwrecks half submerged in the water around them, then rowed to shore. Noa felt ill as he crawled out of the lifeboat into a mob of cheering villagers. The crowds swarmed them, slapping their backs and shaking their hands.

"Thank the tides you're alive! You're safe!" Their nursemaid Bonnie sobbed uncontrollably when she saw them. "I've been worried sick. My boys, you could have died . . . you could have been . . . oh, it doesn't matter! You're here! Dagan, look how your hair has grown! Noa, my dear, you've injured your hand!" she gasped, lifting his bandaged limb.

"He's fine—honestly! We all are!" Dagan tried to escape her suffocating embrace. They would have been subject to her tears much longer if Lana hadn't squeezed her way into the circle.

"Did you bring me back a present?" their sister asked. She was followed by a conspicuous nine-year-old girl goggling at what remained of Dagan's black eye.

Next came Alya, bursting through the crowd of parents straight for Aaron. Holding him with tears in her eyes, she looked over her shoulder and searched for Noa.

"Thank you," she mouthed.

The crowds parted as Titus made his way to his sons, a mixture of relief and joy written on his face. Once they were out of sight from the beach, Titus, Noa, and Dagan let their true feelings come to the surface.

"Forgive me," pleaded Titus as they entered the isolation of the castle gardens. "I did not want the outside world to corrupt you. I knew that once you understood mer-tales were real, you would leave, and I wouldn't be able to protect you. It's why when you were born, your mother and I decided to outlaw any mention of magic. I realize now this was a mistake. But when I thought you were plotting to leave the island . . . and you had the Death King's pendant . . . it terrified me. Please understand, I never meant to do you harm."

"We know why you lied to us," said Dagan.

"Even if you were trying to protect us, it has to stop." Noa made a sweeping gesture in the direction of the village below. "Our people are living a lie. It's time for everyone to know and speak the truth, Father."

Titus was silent as he contemplated this. "Very well. I will announce the truth, and from this time forward, the age requirement to leave the island is abolished."

The boys' breath caught in their throats at what this meant: they could leave the island at will.

"This whole time we could have just asked . . ." Dagan muttered to himself.

"I'm sorry it hasn't been the same between us since your mother passed," Titus went on.

Dagan quietly bowed out, drifting over to a nearby pineapple plant to examine the growing fruit, while Noa was left to remember what the Death King had told him. "It wasn't your fault. You were under the Death King's magic."

Titus studied Noa, his gaze revealing his understanding.

"Magic or not, I want to be better. I should have been there for you."

Titus felt different, vulnerable, but more of a father than Noa could ever remember. Noa thought of what Dakki had said about the Death King's unforgiving past and remembered the decrepit man with a twinge of pity. He didn't want to become that.

"I . . . forgive you," said Noa. He let himself relax into his father's burly embrace, feeling something he hadn't felt in a long time.

The night came slow, blanketing the island in warm darkness. Noa gazed out his bedroom window after a long night of hot food in the banquet hall and tales of their adventures, accompanied by the crew and their families. Ravie had returned home with her mother, but Zuri had decided to live on Ondule for a time to study the new culture, with the assurance she wrote home often, and was enthralled by all the new sights of the island. Awestruck, Zuri couldn't stop gazing at the castle's massive stone walls as she ate, and by the looks of the parents, it wasn't the first time the rest of the children had told their adventurous tales. Noa enjoyed the various sides, each one remembering their voyage differently.

"The map in your chambers . . ." Noa had whispered to Titus, as Zuri explained the woodwork of her treetop village to Bones's interested father. "Why does it have the Death King's symbol?"

"It was given to me before the symbol meant what it means today. You must understand I was young once too, trying to find my place. It took years before I saw the world as my father saw it and became the king I am today."

Noa chewed his bottom lip. "But why does Sulo's castle resemble ours?"

Titus shook his head. "Alas, I'm afraid that is a discussion for another time. For now, let us dine. It is good to have you home."

He handed Noa another mug of coconut mead. Noa allowed himself to drift away on the cloud of his drink, watching Dagan retell his rendition of the escape from Martesia. Noa found Dagan's version the most entertaining. The boy had an undeniable talent for fabricating the facts.

A knock at the door startled him from his memories. Bonnie entered his room, carrying a steaming bowl with a towel draped over her wrist.

"It's straight to bed with you," she said as he used his good hand to wash his face and dry it with the towel. Noa didn't object. His body ached from entertaining, making toasts and greeting each family in an assembly line as they entered the feast. Already his duties as a prince and future king had returned. "Sleep in as much as you like. No school tomorrow."

To his surprise, Noa didn't mind they had canceled school. He glanced at the Ondulian-whelk project on the desk, buried under gifts of fresh ink and new parchment from his father, amazed at how important it once had been.

"Your father doesn't need your attendance at the trial until the afternoon," Bonnie continued.

Noa sat up in bed, wincing as his bandaged hand pressed against his pillow. "The trial is here? Where is King Edjlin?"

"Why, Noa dear, he's locked in the tower."

Noa jumped out of bed. Apologizing over his shoulder, he sprinted down the hall and across the courtyard. He dodged debris from the explosion that had destroyed part of the castle and lighthouse and arrived at the tower out of breath. Exchanging confused glances, the guards let him enter. He was the prince; they couldn't object.

"High seas, what is the meaning of this?" asked Edjlin, pulling the covers over his nightshirt when Noa burst through the door. Even though he was a prisoner, he was still a king—evidenced by the luxuries fitted into the tiny room. "Noa? Is that you?"

Noa panted, lost for words. He felt his pulse pound in his burned arm. How could he tell Edjlin that Weston was the son he'd lost? Where would he start?

"Oh my, this is about my guard, isn't it?" He took Noa's silence as an answer. "When he agreed to spy on Weston, he knew the risks. I told him to stop complaining about the sleeping needles with which you pricked him."

Noa blinked. "Huh?"

"Your father didn't tell you?" asked Edjlin, rubbing his aged eyes. "I had my suspicions luck would turn on me when I trusted that pirate, so I hired someone to inform me of Weston's doings. When I learned what he had done to your ship, it's when it all ended for me. I sent word immediately to Martesia for your rescue mission."

Noa scratched his head. This wasn't the conversation he had planned. "The man I saw you sneaking away with during the Capture the Conch games . . . he was your spy?"

"Yes, I suppose that must have been Willard."

"But—" Noa stammered, "—how did you write letters to communicate when Weston stole all the mailing birds, and they only fly home?"

"I believe you have your dolphin friend to thank for that."

Alya. She had saved them.

Noa still had questions. "Why did you tell my father to *enjoy* the venom if you were asking the Martesians to find us, the only people who could have gotten it?"

Edjlin looked stumped. "Enjoy the venom? I do recall asking him to *destroy* the venom, although I'm not sure how you know that."

Noa wiped his moist palms on his nightshirt. That darn Sirena . . . he could see what Dakki meant when he said many people fought and killed over misunderstood conversations. "Erm . . . I didn't come here to talk about your spy. I need to tell you about Weston."

"My boy, his death is not upon your shoulders. I should never have brought those terrible pirates into your life."

"But—"

"Risking everything to save others is the greatest form of nobility. You risked your life to save your people. You truly are a prince—nay, a king. The day you rule this kingdom shall be a blessed time. My boy, for you, I am eternally grateful. No, please let me explain," continued Edjlin, when Noa protested once more. "My son was about your age when I lost him. He wanted to grow up too fast, and I encouraged it. He shouldn't have been inside the castle when we overturned it. He wasn't supposed to set foot on the island at all. We didn't know until it was too late."

Edjlin looked down at his blankets, needing a moment to compose himself. "Since that day, I vowed vengeance against the Death King. When I realized the venom still existed, I knew it lay with the Death King himself and must be destroyed. I couldn't bear someone using it again. But I have learned the hard way vengeance leads to more pain, and my sentence in Justice Isle will remind me every day what I have done." He glanced solemnly at the bars on the door window. "I did not intend for men to die . . . the pirates, my soldiers . . . I did not foresee my quest would turn to ruin. Yet I needed to destroy the venom for Eric. It was the only way I could repay him for failing to keep him safe."

He leaned forward on the bed. "But you see, Noa, you have done it. You, a mere boy yourself, have avenged my son! The venom is gone. I can never thank you enough. After fifteen long years, I am finally at peace."

Noa stared at Edjlin through the dark, fidgeting with the bandage around his hand. The moonlight cast long shadows over the floor and Edjlin's face, framing his eyes in dark circles.

"You feel at peace with your son?" he asked, after a long pause.

Edjlin nodded. "I have never felt closer to him. It's like he's telling me I can live my life again . . . like he forgives me."

Noa nodded numbly. He couldn't tell Edjlin now, or ever. Edjlin had already lost his son. He wouldn't let him lose his son twice.

"Was there something else?" Edjlin asked when Noa turned to leave.

Noa shook his head and managed to crack a weak smile. "That's all. You said what needed to be said."

───────────

"You didn't tell him?" Dagan asked the next morning. Palm fronds brushed their legs on the jungle path as they walked to the village.

Noa sighed. "It's for the best."

"Becoming Father, are you?" Noa shot him a look of daggers, and Dagan smirked. "Relax! I'm only reeling you in!"

They ducked under a low-hanging mailing pipe, one that had endured a quick repair from recent damage, and Noa caught a glimpse of a message in a bottle floating by as they trudged on. Birds twittered in the treetops, lizards scattered off the path as they approached, and somewhere above them, a monkey screeched. Noa walked with a lighter step. He'd missed this place.

"What did you want to show me?"

Dagan grinned, leading the way into the cobblestone village. "You'll see."

Villagers who recognized Noa and Dagan bowed when they passed. Some reached out in respect to see Noa's damaged hand, but such energy buzzed in the streets that most did not notice the brothers. Noa craned his neck to hear a conversation between children about the blue men. A pair of girls ran past, arguing over whose turn it was to play the mermaid and who would play the unfortunate sailor prey. Larry's Hermit Haven now sold attachable dragon wings for their crabs, and when Noa peered in the store window of Bones's family's toy shop, he found the typical child puppets replaced by miniature fairies with fabric wings. The people of Ondule were embracing the truth faster than Noa had dared to hope.

Dagan pulled Noa away from the toy shop toward a winding jungle path that led to the swimming hole. When they reached the turquoise lagoon, Noa found himself smothered by a wet mob.

"Mr. Blackburn!"

"Noa, you made it!"

"Move over, Pan, it's my turn!"

Arms reached toward him in all directions to hug him or slap him on the back. Every member of his crew, including Zuri, was there. And then came Alya.

"Noa Blackburn, it's about time you came. You picked the wrong day to sleep in."

Noa turned around to look at her. Alya's chestnut hair blew off her neck in the wind, tangling in what Noa imagined she might deem "cravy." A Capture the Conch sack was slung over her tanned shoulder. The others backed away to give them space, and she smiled sheepishly.

"Hi," she said.

"Hi."

Freckles peppered her nose under the sun. He moved in for a hug, and she did too, but neither knew where to put their heads, and they ended up clumsily cheek to cheek.

"Ahem," coughed someone behind them, and they pulled away.

"Noa, we have a proposal we want you to see," said Bones. The others nodded their agreement. "All those for Noa as captain of our Capture the Conch team, say 'Aye'!"

A resounding "AYE!" shouted from every mouth, even from Vim, who wasn't even on Noa's team. Dagan stepped forward and pressed a familiar yellow parchment into Noa's good hand.

"What do you say?" he asked.

Noa unrolled the magical map and smiled at the blue glow appearing on the parchment. A breeze lifted the tips of the fabric and sent soft ripples to the lagoon, beckoning them to enter.

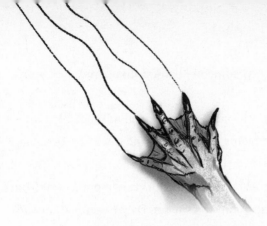

EPILOGUE

In the black liquid, a glow emerged from a nearby jellyfish. It propelled itself backward, lighting a stone wall and revealing the entrance to a ghostly castle. A blue man swam inside, its seaweed hair drifting behind its disproportionately small head, something shiny clutched in its webbed hand. The blue man navigated the castle passages and arrived at an enormous round door. It thrust the pendant into the keyhole. The lock groaned open, and bubbles escaped.

The creature swam into the giant, dark room, searching. Sunken books littered the bottom along with broken chairs and tables. It drifted over them, brushing its webbed hands over their soaked covers.

Searching . . . searching . . .

Its claws snagged fabric in the dark water, and it stopped. It pulled the fabric with both hands. Then it found what it had come for: The blue man wrapped its fishy, blue fingers around the decrepit hand and squeezed hard.

The hand squeezed back.

Acknowledgments

Every time I read this book, I see the hands that shaped it into what it is today, and I am filled with gratitude.

To my beta readers, Allie Smith, Annabelle Begg, Brooke Adams, Charles Hope, Dale Hope, Jane Clayton, Jessica Gibson, Jessica Weaver, Marie Stanford, Matt White, Russel Shaffer, and the English students of BYUI, thank you for your incredible and honest feedback. You were supportive even when my writing was poop.

To Emily Hope, Kyle Rice, and Tony Cox, thank you for diving deeper into the manuscript to help me bring out the true story. My writing grew stronger because of you.

To Brittany Pickett, you are a fantastic critique partner and an amazing friend. Thank you for being there for me through the good and the bad.

To my Mom and Dad, family, and friends who read early drafts and helped with writing queries, and who never stopped believing in me, I love you.

To the cat who played absolutely no role in the making of this book . . . Lily, your death stares during 2 AM writing sessions made life interesting.

M. J. Bogatin, Arielle Eckstut, and David Henry Sterry, thank you for helping me navigate publishing with one foot forward. You're the best!

To my amazing editor, Kelsy Thompson, thank you for

pushing me to explore new ideas and always letting me stay true to the heart of the story. You fought for these brothers, and I love you for it.

Thank you to Mari Kesselring, Megan Naidl, and everyone at Jolly Fish Press for bringing *Sea of Kings* into the world. And to Sophie Geister-Jones and Juan Manuel Moreno, who created the best cover ever! I cannot thank you enough for all you have done.

To my dearest Daniel, this book wouldn't exist without you. Remember June 3, 2012? That's the day we created the idea for this story together. We weren't even engaged yet. And every day since then, you have been the biggest champion for this story. Some of my favorite memories of you are car rides where we talked and talked about this tropical world. Thank you for pushing me to follow my dreams. I love you.

To all those who supported *Sea of Kings* with your excitement and encouraging words, thank you. Whether we have met in person or not, your kindness and friendship have meant more to me than you can know.

Lastly, thank you to my Heavenly Father, because in the end, I am here because of you.

About the Author

Melissa Hope earned her degree in English and is passionate about helping writers improve their craft and connect with the writing community. She escaped the frostbite normalcy of Canadian winters to live in Florida with her family, bipolar cat, and a growing collection of scuba gear.

To learn more about Melissa's books and her free writing tutorials, visit www.authormelissahope.com.